The Art of Fascinating ...
from the 1870s to the present

Could a dusty journal and some California
acreage ensure that Amy, Josie, Harmony and
Arabella, all descendants of renowned Barbary
Coast madam Bella Duprey, would find happiness
with the men they loved? Or was Bella's legacy
destined to disappear unheeded by "modern"
women who thought they knew better....

Heartbreak RANCH

Four complete stories by...
Fern Michaels, Jill Marie Landis, Dorsey Kelley
and Chelley Kitzmiller

"There is something very attractive to men about a madam. She combines the brains of a businessman, the toughness of a prizefighter, the warmth of a companion, the humor of a tragedian. Myths collect about her...."

—John Steinbeck

Heartbreak RANCH

Fern Michaels
Jill Marie Landis
Dorsey Kelley
Chelley Kitzmiller

Harlequin Books

TORONTO • NEW YORK • LONDON
AMSTERDAM • PARIS • SYDNEY • HAMBURG
STOCKHOLM • ATHENS • TOKYO • MILAN
MADRID • WARSAW • BUDAPEST • AUCKLAND

HARLEQUIN BOOKS
225 Duncan Mill Road, Don Mills,
Ontario, Canada M3B 3K9

ISBN 0-373-83325-3

HEARTBREAK RANCH

CONTENTS

Dear Reader,

Three years ago, for our annual retreat, we visited the Quarter Circle U Rankin Ranch in the Tehachapi Mountains of central California.

Little did we suspect as we checked in to our cabin and popped that first champagne cork that a story would be conceived. We learned that Rankin Ranch, first established in the 1860s, and passed from generation to generation, enjoys a passionate history.

The ranch's rich heritage inspired us to create our own characters—dashing men and women who live life to the fullest and seize their destinies with courage and spirit, much like the Rankins. In between hay rides, horseback adventures and games of championship pool, *Heartbreak Ranch* came to life.

For your optimal pleasure, we recommend the stories be read in the order presented.

We hope you enjoy the collection.

Chelley Kitzmiller, Jill Marie Landis, Dorsey Kelley, Fern Michaels

We'd love to hear from you! 20354 Valley Blvd., Tehachapi, CA 93561

THE LEGACY

We gratefully dedicate *Heartbreak Ranch* to the Rankin family. Our thanks also go to Lisa Kimble for her encouragement.

Barbary Coast
San Francisco, California
May 10, 1869

AT PRECISELY TEN o'clock, Arabella Duprey, Queen of the Barbary Coast, left her suite. Accompanied by her eighty-pound white poodle, Toddy, she glided down the hallway then paused at the handrail that overlooked the elaborately appointed gaming hall below.

Oil paintings of nude women covered every square inch of wall space. One was of herself—a life-size portrait, commissioned five years ago when she bought out her longtime employer and became the madam of the Cock O' The Walk.

The enormous, gilt-framed portrait hung directly over the bar, where everyone was sure to see it. Could she help it if she wanted to be remembered throughout the years to come as a beautiful and desirable woman?

Toddy sat panting patiently at her heels as Bella watched the activities below: the croupiers dealing cards and spinning the roulette wheels, the pretty waiter girls serving drinks, the musicians tuning up. And the customers spending their money.

This was her domain and everything was running just as it should. She was proud to be the reigning queen of the Barbary Coast.

A shudder ran down her spine at the thought of how she had jeopardized her business and her future—all for the love of a man.

Sam Heart had played her for a fool.

In the five years since Bella had bought the Cock O' The Walk and become its madam, she had not invited any man to her bed. To do so would have been against the house rules—rules she had set in place to eliminate competition between her and her girls.

She had believed Sam when he pretended to love her. He had even gone so far as to offer her marriage.

But for her daughter, Bella might not have been so gullible.

Six years ago when she had sent Amy away to school, she promised herself she would use the school years to set up a different kind of life for her and Amy. A respectable life, away from the Barbary Coast.

Amy's letter had taken Bella by surprise. Her schooling was finished and she was coming home to help run the Cock O' The Walk. Where had the years gone? There was no more time.

Becoming Sam's wife was the answer to her prayers as well as a dream come true. Except that it was all a lie.

Bella closed her eyes and gripped the rail as she gave up a silent prayer of thanks that she had overheard him boasting about her. He'd been bragging that he would win a bet—a bet that he could sweet-talk her into taking him to her bed. Thank God, she had discovered the awful truth before it was too late. Taking a deep breath, she steeled herself for the night's events. Carefully lifting her skirt out of the way, she started downstairs to greet her customers.

Tonight was the night. Everything was ready. There was no turning back.

Tonight Sam Heart would learn that no one played Bella Duprey for a fool and got away with it.

Tonight he would pay with the one thing he held most dear. His ranch. Heartbreak Ranch.

Once she obtained the deed, she would turn the management of the Cock O' The Walk over to her case keeper and barkeep, Howard Evans, who had been her trusted friend and confidant since she begun working at the fandango palace twenty years ago. By tomorrow morning, when Amy's stage arrived, she would be packed and ready to leave for their new home and their new life—courtesy of Sam Heart.

Always cool and collected, Bella was surprised to be overtaken by a giddy rush of nervousness tinged with excitement. But habit allowed her to smoothly commence her nightly ritual. Upon reaching the land-ing, she paused and nodded to Howard. At her signal, he hit a small, brass Chinese gong at the end of the bar. The room immediately fell into an expectant hush.

"Good evening, gentlemen!" Howard's voice boomed over the crowd, although it was quiet enough to hear a pin drop. "It is my pleasure to present your hostess...the incomparable...the one and only...Bella Duprey!"

She smiled with satisfaction as every man in the room looked up at her. She knew what an arresting sight she made, dressed in a new crimson satin gown, her signature color, now highlighted by the chandelier hanging directly over her head. Her gaze swept the room until she was certain she had everyone's undivided attention. Then, she licked her lips with the tip of her tongue and took a deep breath, knowing how the movement swelled her breasts.

"Gentlemen, I welcome you to ze Cock O' The Walk." She purposely emphasized her French accent.

Immediate applause and cheers rang through the air.

Bella acknowledged them with a slow, regal nod. Before descending the stairs, she gave the big dog beside her a silent signal to sit. When she reached the floor of the gaming hall, she wound her way through the maze of green, felt-topped tables covered with tall stacks of chips and gold and silver coins. She graciously exchanged comments with those she knew and stopped to introduce herself to the few she did not recognize.

Finally, Bella made her way across the room where Sam waited. She silently cursed herself for noticing that he looked particularly handsome tonight in a new checkered wool suit and gold brocade vest. When she reached the faro table where he stood waiting, Sam took her hand and whispered in her ear.

"You're looking especially radiant tonight." He drew her close and discreetly ran his fingertip along the edge of her heart-shaped bodice. "Did you wear this gown for me?" he asked, laughing softly.

"*Oui, mon cher.* For you, Sam. Only for you." She nearly choked on the words as she covered his hand with hers and gently moved his exploring fingers away. "But you will have to wait until midnight when I am through dealing."

"I've waited a long time already. I guess I can wait a few more hours."

She leaned forward, giving him an unobstructed view into the bodice of her gown, then kissed him lightly on the mouth.

"I promise you, it will be a night you will never forget." With that she took her seat at the faro table, opposite Howard, the case keeper, whose look of reassurance betrayed his usual stolid expression. Once she was settled, Howard placed a deck of cards and a dealing box in the center of the table. Bella had always taken pride in running an honest gaming house, but tonight's game called for special equipment. The cards were lightly sanded so that when one card was dropped upon the other, the two appeared as one. The faro dealing box sported an intricately painted face of a tiger. A hole in the tiger's eye allowed the dealer to see the next card up for deal. Bella had only to press a concealed lever to release an extra card. She had ordered the specialty duo so she could turn the tables on any professional gamblers who tried to cheat the house.

"So, gentlemen," she said, smiling a flirtatious smile at each of the men who had hurried to take a seat at her table, "you want to 'buck the tiger,' eh?"

Once she began shuffling the deck, once she felt the cards in her hands, she was able to rein in her emotions and become all business. She cut the cards and put them into the dealing box, confident that everything would come about just as she had planned.

Another of Bella's trusted employees, the lovely waiter girl, Felice, offered everyone at the table drinks on the house. After handing Sam his, Felice gave Bella a discreet nod.

"All bets down, gentlemen," Bella told the gamblers.

She watched Sam sip his drink. The drug Felice had put in Sam's glass would begin taking effect within the hour. An annoying headache, blurred vision and impaired judgment were the first symptoms, followed later by excruciating stomach cramps and eventual loss of consciousness.

Bella relaxed and allowed herself a small, satisfied smile.

Cards ranking from ace to king were painted on the top of the faro table where the players placed their bets. By the end of the first game of twenty-five turns, Sam was winning.

She knew that his run of luck would make him overconfident as he went into the next game. During the next hour, Sam's judgment became so impaired that he played carelessly and was now down to his last few chips. He kept rubbing his forehead and squinting to focus.

"Is something wrong, Sam?" Bella asked solicitously.

He slowly came up out of his seat, leaned across the table and motioned Bella to meet him halfway.

"It seems I've run a little short, my love. Could you extend me a small loan—say a thousand—until tomorrow?"

Bella feigned surprise. It was the moment she had been waiting for. "A loan? Oh, Sam...but I never—"

"I'll pay you back tomorrow as soon as the bank opens."

Shielding her mouth with her hand, Bella replied discreetly, "Sam, I do not doubt you for a second, but it is against the house rules."

"Christ, Bella, you've got more house rules than a dog has fleas. Come on. Be reasonable. My luck will turn. All I need is a thousand." He stretched closer, drew her near until his lips brushed against her ear. "You can trust me."

When he tried to kiss her, she backed away, wagging a finger at him, forcing herself to laugh when what she wanted to do was pull every hair out of his handsome head.

"Very well, *mon cher*," she said, feeling as smug as a cat playing with a mouse. "But, you must understand, I am a businesswoman. You will have to give me something for—how is it you say—for collateral?"

He thought a moment. "I know." He reached into

his pocket, pulled out a gold watch and laid it on the table before her.

"This watch, it is very beautiful, Sam, but it is not worth so much money." Turning her hands over, Bella indicated her helplessness with a shrug, then picked up the cards.

"Just hold on one minute," Sam said, reaching inside his coat. "You want collateral. I've got collateral, dammit."

He pulled a folded paper out of his pocket with a flourish and tossed it across the table.

"There. Heartbreak Ranch. Thirty thousand acres of the finest cattle range in California."

His tone was proud, boastful. Bella knew the drug had altered his good sense. Before he could change his mind, she asked Howard to hand her a pen and ink.

In a voice loud enough for all those gathered around the table to hear she said, "It is against my better judgment to accept this, Sam. I do so only because you insist, you understand." At his nod, she added, *"Très bien."* With icy calm, she shoved the pen and ink toward Sam, then began to count out a thousand dollars in chips.

Sam stared down at the deed for a moment or two as if trying to focus. His hand shook as he scrawled his name across the bottom of the page.

"All signed and legal," he said, thrusting it away from him.

Bella blotted the ink, then refolded the deed. With

her eyes on Sam, she slipped it down the bodice of her gown, between her breasts.

Over the next half hour, Bella made certain Sam regained some of his confidence and some of his money.

"I told you my luck would turn," he crowed, his voice too loud, his forehead and upper lip sheened with sweat. Before the next deal, he bet all his chips on the jack of hearts. The risky bet started a flurry of whispers. Within seconds a crowd gathered around the table. The air crackled with excitement.

A stillness akin to death descended upon the Cock O' The Walk as the crowd waited. Bella made an elaborate show of shuffling the cards, cutting the deck and placing it inside the box. Moving her finger off the tiger's eye, she saw that the next card up was a jack.

Obviously Sam's senses were not yet entirely impaired. He had calculated the odds of being dealt the winning card. Too bad for him that he had not calculated the odds of her discovering his deceit.

Pressing her thumb on the hidden lever, Bella dropped a six on top of the jack and dealt the two cards as one.

The onlookers moaned in chorus when they saw the six. Sam cursed.

"Six wins," Bella declared in a casual tone that belied her elation.

No one had bet on six. Quickly she swept the cards into a pile. "The game, it is *fini.*" Better luck another time."

Seconds later, she and Sam were the only two left at the table. He looked shaken, his dark eyes unfocused, yet haunted. She watched him run an unsteady hand through his hair before trying to collect himself.

With an imploring gaze he stared across the table at her.

"If I didn't know you better—know how honest you are, I'd be real worried right now. Heartbreak Ranch is all I've got."

Her heart tripped over itself. She almost wavered.

Think of Amy's future. Think of what would have happened if you had not discovered the truth.

The legendary Bella Duprey would have become the Barbary Coast's legendary fool.

Sam closed his eyes and groaned.

"Come, *chéri*," Bella coaxed, sidling up close to him. "Let us go now up to my suite."

With both hands planted on the painted tabletop, Sam shoved himself out of his seat and staggered to his feet. "About my deed, Bella..."

"Oui, chéri." She patted her bodice. "I have it right here, next to my heart, safe and sound."

Bella helped Sam up the stairs to where Toddy was waiting. Tongue lolling, the dog bounded down the hall, leading the way.

Once Sam was stretched out on her bed, his head turned sideways against the ruffled satin pillow, she crossed the room and lit the lamp on the table next to the window. When the crimps saw the light they would know the time had come.

Next, she knelt beside the old trunk in the corner

and lifted the lid. Toddy sat down beside her. With a glance toward the man on the bed, she reached in and took out her life's work, a personal journal entitled *The Art of Fascination.* Inside the leather-bound book were the secrets of her success, the information and procedures that had earned her the title of Queen of the Barbary Coast, and had made her a legend.

Lamplight flickered over her meticulously written notes of men's likes and dislikes, their reactions and responses, as well as the various techniques she employed to enhance their sexual pleasure.

With the help of a Chinese herbalist she had developed recipes for wines, potions, elixirs and scents that worked as aphrodisiacs and stimulants.

Her fingers toyed with the springy curls atop the poodle's head. Even he had proved useful—giving her ideas about how to control a man's behavior. Through the years she had discovered that most men responded best to simple commands, just like a dog.

Along with the deed to Heartbreak Ranch, *The Art of Fascination* would be part of Amy's inheritance, which was why she'd written it in English. Bella smiled as she slipped the document into the journal, tucked it in among her other treasures and closed the lid of the trunk.

Sam moaned pitifully and doubled up, drawing his knees to his chest. Bella stood and walked over to the edge of the bed and sat down beside him.

"Poor Sam," she whispered as she smoothed his shining black hair off his forehead. His skin was cold and clammy. He had begun to tremble. He was too far gone to fight her.

Before the crimps came, before Sam lost consciousness, she wanted him to know that she knew of his plans.

"I loved you, Sam," she told him. "I think I'll always love you."

"I'm...sick, Bella," Sam ground out, his teeth rattling. "G-get a d-doctor."

Bella smiled sympathetically, then shook her head. "What you have is not fatal, though I was tempted, believe me."

He stopped writhing long enough to squint up at her.

"What...are you...talking about?"

"The drug I had Felice put in your drink. You're going to get much worse before you get better. Tomorrow, by the time you regain consciousness, I expect you'll be on your way to the port of Shanghai. I hope you don't get seasick on top of everything else." She touched her fingertips to her lips, then placed them upon his mouth. "I will miss you, *mon cher.*"

"You bitch!" He tried to raise himself up on his elbow, but collapsed. "You *poisoned* me?"

"I'm afraid so, Sam. But, as I said, it will not kill you. Although by this time tomorrow, you will wish it had."

He moaned again.

Bella nodded at him. "I know all about your plan to seduce me, to humiliate me. What was it you called me? A two-dollar—no, a two-bit whore? I assure you, Sam, I am worth far more than two bits."

His face twisted. "I would have won that bet, too."

Bella smiled. "I am afraid I will have the last laugh after all."

Toddy growled at a noise outside. Bella got up and walked over to the window. She pulled aside the Belgian lace curtains, then opened the window. Two swarthy figures appeared out of the fog and crawled inside. The smell of sweat, fish and the sea eddied about them.

"He's ready," Bella said, pointing to the bed. "Take him. Quickly. Please." She was trembling so badly she had to grasp the back of a chair for support.

Unable to watch, she pressed her palm against her heart and headed for the opposite door.

"Come, Toddy." He pranced across the room to her side. "That's my good boy," she said, praising the dog in the honeyed tone she used whenever he did exactly as she commanded.

The crimps took hold of Sam Heart and jerked him to his feet. He retched and vomited on his shining black boots as well as the crimps' worn ones, earning himself a rap on the side of the head.

"Damn you, Bella Duprey!" Sam cursed. He struggled futilely as the seamen dragged him to the window. "I hope you go to hell for this," he gasped.

"I think it is you, Sam, who is going to hell."

Her heart breaking, Bella lingered in the doorway with her fingers clutching the brass doorknob. As the crimps shoved Sam Heart out into the night, the man mustered one last burst of energy.

He lashed out, kicking and swearing. The toe of his boot caught on the edge of the table beside the window and sent the kerosene lamp atop it crashing to the floor.

Glass shattered. Kerosene spilled. Immediately, tongues of orange flame licked up the lace curtains, raced down across the polished wooden floor and encircled the wooden chest.

Horrified, Bella screamed and ran toward the fire. She could think of only one thing—saving her precious trunk filled with memories of the past and hopes for the future.

AMY'S STORY
Chelley Kitzmiller

CHAPTER ONE

Barbary Coast
San Francisco, California
One week later

"I GOTTA WARN YOU, missy. There ain't much left to see."

Amelia Duprey sat perched on the edge of the buggy seat, her gloved hands tightly clenched around Toddy's braided silk leash. Despite the warning, when the buggy rounded the curve, she gasped at the sight of the charred ruins of the Cock O' The Walk. It was almost as shocking as coming home from school to the news of her mother's death only hours before.

Howard Evans reined the horse to the side of the road and set the brake. "Hard to take, ain't it?"

Amy nodded, unable to speak. Only the stairs were left standing. As a child, she used to hide behind a potted palm at the top of them and watch her mother greet the customers.

Toddy's whine drew Amy's attention away from the rubble. "I know, boy. I know." She put a comforting arm around the dog and patted his shoulder.

In a sitting position, the curly canine was as tall as Amy.

"I couldn't bring myself to ask you before," Amy ventured, "but...do you know how the fire got started?"

"Well, I—" Howard hesitated, regarding her with a look of uncertainty. "Considering it happened so suddenlike, I 'spect someone knocked over a kerosene lamp."

"Was there a fight?"

Howard shook his head. "Your mama didn't allow no fights. Fact is, everything was goin' as planned— I mean...just fine."

Amy's brow puckered in question but before she could speak, Howard went on to explain.

"She'd finished dealing for the night and went upstairs," he said, his gaze on the ruins. "It weren't an hour later when she come running back down, leading Toddy with one hand, dragging her trunk with the other and screaming, 'Fire!'" He paused and took a deep breath as if to muster the courage to finish. "Everyone panicked and started running every which way. I grabbed the cash box and ran out the side door to go ring the fire bell. By the time I got back, the place was ablaze. Bella weren't nowhere in sight, but she'd tied Toddy up to the handle on her trunk so I figured she was all right." He bowed his head. "I figured wrong," he said on a down note. "She'd gone back inside."

"Why would she go back in?" Amy asked.

"For that." With a glance behind him, Howard indicated the blanket-wrapped bundle in the rear seat. "Next thing I knew she come running out of the building dragging that painting of hers. By the time I got to her she was on her knees gasping for air. I done everything I could to try to save her, but there weren't nothing I could do. She died in my arms."

Thinking about the horror of that night, of the terrible way her mother had died, Amy shuddered. She would never understand why her mother had risked her life to save a painting. But then there was a lot Amy would never understand about her mother, which was exactly the way it was meant to be. Bella Duprey's mystique was part of her success.

Amy turned to Evans. "I'm ready now," she said in a steady voice. "We can go."

He continued to hold the reins still. "I know it ain't my place to tell you what to do, but I owe it to Bella to try to talk some sense into you. It's only been a week since you got here. Seems to me that you should give yourself some time to think about what you want to do with your life before you go off to a ranch you ain't even seen. Your ma left you more than enough money to see you through. And you'd have even more if you decided to sell the property."

"Sell the ranch? Oh, no, Howard. I couldn't possibly sell it," she said, shaking her head. "Settling down on a ranch was Mama's dream. I know you think I'm acting irrationally, but I really have thought things out. If I don't like what I see, I can always come back here."

"I know all about your mama's dreams, believe

me. But things are different now," the gray-haired man argued. "It's not up to you—"

Amy placed her gloved hand over his. "Howard, Mama gave me everything I ever wanted. I don't know if it's possible, but I have to try to make her dream come true."

"You're just as stubborn as Bella was," he said with a rueful smile, then snapped the reins.

Minutes later they arrived at the stage station. Two burly men hefted Amy's trunk and her mother's smaller one to the top of the coach. When they reached for the painting, she cautioned them to take extra care and watched as they stood it upright between her trunks.

Satisfied it was secure, she led Toddy around to the side of the coach. "Up, boy," she commanded, patting the floor. Toddy needed no urging. He jumped up into the Concord and sat down. "He's the smartest dog I've ever seen," she said, turning to Evans.

"Bella was plumb crazy 'bout that fool dog. Spent a lot of time training him." He reached into his pocket and pulled out a piece of paper and a small cloth bundle. "Here's a list of basic tricks and commands you need to know right off to make him mind you. And here's some of his favorite treats. Your mama made them special. He'll do just about anything to get one, so you best hide them where he can't see or smell them or he'll drive you crazy with his beggin'. Everything else you need to know 'bout him is in Bella's journal. You should know, Missy, that your mama put a lot of work into that journal. I believe she intended it to be useful for you one day, although I'm not quite sure how. As far as I know, it's just full of dog commands." Evans regarded Toddy with a look of dismay. "To hear Bella talk about that animal, you'd think he was human. Claimed he was the best thing that ever happened to her. Said he taught her more about men than all the courtesans in France." The moment the words left his mouth, he reddened with embarrassment.

"Is that so?" Amy barely managed to hold back a smile. "In that case—" she lowered her voice to a whisper "—he'll be quite an asset because I know nothing at all about men." With that, she lifted her skirt and climbed up into the coach.

A red-faced Evans stood at the stage door until she was settled. "If you need me for anything—anything at all—I'll be working downtown at the What Cheer House."

The moment had come. Amy didn't speak for fear she would cry. She had known Howard Evans all her life and thought of him as the father she never had.

"Thank you for loving Mama and taking care of her all these years." She tried to stem the welling tears but could not. "I know in her own way she loved you, too."

"That she did, honey. That she did." Howard squeezed her hand, then stepped back as the Concord lurched forward.

IT WAS NOON when the stage pulled into Havilah, a busy mining town high in the Tehachapi Mountains.

It stopped in front of the Golden Gate Hotel. As the passengers disembarked, the hotel proprietor, Leopold Wattiez, announced that he provided the best accommodations in town along with French-cooked meals.

Amy decided that a French-cooked meal was exactly what she needed before continuing on to the ranch. She tied Toddy to the post next to the water trough and went inside.

"Voilà!" said the rotund cook a few minutes later, as he set the plate down in front of her. Amy was hard-pressed to see what was French about the roast beef and potato dish, but she kept her thoughts to herself. Recalling some of the French phrases her mother had taught her, she praised his efforts and earned a beaming smile plus all the information she needed about the town, where to shop and where to hire a wagon and driver.

Not knowing exactly what supplies she would need, she decided to buy a little of everything so she wouldn't have to come back for a while. Then she hired a boy with a spring wagon to load up her things and drive her out to the ranch.

An hour later, they came within view of Heartbreak Ranch.

"I ain't been out here for a long time, but I'm purty sure this is it," said the boy, pointing a finger.

Amy gasped in delight at the small white house surrounded by ancient oaks and emerald green hills covered with bright orange poppies, blue lupine and owl's clover. Dozens of fat steers stood grazing, not even looking up as the wagon drew close.

It's Mama's dream come true, she thought, wishing her mother were here to share this moment with her.

Riding in the back of the wagon, Toddy ran back and forth, barking with excitement.

"Toddy, quiet," Amy commanded, then realized he probably thought the steers were big dogs and wanted to chase them. Until he got used to them—and they to Toddy—she'd have to tie him up.

The closer they got, the more Amy saw that the house's beauty was an illusion, caused by distance and wishful thinking. Up close, it was nothing more than a tumbledown shack. Overcome with disappointment, she now felt relieved that her mother wasn't there to see her dream shattered.

So this is Heartbreak Ranch. She shook her head. She'd wondered about the name. Now, she knew. It broke her heart just looking at it—the chipped and peeling whitewash, the dilapidated front porch, the weatherworn door branded with a broken heart. Maybe she should have taken Howard's advice and stayed in San Francisco.

"Where do you want me to put your things?" the boy asked.

It was on the tip of her tongue to tell him to turn the wagon around and head back to Havilah. Instead, she surprised herself by saying, "Anywhere will be fine." Before she could change her mind, she climbed out of the wagon. Toddy leaped out of the wagon bed, nearly toppling her in his excitement to get down. She grabbed his leash and gently commanded him to settle down, but it was an effort in futility. Straining against his leash, he pulled her across the yard to the house, where he used his long nose to push the door open.

The inside of the house was even worse than the outside. Thick dust and dirt covered everything. A stack of old newspapers lay on the table, the edges chewed away. The furniture—what there was of it— was crudely made and the earthen floor was covered with animal droppings and litter.

The thought that this was her legacy made Amy groan. "Oh, Toddy, I don't know...."

"That's the last of it," the boy said, walking up behind her.

Only when he held out his hand, did Amy remember that she needed to pay him. She reached into her reticule, pulled out three coins and dropped them into his palm.

"Much obliged, ma'am. Let me know if you need me for anything else, you hear?"

Amy could only nod. The fact was, she needed so much she didn't know what to ask for first. Dazed, she stared after him as he climbed into the wagon and released the brake. He was beyond shouting distance when she thought to ask how she was supposed to contact him.

Toddy snapped her out of her thoughts when he jumped up on his hind legs and dropped his big paws on her shoulders.

"Good grief! What are you doing?" she asked, struggling to push him off. "Down, Toddy. Get down."

She barely finished speaking when a raccoon scampered out of its hiding place and ran between them, then out the door.

Amy screamed and jumped back.

Toddy yipped and lurched forward, yanking his leash out of her hand. He ran after the creature at a full gallop.

Amy chased him, yelling for him to stop. Finally, the raccoon darted up an oak tree and sat on a branch looking smugly down at the dog.

"Bad dog!" Amy scolded between gasps. She tried to pull him away from the tree, but he fought her every step, twisting and turning, barking and yipping. She had no idea how to control the animal. Nothing on the list Howard had given her covered chasing raccoons up trees. Remembering that his other commands were in her mother's journal, she decided to look them up at the first opportunity. On her way back to the house, she stopped at the pile of baggage and supplies and opened her satchel. She pocketed a handful of Toddy's bite-size treats, thinking they might come in handy if Toddy gave her any more trouble.

Looking up at the sky, she figured she had about an hour before nightfall. After her town meal, she wasn't hungry, which meant she wouldn't have to tackle the kitchen area just yet. That was a relief, since it was the dirtiest.

She supposed the first thing to do was to put the bedroom in order so she would have a clean place to sleep. She tied Toddy to a porch post and fed him the leftover beef she'd saved from her supper.

It took less time than anticipated to clean the bedroom and make up the bed. As soon as she finished, she went outside to get her mother's painting. Having already decided against hanging it in the main room because of the difficulty she would have explaining it to anyone who saw it, she opted for the bedroom.

Lifting the heavy, gilt-framed, life-size nude up to the nail above the bed proved to be a challenge. It took her three tries before she succeeded, then she jumped down off the bed and stood back to admire her efforts.

"You're home, Mama," she said, feeling a little foolish talking to an inanimate object. "I know it's not exactly what you had in mind, but I promise you that one day it will be everything you dreamed of and more."

A pistol shot interrupted her one-sided conversation.

Amy shrieked, jumped back and flattened herself against the wall next to the window. Outside, Toddy barked furiously. *Dear God, don't let him get shot.* Cautiously, Amy sidled up next to the window and peeked out. At first, all she saw was Toddy fighting against his rope. Then she saw a half dozen men on horseback galloping toward the house, their guns drawn. Who were they? What did they want? She looked around for something to use as a weapon, then realized the futility of it. If they meant to do her harm, she was virtually at their mercy.

As she waited, something drew her gaze to the painting. *Be brave, chérie. I am with you. I will always be with you.*

Outside, an angry voice called out, "Whoever you are, get out here."

Amy straightened her spine, smoothed back her hair and headed for the door.

The riders, still astride their horses, formed a semicircle several yards from the porch step. The sun had slipped below the horizon making it impossible for her to see their faces clearly.

"Who are you and what do you want?" In spite of her resolve, her voice cracked.

One of the six nudged his horse a step forward. "Name's Walker Heart and you're trespassin' on my property."

"There must be some mistake," Amy replied without hesitation.

"Damn right there is," the man rejoined. "And you made it. Now get the hell off my land."

Amy gasped. No one had ever spoken to her in such a crude manner. Forgetting to be cautious, she stomped out onto the porch, where Toddy's loud, insistent barks provoked her all the more.

"Toddy, quiet," she commanded so sternly that the curly, white canine lay down and put his head between his paws. "And you, Mr. Heart," she said, pointing an accusing finger, "I'll thank you to mind your language. You happen to be speaking to a lady."

Walker Heart's eyes widened in surprise at the blue-eyed blonde decorating his front porch. From a distance she hadn't appeared to be anything special— just another squatter's wife. He'd ordered the last squatters off his property a month ago and threatened to shoot them if he ever saw them on his land again. He was sick and tired of folks trying to take what didn't belong to them and had decided to get tough even if it meant gaining a reputation as a bully.

Damned if she isn't the prettiest woman I've ever seen, he thought. *And the maddest.* Feet slightly apart, arms akimbo, she looked ready to do battle. But so was he. He rearranged himself in the saddle and leaned forward over the saddle horn. "I'm only gonna to tell you one more time. This is my land and I want you off it. Now."

His land. Amy's heart sank. Was it possible that this wasn't Heartbreak Ranch after all? Had the boy made a mistake and brought her to the wrong ranch?

She was about to tell the rude Mr. Walker Heart that she would gladly leave if she had the means to do so when a thought struck her. *Heart* was the name on the deed.

"Are you related to a Sam Heart?" she ventured, hoping two and two would make four.

Walker cast a sideways look at the Indian next to him, then turned back to her. "He's my pa."

"Oooh." She unconsciously drew the word out as far as it could go. It was a relief to know she was right where she was supposed to be. But why didn't Walker Heart know it? Wouldn't his father have told him that he'd sold their property?

"What's that supposed to mean?" he asked, nudging the brim of his hat back off his forehead.

He was so arrogant. So cocksure. So infuriating. If he wasn't so mean and nasty, she might feel sorry for him and regret having to be the one to tell him he no longer had a claim on Heartbreak Ranch. As it was, she felt a sort of perverse satisfaction.

"I believe the mistake is yours, Mr. Heart," she said with all the haughtiness she could muster. "I am the new owner of Heartbreak Ranch."

Walker gave a sarcastic chuckle. "You expect me to believe that? What do I look like, a fool?"

Amy's eyebrows arched to a peak. A fool? Him? Actually she had a different word in mind but was too much of a lady to utter it.

"I would not make such a claim if I didn't have the proof. It's in my trunk—a deed signed by your father." She expected some sort of reaction but none surfaced. "If you and your men will move your horses out of the way, I'll get it and you can see for yourself."

Nobody moved.

Amy waited a moment longer. If they thought they were going to intimidate her, they had another think coming. She untied Toddy and walked toward them.

Walker stared down at her, his horse's reins held loosely before him. He'd seen and heard enough and was getting angrier by the second. It was inconceivable that his father would sell the ranch. To anybody. For any price.

He had to admit that when his ma died, things did change some between them. There were clashes of will and disagreements. Then his pa started going up the road to Havilah on Saturday nights. More than once Walker found him sitting at the faro table, too drunk to make it home on his own. And there was that woman, Jersey Lil. A whore. Every man in a fifty-mile radius had bedded her.

But the one thing he and his father had always agreed on was how to run Heartbreak Ranch. Someone would've had to put a pistol to Sam Heart's head to get him to sign over the deed.

Amy stopped a few yards short of the horses. Neither Walker Heart nor any of his gunmen had moved so much as an inch. She could be patient to a point and she had reached it. But as she stared at Walker Heart she wondered what she could do against a thousand pounds of horse and two hundred pounds of man?

She *could* take the long route, walking in a circle around them, then behind them to her trunk.

What would her mama have said about that? Amy could think of several things and decided that the long route was not an option.

She *could* call on whatever chivalry they might possess and plead prettily for them to move.

Her own instincts told her that was out.

Ironically, it was Walker Heart's horse who offered a possible solution. The closer Toddy got the more skittish the horse became.

The horse has probably never seen a dog like Toddy, she realized. *I wonder what would happen if Toddy showed him one of the little tricks?* Amy had studied Howard's list and knew what tricks he was capable of doing.

Pulling Toddy along beside her, Amy advanced a

few more feet, then stopped and looked up at her tormentor. Until this moment, Walker's face had been hidden by the evening's shadows and she'd only imagined what he looked like. But up close, he didn't look anything like the ogre she'd thought him to be. He was a handsome man but not in the typical smooth-featured way. His was a handsomeness honed by sun and wind and toughened by hard living. It appealed to her in ways she'd never dreamed. A blunt jaw, sharp cheekbones and a slightly crooked nose added character. Beneath his dun-colored hat, his brown hair was a bit too long, as were his sideburns.

But it was his eyes that gave her pause and caused her to reconsider her plan to make him move out of her way. It wasn't just their color—a light, clear blue—but the way they watched her in narrowed speculation.

The same voice she'd imagined hearing coming from the painting came to her on the breeze, encouraging her.

Stay calm. He is, after all, only a man.

She reached into her pocket for one of Toddy's treats, then gained the dog's attention by holding it in front of him. "Dance, Toddy...and sing. Sing pretty."

The big white dog reared up on his hind legs, yipping and howling like a coyote. With his front paws waving up and down, he danced around in a circle.

Amy had thought only to frighten Walker's horse enough so it would move. Instead, bedlam.

All six horses panicked and broke from their riders'

control, bucking, kicking, tossing their heads. Afraid she and Toddy would be kicked or trampled, Amy yanked on Toddy's leash and made a dash for the pile of baggage and supplies. Between the horses' whinnies and snorts, she heard human cuss words so hot they could sizzle bacon.

It took Walker several minutes to regain control of his horse, and his men slightly longer. By the time he dismounted and tied the animal to the hitching post, he was obviously angry.

Amy nearly panicked when Walker strode toward her. The jingle of spurs punctuated his every step like a death knell. Her eyes widened and her stomach flip-flopped when he chomped down on the fingertip of his glove and yanked it off. If ever she wanted to run and hide, it was now.

Toddy took a protective stance in front of her and growled a fierce warning.

"If that overgrown lamb bites me, I'll truss him up like a Christmas turkey and roast him for supper."

Amy stiffened. "He's a French poodle," she retorted in defense of the insult. "Trained to maim on command," she added quickly, feeling a desperate need to boost Toddy's too soft image.

Walker stopped as she hoped he would.

"Call him off and show me this deed you say my pa signed."

Keeping her eyes on Walker and her hold on Toddy, Amy opened the trunk and took the deed from inside her mother's journal. "It's quite legal, I assure you," she said, slapping it into his outstretched hand.

Walker unfolded the document, then lowered his gaze to the signature line. There was no mistaking his father's handwriting. The bold scrawl was entirely his own. Following the name was the date. May 10, 1869. Only two weeks ago, Walker realized. His father had left for San Francisco six weeks ago with the intention of settling a boundary dispute. Once the error was corrected, a new deed was to have been drawn up.

Walker read the document from top to bottom looking for something that would tell him why his father sold the ranch. There was nothing. Nothing at all.

He looked at Amy, thinking he should be able to see something in her demeanor to tell him she was lying. But he didn't. Switching his gaze to the dog, he reminded himself that looks could be deceiving.

Walker's eyes narrowed to slits. "My pa—did he owe you money or somethin'?"

Amy shook her head.

"Then did he make you promises...in exchange for...you know...services?"

Amy's brow knitted in confusion. "Services? What kind of—" A gasp escaped her lungs in a whoosh of indignation. "How dare you imply such a thing!" She plucked the deed from his hand. "For your information I've never even met your father."

Taken aback, Walker cocked his head. "You never met him and yet—"

"I inherited the ranch from my mother," she cut in, resenting the need to give him any kind of an explanation after what he'd just said.

Walker removed his hat and slapped it against his

leg, drawing Amy's attention to the ominous looking six-shooter that was strapped there.

"You inherited it from your mother," he parroted. "Did my pa owe your mother money, or—"

"I have no idea," Amy returned. "She died in a fire only hours before I arrived home in San Francisco." Amy bent her head forward. "All I know is that the deed was among the things she left me."

Walker scratched his ear as he considered her words. He found himself almost believing her. But there were still too many unanswered questions— questions that she either had no answers for or wasn't going to answer because she was hiding something.

"So it's just you and your...uh...dog, right?" At her nod, he added, "You know anything about workin' cattle?"

Working cattle. Amy's bravado faltered. "I figured I'd get myself settled, then make some inquiries as to what I'd need to do."

When a chorus of laughter rang out around her, she realized how impossibly foolish she must have sounded. Until now, she'd never even given a thought to how she was going to care for the cattle, let alone *work* them. But she'd be the last one to admit to Walker Heart that the only thing she knew about cattle was that she liked her beef cooked medium rare.

"What did you say your name was?" he asked, changing the subject.

"I didn't. But it's Amelia—Amy Duprey."

Walker put his hat back on and pulled the brim low. "All right, Miss Duprey. Me and my men are gonna ride on out of here, but don't make the mistake of thinkin' that you've seen the last of me or that I'm givin' in." He turned away from her, walked over to his horse and mounted up.

Amy didn't know what to say, so she said nothing at all. Was he making a promise or issuing a threat?

Gathering his reins, Walker wheeled his horse around and rode up next to her. "Deed or no deed, lady, Heartbreak Ranch belongs to me." He touched his hat brim in mock salute, then spurred his horse into a gallop. His men followed.

The horses kicked up a cloud of dust that forced her to run into the house. By the time it cleared, the riders had disappeared.

CHAPTER TWO

As SOON AS WALKER returned home, he drafted a message to John Drum, hiring him to find his father. Walker had known Drum since they were boys together in Philadelphia. Drum had hired on with the Pinkerton Detective Agency and was currently based in San Francisco. Walker wrote him about his pa's traveling plans and all that he'd learned today. Tomorrow morning he would have his foreman ride down the mountain to the Bakersfield telegraph station and send the message over the wire.

Walker leaned back in his big cowhide-covered chair and placed his booted feet atop his desk. Crossing his arms in front of him, he stared across at the massive oak bookcase and tried to recall anything unusual his pa had said or done before he'd left. Walker could think of nothing.

If he didn't hear from his father in the meantime, then in a couple of weeks Walker would know for sure what was going on with his pa. He hoped for the best, a logical explanation for what had happened. But the realist in him feared something was seriously wrong, and he suspected that Miss Amelia Duprey, for all her outward innocence, knew more than she'd let on.

Meantime, Walker decided to keep a close eye on the picture-pretty miss to make sure she didn't venture over the big hill and discover the new Heartbreak Ranch homestead. The last thing he wanted her to see was the fine house built of sugar pine, the bunkhouse and numerous corrals and outbuildings. As it stood now, she thought the branding shack, built when his ma and pa settled in Walker Basin, was all there was.

EARLY THE NEXT morning, minutes after his foreman rode off to send the wire, Walker saddled up and headed over the hill. He'd spent a restless night thinking about Amy Duprey. Was she telling the truth? Or wasn't she? Either way, she had legal title to *his* land and he'd be damned if he was just going to sit back and let her have it without a fight. If, in fact, his pa had sold out to her mother, Walker would buy the ranch back. Heartbreak Ranch meant too much to him to lose it, especially to a woman who no more knew how to run a cattle ranch than he knew how to sew.

And if spending half the night thinking about her wasn't enough, he'd spent the other half of the night dreaming about her. Dreaming about what they could do together. His dreams had ended abruptly when he squeezed his pillow so hard the seam popped and all the feathers flew out. He'd had a devil of a time explaining that one to the housekeeper. Even now, wide awake, the lingering memories of that dream made him ache.

Sometime later he reached the top of the hill and looked down on the shack. Smoke billowed out of the chimney. Huge white clouds of smoke. Not only was it coming out of the chimney but it was seeping out through the cracks in the door and from between the shutters.

He spurred his horse and galloped toward the shack.

Blinded by the smoke, Amy finally found the door and stumbled outside onto the porch, coughing and choking. Not seeing the step, she pitched forward and landed in a sprawl on the ground.

Tied to the porch post, Toddy fought against his leash but was unable to break loose and come to her.

Walker reined his horse to a sliding stop, leaped off and ran to Amy's rescue.

"Are you all right?" he demanded, lifting her to her feet.

She could only wheeze, cough and choke.

"Take deep breaths." He stood facing her, his hands on her arms, holding her up. "Come on now. Relax and breathe real deep." He helped her across the yard to the well, then used his body to pin her up against the rock wall. He drew water, filled the dipper and held it to her lips. "Drink."

She raised her hands to encircle the dipper and slowly sipped the water.

Deciding she'd had enough, Walker took the dipper and dropped it back into the bucket. Her breathing was still ragged and she looked utterly exhausted.

Before he knew what he was doing, he drew her against him and wrapped his arms around her trembling body. He could feel her heart pounding against his own. "Give yourself a minute or two and you'll feel better." He nuzzled his chin into the wavy golden hair atop her head. It had been a long time since he'd held a woman and he couldn't remember ever comforting one. He was glad he'd been there for her when she needed him. No one had ever needed him.

The nearness of her reminded him of last night's dream. And in less time than it took to rope a steer, he was hotter and harder than a branding iron.

"I'd better get inside and see if any damage has been done." He pushed her back, making certain she could stand on her own. Then he wet his kerchief, wrapped it bandit style around his nose and mouth and headed into the shack.

Amy leaned against the well for support as she watched Walker Heart enter the smoke-filled house. The fact that he had come to her rescue told her he wasn't as heartless as he had appeared yesterday. That he had held her so tenderly, comforted her, then shoved her away from him with such force, told her something else—that he was attracted to her. Attracted to her more than he would probably care to admit. She knew she wouldn't have been able to interpret his behavior if she hadn't had a mother who specialized in understanding why men acted as they did.

Amy smiled to herself. There wasn't much her mother didn't know about men. But what about women? What would her mother have called that fluttery feeling she'd experienced when Walker nuzzled his head into her hair?

Nerves, she told herself. Just nerves.

Before she had time to contemplate the matter further, the house's wooden shutters flew open one by one and a moment later Walker came back outside. Striding toward her, he untied his kerchief and wiped his face and eyes.

Amy took a step toward him. "I want to thank—" she croaked, her throat sore from coughing.

"What in hell did you put into that stove?"

"Wood." She shrugged her shoulders. "Just... wood."

"Show me where you got it."

She had only to point to the pile of wood stacked neatly against the side of the house.

Walker walked over to it and picked up a halved log, then motioned her over. "Don't you know the difference between green wood and seasoned wood, for God's sake? You don't burn green wood unless you're fixin' to send up a smoke signal."

Amy wiped a weary hand across her brow. "I'm sorry. I've never made a fire before. The servants at boarding school made them." She scrutinized the piece of wood in his hand. He'd said it was green wood, but for the life of her she couldn't see that it was anything but brown. "Is everything all right inside?"

"More or less."

"Then...I didn't actually start a fire?"

He shook his head. The only fire she'd started had been the one inside him and he had a feeling he was going to play hell putting it out.

"It's a good thing you came by when you did."

"Yeah, a real good thing."

"I was trying to boil water for washing all those dirty pots and pans someone left behind."

"Well, now you'll have to wait until the green wood burns up before you put in anything else."

"Forgive me, but I'm a little confused. What color is the wood I'm supposed to use?"

"Color?" he asked, incredulous. He saw that she was serious and said, "Come with me." He led her around the back and showed her the pile of seasoned wood.

After examining the *seasoned* wood—which was exactly the same color as the *green* wood—she went around to the front of the house, sat down on the porch and put her arm around Toddy. There was nothing to do for now but wait until the smoke cleared.

Walker leaned negligently against a post, his thumbs hooked in his belt loops. "What else are you plannin' on doin' today?

Amy answered without thinking. "I...ah...I'm going to finish cleaning the place up, then unpack my trunks and put the supplies away. Why?"

"Because I was wonderin' if I should stay around to protect my property."

"Protect it from what?"

"From you." With that he pushed himself away from the post and strode past her.

Gritting her teeth, Amy watched him mount his horse and ride up the hill.

"It's not *your* property," she called after him,

knowing he probably couldn't hear her. "Of all the arrogant, overbearing...maddening.... You, Mr. Walker Heart, are everything my mama warned me about!" It was true. Walker Heart epitomized the kind of man Bella had warned her about—for all sorts of reasons. But he was also the kind of man Bella had loved to tame, using methods only she knew because she had invented them. Amy couldn't imagine anyone taming Walker Heart.

He'd be quite a challenge. She shook the thought from her head, only to have another even more provocative one take its place. *I wouldn't mind taking up the challenge.*

WALKER'S HORSE grazed nearby while he made himself comfortable, sitting halfway down the hill with his back against a boulder. He removed his field glasses from their leather case, flung the strap over his head and focused the lenses on the shack. He'd convinced himself that he needed to keep an eye on her, even though he knew she wasn't likely to venture over the hill, especially once it got dark. Even she had more sense than that.

So why was he there? He wasn't sure. Something about her called to him, like a siren singing to a seaman, only Walker wasn't about to let this siren lure him to destruction. He'd meant what he'd said. Deed or no deed, Heartbreak Ranch was his.

AFTER THE SMOKE cleared, the only work Amy managed to accomplish before dark was to drag her trunks and supplies inside. She didn't want to leave them outside a second night.

Rather than add any more wood to the stove—seasoned or green—she used cold water right out of the bucket to bathe. Each time she touched the cloth to her skin, she thought up another witty retort that would have neatly countered Walker Heart's sarcastic statements and questions. If only she'd thought of them earlier when they would have done her some good. Next time, she promised herself, she'd be better prepared.

Finished with her ablutions, Amy readied pen, ink and paper, then crawled into bed and sat up against the iron head rail. She started to make a list of all the things she had to do tomorrow: scrub the kitchen, cookware and utensils; shelve and organize suppl— Her pen rested on the *l* as her mind wandered. *How awful for Walker to learn from a perfect stranger that his father had sold the ranch. What kind of father would do such a thing?* She focused her attention and rewrote the last word because a pool of ink had obliterated the letters. Then, she added: rearrange the furniture— *Is there a Mrs. Walker Heart? Little Hearts with sandy brown hair and blue eyes?*

A moment later she shook her head. Impossible. She hadn't seen anything to indicate a family had lived in the house. As far as she could tell, the only inhabitants had been a few mice and a raccoon, which left the question, if Walker Heart didn't live here, where did he live?

"What do I care?" she asked herself, pretending

not to care. Much to her surprise she realized she really did care.

She leaned forward and twisted around to look behind her at her mother's portrait. "I wish you could tell me just exactly how you acquired Heartbreak Ranch," she said, staring into her mother's violet eyes, eyes so like her own. "Did you buy it or did you get it as collateral for a gambling loan?" She knew gamblers put up everything from property to racehorses for collateral.

Might she have written something about how she'd acquired Heartbreak Ranch in her journal?

Setting pen and paper aside, Amy got out of bed and opened her mother's trunk, releasing the scent of lemon verbena. Inside were a dozen or more bottles, some labeled in English, others in Chinese. Most of them were filled with liquids; others appeared to contain dry ingredients. Hidden within the fabric of a magnificent blood red velvet gown was a faro dealing box. She ran her fingers over the painted tiger face, then its eyes.

"Emeralds." She stared at the twin jewels, then laughed. They couldn't possibly be real. If they were, Howard would have told her about them. Next came a jewel-studded dog collar, which served to confirm her belief that the tiger's eyes were fake, since the stones in the dog collar were almost as large, and nobody—not even Bella Duprey—would go so far as to put real jewels in a dog's collar.

The journal was at the very bottom of the trunk. Howard had told her that the journal could be useful to her one day. What a magical tome it would be if it could give her the answers she needed now. Flipping through the pages, Amy saw that the journal was divided into four sections, each with its own title: "Captivating Your Man"; "Toddy's Tricks and Commands"; "My Life— Bella Duprey"; and "Recipes for Romance and Other Concoctions." The first seemed to be a manual on how to handle men. The second and smallest section was devoted to Toddy. And the third was a sort of diary of her mother's life, beginning when she left France and came to San Francisco with fifty other courtesans to find their fortunes. The fourth was nothing but recipes.

Later, when time allowed, she would read it in its entirety, but right now she needed specific information. She leafed through to the last entry of the diary and began reading.

May 10
Tonight is the night. Everything is ready. There can be no mistakes and no turning back. The crimps will come for Sam at midnight and carry him off to some faraway port. If only he had loved me as I loved him.

"Oh, my God! Mama had Sam Heart shanghaied!" Amy slapped the journal shut, then pressed her palms against the front and back covers as if to keep the incriminating words from escaping.

The noise awakened Toddy, who had been sleeping

on the bed next to her. He bolted to a sitting position and stared at her expectantly.

"Why, Toddy? What would possess her to do such a terrible thing?" The poodle curled his upper lip and showed his fangs. "Toddy Duprey! Shame on you." With a whine, Toddy got down off the bed and crawled beneath it.

If only he had loved me as I loved him. The words reverberated in Amy's head. Somehow Sam Heart had achieved the impossible; he had made her mother fall in love with him. But what on earth had he done to hurt her?

Reopening the journal, Amy flipped back until she found the first entry mentioning Sam Heart.

April 5
His name is Sam Heart and he is *très magnifique!* Every night he comes to my faro table and makes love to me with his eyes. Felice, she has tried to entice him, but he tells her he wants only me. I have told him my services are no longer for sale but he insists that I make an exception for him.

Amy read on—word for word—to the end, which she read once again, but only now fully understood.

Sam had played her mother for a fool. He'd told her he loved her and wanted to marry her, when in truth what he'd wanted was to win a bet—a bet that he could get her to do what no man had in five years: break the house rule and take him to her bed.

Amy closed the journal and stared at the wall, tears blurring her eyes. She didn't have to read between the lines of those last entries to know how much it had hurt her mother to end her relationship with Sam. Every word echoed her sorrow and pain. But it still didn't excuse her actions. Amy had grown up on the Barbary Coast and knew that once a man was shanghaied, he was usually never seen again.

"Oh, no!" she said suddenly. What would Walker do if he found out? It was a question she didn't want to contemplate. "He won't find out because I'm not going to tell him," she told herself.

Filled with her mother's righteous indignation, Amy had no difficulty convincing herself that she was justified in keeping what she knew of Sam Heart's disappearance a secret and in maintaining ownership of Heartbreak Ranch.

At length, she turned down the light and waited for sleep.

But sleep eluded her. She tossed. She turned. She pounded her pillow. She pulled the covers up to her chin. She pushed them down to her knees.

When she felt Toddy's hot, moist breath on her face, a signal that he had to go outside, she was glad to leave her bed. He yipped once and ran to the door, tail wagging.

"All right, I'm coming."

She lit the lamp, carried it to the other room and set it on the table. When she opened the door, a cool breeze billowed her nightgown.

Toddy ran outside and headed for the closest tree.

WATCHING THROUGH his field glasses, Walker felt his
breath catch in his throat when he saw Amy Duprey
standing in the doorway. God, she was beautiful.
Beautiful all over. Her honey-blond hair fell around
her shoulders in shining waves. The lamplight behind
her filtered through her nightgown, silhouetting her
slender body and revealing far more than he should
be seeing, but not nearly as much as he would like to
see. He adjusted the focus until her image appeared
sharper.

Maybe if he hadn't held her in his arms and didn't
know just how good she'd felt, he wouldn't be driving
himself crazy wanting to do it again. There was no
forgetting those womanly curves or the way her body
seemed to fit his as if she were made for him, for him
alone.

"Toddy! Where are you, boy?" she called, a brisk
breeze lifting her nightgown well above her knees.

Walker nearly swallowed his tongue when she
pushed the fabric down and poked it between her legs.
A low moan escaped him and he was forced to shift
his position to ease his ache—an ache that was not
only physically painful but damned unnerving. He
had never reacted to a woman this intensely before.

"Toddy!"

The answering bark drew Walker's gaze away from
Amy to her big, dumb beast of a dog...who was
charging up the hill after him.

"Oh, no!" Walker jumped to his feet and ran for
his horse. "Hold still, you fiddle-footed knothead or
I'm gonna trade you in for a mule." He grabbed the

reins and yanked the animal into position, then leaped into the saddle and galloped up the hill.

From where she stood in the doorway, Amy couldn't tell what Toddy was after, but whatever it was, he scared it away.

"Good boy," she congratulated him as he came prancing back. She reached out her hand to pat his head and noticed he was carrying something. "What have you got in your mouth?" He sat down in front of her and gave up his prize to her open palm. "It's…why, they're field glasses." She looked at Toddy. The dog cocked his head and barked as if to confirm her conclusion.

Amy's gaze flew to the hill. No one had to tell her whose they were.

Grabbing Toddy's collar, she jerked him inside and slammed the door so hard the shutters rattled.

NEAR DAWN, Amy gave up trying to get any sleep and started cleaning the kitchen, attacking the built-up grease and dirt with a vengeance. It didn't take her long to realize how little she knew about house-keeping.

By noon, she had managed to finish her cleaning and was struggling with her first attempt at baking. She'd heard that biscuits were a basic and had brought a recipe with her. So far she'd made two batches, used up half her flour supply and still didn't even have one edible biscuit. Batch number three was nearly ready to come out of the oven and it looked promising, but no matter how it turned out, it was going to be her last. All that kneading had worn her out.

After two ruined batches, Amy knew that brown on top meant burned on the bottom, so this time she took them out before they browned. She pulled the pan out of the oven, shut the door and used her towel to flip one over.

"Perfect!" she exclaimed in excitement. Her stomach growled in anticipation.

Toddy sniffed the air and woofed.

While she was turning to set the pan on the table, the front door swung open and banged against her arm, sending all twelve perfect biscuits flying into the air.

"Miss Duprey? I heard you yell and I—"

Amy stood watching the biscuits fall, bounce, then roll across the floor.

Toddy ran toward the door barking, then abruptly changed direction when a biscuit rolled past him.

Fighting to control her temper, which had become particularly volatile since meeting Walker Heart, Amy resisted looking at him as she spoke. "I don't suppose you could have knocked," she said in an even monotone.

Walker's gaze darted from Amy to the floor to Toddy, who was pawing at a steaming biscuit.

"I...uh...told you. I heard you yell. I thought somethin' was wrong."

"Something *is* wrong, Mr. Heart," she said, gritting her teeth. "Something is very wrong."

"Yeah, well, I'm sorry about your biscuits, but it's

not like you can't whip up another batch lickety-split." He reached down, retrieved one off the floor and inspected it. "Kind of puny, don't you think?" Grinning, he added, "Looks to me like you got more flour on you than in the—" He broke off, his gaze having lifted to meet hers.

Eyes narrowed and nose pinched, Amy scowled at him, silently daring him to continue.

Walker's cocky expression curdled. He looked beyond her to take in the flour-covered kitchen and the refuse bucket full of black-bottomed biscuits. He glanced down at the biscuit in his hand and appeared to give it serious thought.

Much to Amy's surprise, he brushed it against his chest, then bit into it and started to chew. "They're small, but tasty," he mumbled, his mouth full.

Amy flashed him her most brilliant smile. "Well, then, in that case, why don't you sit down and I'll get you some more." She shoved Walker into the closest chair, then went around the room picking up biscuits and dropping them into her apron.

Toddy had eaten one biscuit and had another one in his mouth, ready to carry it away, when Amy shouted for him to stop. "Give that to me," she commanded. He dropped the biscuit into her hand and crawled under the table.

Out of the corner of her eye, Amy saw Walker start to get up. "Sit," she ordered, in the same tone she'd used with Toddy.

Walker sat.

Emboldened by her anger, Amy removed the biscuits from her apron and set them down, one by one, on the table in front of him.

"You like them?" she asked, mischief sugaring her voice. "Then eat them."

Walker looked down at the dirt-smudged biscuits and swallowed. "I'm really not very hungry. Cookie just finished serving me and the boys some leftover stew."

"Cookie?"

"Yeah. Damned if I remember what his real name is. He's the cook so we call him Cookie."

"And where does Cookie do his cooking?"

"Yonder, over at the—" He cut himself off, suddenly realizing he was about to give his secret away. To cover his mistake, he started coughing. He'd have to be more careful in the future. If she got wind that the real ranch house—a house ten times the size of the branding shack—was only a mile-and-a-half away, she'd be harder to uproot than an oak tree.

Amy sat down across from him and folded her arms in front of her. "You were saying?" she prompted.

Walker made a fist, pounded his chest and cleared his throat. "Me and...the boys, we got us a cow camp...over yonder."

Toddy came out from under the table and sat down in front of Walker. Walker stared at him. Up close he didn't look like a lamb, he decided. His nose was too long...and those ears! What he did look like, Walker wasn't sure.

"What's he want?" he asked when Toddy lifted his paws.

"He's hungry. I expect he wants a biscuit."

"If I give him one, he won't come chasing after me when I leave, will he?"

"You mean like he did last night?"

Walker's eyes narrowed. "What are you talking about?"

Amy stood up and closed the door. Behind the door, hanging by the strap from a nail were his field glasses. She lifted them off and walked over to him, the glasses swinging back and forth like a pendulum.

"I believe you left these behind," she said, dropping them into his lap. "Toddy found them and brought them to me."

Walker picked them up, slung the strap around his shoulder and jumped to his feet. "I can explain," he said, reaching for her.

"Don't touch me, you—you Peeping Tom!" She turned away and he grabbed her arm.

"All right. I admit I was watchin' you, but dammit, Amy, I have a right to know what you're up to. Sure as I'm standing here, there's something fishy about my pa signing Heartbreak Ranch over to your ma, and I think you know what it is!"

Amy stiffened. "I don't know anything more than what I told you," she returned in a tone that was anything but convincing.

He released her. "So you say, which is why I wired a friend of mine, a Pinkerton man, to take the case."

"A Pinkerton man?" Amy's throat felt dry. "You hired a detective?"

Walker's eyes narrowed. "Yeah. It seemed the only way to find out what's going on with my pa."

His words were followed by a stern silence. Amy had to stop herself from filling in the void with a confession. Only by force of will did she succeed.

Walker drew a breath. "So that's where we stand."

Stand? Amy felt as if her knees were going to buckle. A Pinkerton man! She'd heard how efficient they were at tracking down outlaws and train robbers and how cold they could be when it came to dispensing justice. What were the chances of the man discovering that Sam Heart had been shanghaied? Better than the chances that he wouldn't!

Amy clasped her hands, trying to think. According to the journal, only Howard Evans and a pretty waiter girl named Felice had known of her mother's plan. Amy was certain Howard would never say anything, but what about Felice? Obviously, her mother had considered Felice to be a trusted employee, but was she?

"I expect an answer in a couple of weeks," Walker said, breaking the tense silence. Amy frowned at him, distracted from her thoughts. "Until then, I intend to continue running this ranch the way I always have."

Amy managed a stiff nod. "Of course," she replied. A couple of weeks. It wasn't much time and yet she knew it would seem like a lifetime.

It will be all right, ma chère. *You must trust your mama.*

Amy glanced over her shoulder, half expecting to see her mother standing there, poised and in control.

But Bella was gone. And wasn't coming back. Amy had to accept that, no matter how she felt, or what she thought she heard.

Trust me, my Amy. I will always be here for you.

Amy's body tensed. "Did you hear anything?" she asked. Without waiting for an answer, she crossed the floor to her bedroom, opened the door and peered inside. The only sign of her mother was the painted image above her bed.

"No," Walker answered. "Why?"

Hearing the jangle of Walker's spurs, Amy quickly pulled the door closed. Like a dutiful sentry she stood in front of it. "My imagination," she said with a shrug of her shoulders, hoping her air of nonchalance would divert him. She could not allow Walker to see the painting. The picture represented her mother's life—first as a prostitute, then as a madam, who had bedded so many clients that she didn't know who Amy's father was.

Walker simply wouldn't understand.

"What's in there?" He took a step toward her.

Panic rose inside her but she forced herself to appear calm and stepped directly in front of him, blocking his path. "It's just my bedroom," she told him, as if that was explanation enough. He hesitated but a moment, then moved to go around her. "I beg your pardon, Mr. Heart," she said, placing her hand upon his chest to halt him, "but some things simply aren't done. You do not enter a lady's bedroom without an invitation." The words were no sooner out than Amy realized exactly where the reprimand had come from.

Her mother had taught all her protégées that rule—
no customer was allowed entry into a girl's bedroom
without explicit permission. Such formality was intended to eliminate disastrous surprises, as well as
protect what little privacy the girls had.

Much to Amy's relief, Walker didn't argue. He
seemed at a loss for words, even embarrassed.

"Well, I...I guess I'd better go."

"Yes, I guess you'd better."

He strode to the front door, then jerked it open.
"Thanks for the biscuits," he said over his shoulder,
though he didn't sound thankful at all.

Amy pursed her lips in a tight smile. "My pleasure."

She followed behind him, then stood on the threshold, watching as he slowly made his way to the edge
of the porch. He stopped before he reached the steps
and looked north toward Havilah. After a moment, he
turned and faced her.

Amy raised a defensive brow. "Yes?" she
prompted. "Was there something you forgot?"

He looked her square in the eyes. "Yeah," he said.
"My backbone." Walker wrapped his hand around
the porch post. "Look, I'm not real good at tea and
biscuit manners, but I'm no monster, either. The reason I rode down here was because...well...we got off
to a bad start the other day and now...well, here we
go again. It seems we can't talk without gettin' all
riled up at each other."

Was he apologizing? Amy searched his handsome
face but couldn't seem to get past his eyes. Such

beautiful eyes for a man. So expressive. A girl could lose her heart just gazing into them.

He nudged his hat up his forehead. "So anyway…I got somethin' to say and I don't want to leave here till I've said it."

He wasn't apologizing, she realized. But he seemed to be making a genuine effort to talk to her in a reasonable manner, which was better than sarcasm and a Pinkerton threat.

"All right. I'm listening." Curious but guarded, Amy crossed her arms in front of her and leaned against the door frame. She avoided looking into his eyes.

Walker sat sideways on the porch rail, his right leg bent at the knee. "I don't know anything about you 'cept what little you've told me and what I can see with my own eyes," he began. His gaze ran up, then down the length of her body as he spoke. "And what I see is you're a lady. You'll never make it out here on your own. Ranchin' and cattle—that's men's work. I've only known one woman cattle rancher, and believe me she was no lady."

"Mr. Heart—"

"Call me Walker," he interrupted, "and let me finish." His polite insistence cut her off and kept her quiet. "I don't want you to take this wrong—like I'm tryin' to scare you off or somethin'." He removed his hat and set it on the crook of his knee. "Heartbreak Ranch…well, it's…my life and I'm not going to give it up without a fight."

"I don't blame you," she replied. She had been

here only a few days and already she had fallen in love with the vast expanse of grazing land and the surrounding mountains. She could imagine how he felt, thinking he might lose it all and not even know why. She looked away, feeling guilty for her deceit.

"What's wrong?" He left the porch rail and came toward her.

Amy took an unconscious step back. "Nothing's wrong." But, in truth, Walker's honest admission of his feelings left her drained of all energy and fight. "I'm just tired. I didn't sleep particularly well last night."

"Sure you're not comin' down with somethin'?"

"I'm sure." She stood up straight as if to prove her point. He took another step toward her, forcing her to look up at him.

"I just want to add one thing," he said. "The other day…I said some things…implied some things about you and your ma that I shouldn't have."

Those implications, still fresh in her memory, sent a surge of anger through her. "Don't insult me by saying you didn't mean them," Amy snapped, her chin jutting forward with wounded pride. She stared at him, her gaze narrowing. "But tell me, Mr. Heart— I mean, Walker," she corrected herself. "Do you still think I look like the kind of woman who would offer her—what did you call them?—oh, yes, services in exchange for money? Look at me closely and tell me what you see, because if I do—if I do look like that kind of woman, I— I—" She stopped midsentence, mortified to realize he was doing just as she had asked—looking at her. Intently looking at her. Amy's mind went blank as her body grew hot. Just because she'd told him to look at her didn't mean he had to do it like that, with such fervor. Point lost, she had no idea how to continue.

His eyes actually glimmered. What did he see for heaven's sake? It was a sure bet he wasn't seeing the proper, sophisticated, young woman she'd intended him to see. Feeling suddenly breathless and light-headed, she lifted her bodice away from her skin. She could feel her face redden beneath his scrutiny and told herself to turn and walk away, but somehow she couldn't seem to make herself take that first step.

Walker took it for her. One step closer brought them toe to toe. Amy watched as he raised his hand and cradled her chin between his fingers. "You want to know what I see? I see a smart and beautiful young woman who's too stubborn and independent for her own good." His eyes were so light blue they appeared silver. She could see herself on their glittering surface.

"Walker? There's something I need to tell—" The words died in her throat. She couldn't do it. Not now.

Walker was mesmerized by the contrast between his rough, suntanned hand—the hand he used to tie up calves and cock a pistol—and her soft, ivory face. To think that she was that same creamy white all over stirred him in ways he had never experienced with any other woman.

"I don't want to talk anymore," he said, bending his head toward hers. He hadn't meant to kiss her, but he couldn't help himself. Not even a saint could have resisted such a vulnerable and bewildered look. And there was one other thing. He'd seen it in her eyes the moment he'd gotten down off his horse and confronted her that first day. She was attracted to him. She probably wouldn't admit it—even to herself—but there were some things that eyes couldn't hide.

The emotions that came with kissing her took him by surprise. He wasn't sure what he'd expected, but it sure wasn't this all-consuming need to hold her against his body and never let her go. He moved his hand away from her chin and explored the soft contours of her jaw and cheek and realized how delicate she was—like the spring poppies that grew on the hillside.

His mouth moved over hers gently yet insistently, coaxing her lips apart, tasting the sweetness just within. When he felt her tremble, he moved his hand around behind her head, steadying her. She opened her mouth to him, moaning softly, pleading unintelligibly for him to stop, even as she stretched up and twined her arms around his neck. Like a schoolboy, he shivered with excitement, but then the man took over and he pulled her close.

The last thing Amy had expected from this day was to find herself in Walker Heart's arms. What had she said to bring it about? What had he said? For the life of her she couldn't think of a thing, but with each passing second it mattered less and less. Nobody had ever kissed her like Walker was kissing her, as if she were revered, cherished. There was tenderness in him that confused her, that could almost make her believe he was in love with her.

In some distant region of her mind, Amy knew that was impossible. Walker Heart couldn't love her. She was his enemy.

Yet, there had to be something there. No man could kiss a woman the way he was kissing her and not feel *something* for her.

"God, Amy, you have no idea what you're doing to me," he whispered, his lips exploring her neck.

You have no idea what you're doing to me, she repeated to herself. It wasn't just the kiss or the way he was holding her; it was more than that. It was a sense of well-being, of closeness and of joy. She'd never experienced feelings like these before.

"Walker." It took every bit of her will to push her hands against his chest. But she had to stop him— and herself—before things got out of control. She knew if she didn't stop him now it might be impossible to stop him later. He held her a moment longer as if to test her. She remained firm, then took a step backward, breathing heavily. "I think you'd better leave," she said, her heart aching under her breast.

His hands slipped away. "I think you're right."

CHAPTER THREE

AMY KEPT HER MIND busy by doing what she could to fix things inside and outside the house. But there was a lot that needed doing and a body could only do so much without new lumber, whitewash and muscle.

Most of all the roof needed fixing. It was full of acorn-size holes, as was the wood siding. The whole house seemed to be a haven for an army of tireless, redheaded woodpeckers. A long-dead oak tree standing nearby served as their multilevel home, though Amy would have sworn they rarely used it. The birds spent the mornings pecking holes in the roof, the afternoons pecking holes in the siding and the evenings feeding their screaming babies—a whole new generation of wood-pecking pests.

The days went by quickly, spent chasing the birds away and doing chores. It was the nights she dreaded, when there was nothing to occupy her mind, nothing to keep her from thinking about Walker Heart, his words, his kiss, his embrace, his desire for her. Her desire for him. Each night loomed longer and lonelier than the one before it.

It had been two weeks since Walker's last visit but it seemed much longer. Toddy by her side, Amy sat on the porch step, arms wrapped around her knees, watching the most spectacular sunset she'd ever seen. The sun's last rays ignited the low clouds clustered over the Tehachapi Mountains, setting them ablaze with bright orange light. It was the kind of sunset poets wrote about, to be appreciated by lovers, not by a lone woman and her dog.

Amy put her arm around Toddy and pulled him close. "Oh, Toddy, what have I gotten myself into?" Toddy licked her hand and she reached up and scratched him behind his ears. "I can't stop thinking about him no matter what I do." Toddy stared at her, head cocked to one side as if considering her dilemma. He made a funny, whiny sound that made Amy smile. "You're right," she said. "I'm feeling sorry for myself." She kissed him on the snout, then got up. "Come on, boy. Time for supper."

Amy took one last, wistful look at the disappearing sunset, then stepped into the shack.

A THUNDEROUS NOISE pounded the roof. Amy woke with a start and bolted upright. Toddy scampered out from under the covers and barked.

The pounding continued, but it didn't sound like any thunder she'd ever heard. The woodpeckers? No, it couldn't be. Even if they all attacked the roof at the same time, they couldn't make that kind of noise. A hailstorm maybe?

Amy sprang out of bed and ran barefoot into the other room. Dirt and dust fell like heavy snow from the ceiling onto the table, the chairs—everywhere she had spent so much time cleaning. Fearing the roof might collapse at any second, she caught hold of Toddy's collar, opened the door and ran outside.

It was with something like dismay that Amy saw there was no army of birds, no dark, thunderous storm clouds, no hailstorm. Nothing! What then? An animal? She shrank back toward the door, pulling Toddy with her. Maybe the raccoon had come back and was on the roof. Or maybe something bigger—like a bear! Not wanting to take any chances, she turned to run inside.

The pounding stopped.

''Amy. You finally up?''

Both Amy and Toddy looked up and stared at the porch's overhang as if they could see the speaker through the wood and shingle.

Not a raccoon. Not a bear. But a polecat named Walker Heart!

Toddy let loose with a series of howls and Amy stomped down the porch step into the open. A few paces out, she turned, shaded her eyes and glared up at Walker who was straddling the peak of the roof.

''Mornin'.'' Walker lifted a gloved hand. ''I know it's a mite early, but I wanted to—''

''Quiet!'' Amy shouted at Toddy to stop his howling. Much to her surprise, the command silenced both Toddy and Walker. ''What are you doing up there?''

Walker grinned. ''Fixin' the roof.''

''But it's—it's barely even light out.'' Amy gestured at the sun, just beginning to creep over the horizon.

"It's a big job. I needed to get an early start."

"Well, you've certainly done that. I don't suppose you could have given me some warning?"

"I told you that until I heard from the Pinkerton man, I was gonna run this ranch the way I always have. The roof has to be fixed before the next brandin'."

Amy bristled at the reminder of the Pinkerton man, ignoring most of what else he said. Second to Walker's kissing her, she'd thought of little else. "You still could have had the courtesy to tell me," she snapped. "I spent a lot of time cleaning things up, and now, because of your hammering, there's dirt all over everything."

"So I see," he intoned, his gaze traveling downward.

Confused by his answer and his too-intimate expression, Amy bent her head and looked down at herself. It wasn't the dirt that made her draw in her breath, but that she was wearing her nightgown.

She could have screamed. *Would* have screamed if she hadn't been so embarrassed. She grabbed Toddy's collar, made a dash for the house, then bolted the door behind her.

"I should have known he'd do something like this," she said, looking down at Toddy. "He probably thinks if he makes our lives miserable enough we'll just pick up and leave." Toddy gave a low growl that Amy interpreted as agreement. She shook her head and patted him comfortingly. "No, don't worry. We're not leaving. We have every right to be here. Sort of.''

Feeling calmer after her talk with Toddy, she dashed around the house gathering up all her personal belongings, then piled them in the bedroom and covered them up. She draped a blue checkered tablecloth over her mother's painting and spread an old blanket over her bed quilt. The journal lay on the trunk beside the bed. She hadn't had time to read it in its entirety, but perhaps today would be the day since she could do little else thanks to Walker.

Moments later Amy left the house carrying a blanket, a food basket and the journal. Toddy prancing by her side, she marched like an infantry soldier toward a grassy knoll near the corral. Considering Walker's curiosity of what was in her bedroom, she wanted to stay close enough to the house to keep an eye on him.

''Hey! Where are you going?'' Walker called after her.

Amy jutted out her chin and kept walking, her sights set on an oak tree. The tree's leafy branches would provide shade and its trunk would make a solid backrest. She laid her blanket beneath the tree and sat down.

''Sit, Toddy.'' As soon as he sat, she removed his leash, confidant he'd stay close. Two days ago he'd learned his lesson about chasing cattle when one of them chased him. Since then, he'd been content to observe them from afar.

After situating herself, Amy opened the journal to

the section entitled "My Life—Bella Duprey" and
began reading.

My darling Amy,
If you are reading this, it is because I am unable
to educate you in the Art Of Fascination. It is
not my wish that you follow in my footsteps and
become a courtesan. I want more for you than
that. I want you to have a home, a husband and
a family—all the things I never had. Because I
know you want this, too, I have written this journal in the hopes that it will help you attract, manage and keep the man you love.
Here, in these pages, you will find the secrets of
my success—methods and techniques in the art
of understanding and pleasing a man. Some of
them may shock you. Others you may find
laughable. But trust me, done properly, they all
work! One word of caution—if you are not de-
sirous of a particular man's attentions, be wary
of casual experimentation.

Amy hadn't realized that the journal was written
specifically for her, although Howard had suggested
as much. That her mother would go to so much work
for her benefit brought a smile to her lips and tears
to her eyes.
She turned the page and was immediately engrossed in her mother's writings. She read that her
mother had made a habit of observing men—their
likes, dislikes and responses. With this knowledge,

she felt she could assess a man's temperament as well as determine the best way to enhance his sexual pleasure. Each page confirmed just how dedicated her mother had been to her profession. She'd left nothing to chance. After purchasing the Cock O' The Walk, she'd hired a Chinese herbalist to help her develop aphrodisiacs, elixirs and potions to soothe the mind, heal the body and heighten sexual pleasure.

This explained the bottles in the bottom of the trunk.

Amy skimmed through the pages of the recipe section, thinking of them as witches' brews. Then a thought crossed her mind. Might there be a potion she could mix up and use on Walker to soften his heart? She quickly turned the page, chiding herself for even thinking such a thing. If there was such a magical formula, she could never bring herself to use it.

Amy figured it was well past noon by the way the shadows fell. She had to read only another twenty pages or so of the journal and she'd be finished. Tired of sitting, she stretched out on her stomach and propped herself up on her elbows.

Toddy lay down beside her and rested his long nose between his front paws.

To become accomplished in the Art of Fascination, you must be willing to explore even the most unconventional methods. Several years ago an idea came to me quite by accident, after a devoted gentleman friend gave me Toddy.

Curious as to how Toddy figured into things, Amy leaned closer to the page, not wanting to miss a single word. Nothing could have surprised her more than to read her mother's theory that a man could be trained in much the same way as a dog. She laughed out loud at the ridiculousness of it but continued to read—page after page of instruction on how to correct a man's behavioral problems with training methods similar to those used for a dog.

It is all in the communication. You must make very clear what you want. And use short commands because men, like dogs, sometimes get confused.

Now Amy knew what Howard meant when he said Toddy taught Bella more about men than all the courtesans in France.

"Toddy, sit," Amy said, putting her mother's theory to test. The big poodle sat down. "Good boy," she congratulated him. "Speak." He began to bark. "Quiet," she told him and he stopped.

It was then she remembered that this morning she had seen for herself how commanding Toddy to be quiet had inadvertently silenced Walker as well. And when Walker had ruined her only decent batch of biscuits, she'd ordered him to sit and he'd sat!

"Good heavens!" she whispered, stunned. Her mother's theory did indeed appear to work, but— How awful! How demeaning! She could never bring herself to use such underhanded tactics to—

Uninvited, a trio of recent and rather demeaning events popped into her head: Walker refusing to move his horse so she could get the deed from her trunk; Walker chastising her for not knowing the difference between green wood and seasoned wood; and Walker inspecting her biscuits, then having the audacity to call them puny.

One corner of her mouth drew taut and her eyes narrowed to slits as she gave in to her devilish thoughts…and the delightful possibilities.

She went back to the first line where Toddy was mentioned and pored over the lessons, laughing even as she committed them to memory.

It was late afternoon when she finished and started back to the house. Approaching the corral, Amy stopped short when she looked up and saw Walker standing on the roof unbuttoning his shirt. She went breathlessly still as she watched him peel it off. His sweat-slick arms were heavy with muscle, and a dark thatch of hair covered his chest, narrowing as it ran down his stomach and disappeared into his pants. He looked hot, tired and entirely too appealing for any man to look, especially after a day of hard physical labor.

"I'm just about finished," he said, crumpling the shirt into a ball, then tossing it down. "Here. Catch."

Hypnotized by the wide expanse of Walker's chest and the rugged breadth of his shoulders, Amy didn't see the garment until it dropped on top of her head. While fighting to get it off, she heard Walker laughing. She threw the shirt to the ground and glared up at him.

His laughter stopped abruptly when he lost his footing. Amy's mouth opened to shout a warning but nothing came out. She watched fearfully as he struggled to maintain his balance, his arms windmilling. In the end, he was unable to save himself and gave in to the roof's slippery slant.

The ground under her feet seemed to vibrate with the force of his landing.

"Walker!" She hiked up her skirts and ran to his side.

Flat on his back, spread-eagle, he lay still as death. In a panic, she knelt beside him. "Walker?" His eyes were wide open but he didn't seem to see her. "Walker, oh, no, please." Amy looked him over for signs of broken bones and blood, but there were no visible injuries. With shaky hands, she carefully turned his head toward her. "Walker, please say you're all right."

He lifted his hand and clasped it around her arm, squeezing tight as he gulped air back into his lungs.

"I—I'm all—right," he managed at last, releasing his hold on her arm. "Just got…the wind… knocked—" He started to cough.

Amy bowed her head and thanked God. For all the anger and mistrust between them, she didn't wish him harm. When she looked up again, she saw Toddy standing next to Walker's head. In an uncharacteristic display of affection, he licked Walker's face.

"Get him...stop—" Walker sputtered between gasps.

"Toddy! Don't do that," Amy commanded, but instead of obeying her, he did it again.

"Damn dog... I'm gonna—kill—" Walker choked out as he rolled over onto the hem of Amy's skirt.

"Toddy! No!" Amy shouted.

Toddy turned and headed for the house, his tail between his legs.

"I'm sorry. He must really like you." She looked down and saw Walker's head lying on her skirt in the junction between her thighs. She took in a startled breath, then tried to hide her shock when he glanced up at her.

"Just give me a minute," he said, as if reading her thoughts.

Unable to speak, she could only nod.

Minutes later Walker was breathing more normally. He made a face as he lifted his head off her skirt and raised himself on one elbow.

"Let me help you," Amy offered, reaching toward him. She wasn't sure how much assistance she could give, considering he probably outweighed her by a hundred pounds or more. But she would do what she could.

"No. Leave me be."

Amy ignored him. "Oh, don't be silly." She jumped to her feet, bent down in front of him and was reaching toward him when he swore at her under his breath.

"I said leave me be." He waved her away, then,

amid grunts and groans, rolled to his knees and began easing himself up.

Hands clenched together against her heart, Amy watched his struggle and felt his pain almost as strongly as if it were her own. Why he would refuse her help, she could only guess. Masculine pride, perhaps. Or maybe just bullheadedness. Whatever the reason, it simply wasn't good enough.

He was halfway between a stoop and a stand and making poor progress when Amy bent down in front of him, wrapped her arms around his bare middle and helped lift him to his feet. Even after they were standing, she continued to hold him close to her, afraid to let him go.

With her cheek pressed against his chest, she could feel the vibration of his voice, hear the rapid beating of his heart. Memories of another day—of him holding her, kissing her—flashed through her mind. She closed her eyes and let the memory envelop her.

"I thought I told you to leave me be," he said in a tone that effectively ended her daydream.

She pulled back to look up at him. "So you did, but it happens that I don't respond well to being ordered around."

"I've noticed."

She smiled, pleased with herself that she'd stood her ground.

Amy released him then and took a step backward. "Can you walk?"

"Yeah. No. I don't know. My back hurts like a son of a—!"

"Walker Heart! I will not tolerate cursing!"

"For God's sake, Amy! This is no time—" Whatever he was about to say ended when he took a step forward and faltered.

Amy saw the difficulty he was having and moved around to his side. "Put your arm around my shoulder and lean on me." When he didn't make a move to do as she suggested, she did it for him. "Now, then, let's take it real easy. One step at a time."

Once they were in the house, Amy steered Walker toward the bedroom. She maneuvered him through the door, then propped him against the door frame.

"Stay here a minute. I have to take the blanket off the bed."

"Don't go to any extra trouble for me." He took a step forward.

"Walker, stay!" she shouted, halting him before he could take another step. Amy didn't have time to ponder the fact that she'd used a dog command to get him to listen to her, because the second she turned around, she confronted the blue-checkered tablecloth covering her mother's painting.

She froze, her heart racing, as she tried to think of what to do. Short of ordering him back outside, then telling him to mount up and ride out, there wasn't anything she could do, except hope for a miracle that he wouldn't ask what she was hiding.

Taking a deep breath, she took the debris-covered blanket off the bed, then started fluffing the pillow.

Walker made a sound in his throat that was a combination of impatience and pain.

Keep the training lessons short. The journal's lessons came to her unbidden, but she didn't shut them out. If ever she needed help on handling a man, it was now. And whether she approved of the method or not, anything was preferable to his seeing the painting and discovering her secrets. *If you work with him for too long at one time, he'll become bored and won't respond at all.*

Amy hurried to finish.

"Ready?" she asked. He growled an indistinguishable answer and pushed off the door frame as she started toward him. "Wait for me," she said, ducking under his arm. Amy gritted her teeth as she prepared to bear his weight, but instead he dropped his arm from around her shoulders and moved forward on his own.

"Walker Heart!" She brandished his name like a weapon and slipped around in front of him, splaying her hands flat against his chest to prevent him from taking another step. "You're going to do as I say or else!" she threatened, her voice throbbing with anger and frustration. Too late she remembered her mother's cautionary note.

Never lose your temper. Yelling and stamping around in anger will only make things worse, and he'll be reluctant to respond to your training.

"I—I'm sorry," she offered, hoping to undo any damage she might have caused. When she realized she was speaking to his chest, she tilted her head back and looked up. His expression was tight with strain.

"I really must insist that you let me help you. One wrong move and you could hurt yourself even more."

Believing that she had appealed to his common sense, Amy tried again and this time found him slightly more cooperative. Still, getting Walker into bed was no easy task. He was not a small man and pain made him inflexible.

Muttering an oath, he sat down on the edge of the bed.

Turning, lifting, pushing and pulling, Amy managed to lay him down.

"There now. That should do it," she said, adjusting the pillow beneath his head.

"I can't lie here like this," he complained. "I feel like a corpse. I need pillows to prop me up."

She shook her head. "What you need is to lie flat."

"You a doc?" he snapped.

"No, but I often helped my mother take care of her girls. They were always straining their backs and—" She broke off, the reality of what she'd said hitting her like a slap on the face. She glanced down at Walker and was relieved to see that he wasn't paying her any attention. He was too busy trying to get himself comfortable.

Admonishing herself for always saying the first thing that came into her head, Amy moved to the end of the bed, grabbed his left boot and started to tug.

"Hey!" he shouted. He shook his foot lose of her hand. "The boots stay on."

Remember who is in charge. Be confident in your authority.

"Not in my bed they don't," she said in a voice that brooked no argument. Before he could respond, she grabbed his boots by the heels and tugged them off. "I'll just leave them by the door."

"Thanks," he replied to her back as she set the boots on the floor.

A moment later she was back, pulling off his socks. She tossed them on the floor next to his boots. Coming around to the side of the bed, she leaned forward and started toward his belt buckle.

He grabbed her hands in midmotion. "If you want to take my pants off it's fine with me. But I think I should warn you that I'm not wearin' anything underneath."

Amy snatched her hands away. What on earth had she been thinking? Obviously, she'd gotten carried away with her nursing duties. His smug expression mocked her, but she refused to let him see her mortification.

"Thank you for the warning. It didn't occur to me that you wouldn't be wearing any—I mean—I just wanted you to be comfortable."

"I'm as comfortable as I'm gonna to get, considerin'." He gave her a disgruntled look, then turned his face toward the wall.

"Good. That's…good."

Without another word, Amy fled the room and closed the door behind her.

CHAPTER FOUR

WALKER WAS HALF-ASLEEP when Amy bustled back into the bedroom, making more noise than a bunkhouse full of booted ranch hands. He cracked one eye open and saw her set a washbasin down on the trunk beside the bed. Wearing a starched white apron with a towel draped over one of her shoulders, she dipped a cloth into the basin, then rubbed it against a large cake of soap. He waited until she was leaning over him, her hand inches above his face, then he opened his eyes wide and glared at her.

"What the hell are you doin'?" He gave her an accusing look.

Amy bristled like a porcupine. "I was about to clean some of the dirt off you. I guess I'd better start with that mouth of yours." He intercepted her hand before she could stuff the soapy cloth into his mouth.

"I'm a little past that age, don't you think?"

"Apparently age has nothing to do with bad behavior."

"Bad behavior, huh? If you're bent on tryin' to change me into somethin' I'm not, you can forget it. I am the way I am. I spend my days and sometimes my nights with ornery steers and cuss words are the only language they understand."

"All I ask is that you make an effort not to swear in front of me. Now, if I may proceed?"

"With what?"

"Cleaning you up."

"No thanks. I'd like to try to get some shut-eye."

Before he knew what she was about, she swiped the cloth across his chest, then held it for him to see. It was filthy.

"Do what you gotta do," he said, resigned.

Amy gave him an indulgent smile as she stretched out her arm and pushed his hair back from his forehead. He watched her closely as she performed the task of washing his face and wished, not for the first time, that things could be different between them. But until he heard from the Pinkerton man, he needed to keep his guard up.

"As soon as I'm through, we'll see about getting you home. I'll take your horse and go tell your men you're here—"

"No!" he replied sharply. That would be all he needed. If she found out he'd been keeping the truth from her about the real homestead, she'd never give up the deed.

Amy laughed lightly. "Well, you can't stay *here*."

"Why not?"

She seemed to flounder before his questioning gaze. "Well, because you can't. It wouldn't be right...you and me together...all night long. There's a matter of propriety, you know. People would talk and my reputation would be ruined."

"What people?"

"The neighbors."

"What neighbors?"

Amy pulled back and stared at him. "There aren't any neighbors?"

"This is a big ranch, Amy. The closest ones are in Havilah. Nobody's gonna find out if we don't tell them."

"But—"

"No buts. I'm stayin' and that's that. Besides, nobody can ride Outlaw but me. He'd buck you off even before you got in the saddle." She was silent, defeated, he hoped. "Don't look so glum. It's only for one night. Come mornin' I'll be right as rain and back up on top of that roof."

Amy rolled her eyes. She wished she shared his optimism, but conversely, she thought he'd probably feel worse than ever come morning.

Weary of fighting him on every issue and weary of standing and leaning over him, Amy sat down on the edge of the bed and devoted herself to the task at hand. She washed his neck, arms and upper chest. She couldn't help but admire his well-developed muscles. His physical presence not only filled the bed but filled the room, creating a sexual awareness in her that she'd never experienced before. The thought that he would be spending the entire night in her house, in her bedroom, in her bed, caused beads of perspiration to break out on her upper lip.

Wishing she'd never started bathing him in the first place, Amy hurried to be done with it. As she moved the cloth in a circular pattern down his stomach, her thumb came in contact with the top edge of his belt buckle. Remembering his warning, her hand slowed.

She slid her gaze to his face and saw that his eyes were closed. He appeared totally relaxed, which struck her as ironic since he'd made so much fuss about being bathed. Determined not to let her thoughts about what he wasn't wearing beneath his pants get the best of her, she carried on. Moments later, her hand was once again at the bottom of the circle near the buckle. Before she could talk herself out of it, she pressed down lightly and ran her thumb below the buckle, touching skin she couldn't see.

She inhaled sharply as a surge of fiery heat raced through her body. Unable to fathom how so simple an action could cause such an alarming reaction, she stared at her hand as if it had betrayed her.

WALKER WATCHED her from beneath lowered lids, fascinated. Emotions flitted like evening shadows across her face, one after another. Determination, confusion, surprise. Desire. A man would have to be stone-blind not to see it and pushing petunias from six feet under not to feel it. When her hand slowed, he knew she was remembering what he'd said about not wearing anything under his pants. Had she thought him awake, she wouldn't have gone anywhere near that belt buckle. But because she thought him sleeping, she not only went near it, but below it. In fact, another inch and she would discover the profound effect she was having on him.

He closed his eyes and waited to see what she

would do next. He was disappointed when he heard the sound of her rinsing out the cloth. When she again touched him with the cold cloth, he flinched and pretended to come awake.

"I'm almost finished," she said, a worried look upon her face.

For some inexplicable reason he felt compelled to guard her secret. "I must have nodded off."

"Rest *is* the best thing," she answered in a breathy voice. "I think I'll go see about fixing something to eat. I imagine you must be hungry."

"Starved," he said, meaning it far differently from how she would take it.

Seconds after Amy left the room, Toddy walked in, stood beside the bed and looked at him with expectation.

Walker eyed him suspiciously. "What do you want?" Damned if that wasn't the silliest-looking dog he'd ever seen. Toddy whined softly, then sat back on his haunches and lifted his right paw as Walker had seen him do with Amy. "No. I don't wanna shake hands," he mumbled beneath his breath.

Toddy cocked his head and whined again. Walker glanced toward the open doorway and saw Amy standing at the table, her back to the bedroom. He slid his hand over the edge of the bed, grabbed Toddy's paw and gave it a quick shake.

"All right now, outta here," he whispered gruffly, jerking his hand away.

Hanging his head as if he'd been reprimanded, Toddy got up and walked toward the door. He stopped near the threshold, looked back toward the bed, then lifted his leg and peed on Walker's boots.

AMY COULDN'T GET Walker's belt buckle off her mind. While stoking the fire for her stew pot, she reflected upon what she'd done and vowed not to let anything like that happen again. The journal had warned her about the dangers of casual experimentation and now she knew why. It worried her to think that if she hadn't been so afraid he'd wake up and catch her, she actually might have gone lower.

Amy backed away from the fire, the heat suddenly unbearable.

As the stew cooked, Amy went outside and corralled Walker's horse. She considered ignoring Walker's warning that nobody could ride Outlaw except him, but she didn't have enough confidence in her horsemanship to take the chance.

On her way back to the house, she picked up the things she'd dropped when Walker fell off the roof. She would have to be careful not to let him see the journal. If he ever read it, there was no telling what he would do.

Walker was snoring softly as Amy entered the house. She tiptoed into the bedroom, put the journal back in the trunk and left the room.

Not a minute later, he woke up.

"Amy?"

"I hope you're hungry," she answered from the kitchen. "I've got enough stew to feed a house full of hungry whores." The second the words were out, she gasped, then clamped her hand over her mouth. In spite of her boarding school education, there were a few of her mother's expressions that she just couldn't seem to stop herself from saying.

"What did you say?"

Amy could hear the uncertainty in his voice and knew he wasn't sure he'd heard her correctly.

"I said, I've got enough stew to feed a hungry horse." She stood next to the table, gripping the back of the chair, awaiting his answer. None came. It was Toddy's cold, wet nose nudging her elbow, reminding her he was hungry, that got her moving again.

"Just a second," she told him, then ladled out a generous portion of stew into a bowl and set it on the floor. When it came to suppertime, Toddy was a beggar who turned into a thief if he didn't get fed right away.

Once Toddy was settled, Amy looked around for something she could use for a tray. She found an old wooden box lid and covered it with a blue-and-white checkered napkin, then spent several minutes arranging and rearranging a large bowl of steaming hot stew, a knife and spoon, two perfectly browned biscuits from yesterday's baking, and a cupful of rich black coffee.

Walker looked up when she came into the room. "Let me set this tray down, then I'll help you sit up." She was prepared for him to be difficult and refuse her help as he had earlier. This time, however, he didn't make a move, but waited patiently for her assistance.

Was he in too much pain to be difficult? Or was his good behavior a direct result of the dog training commands she had used earlier? Her lips pursed with a smile that threatened to take over her face.

Sitting Walker up proved almost as difficult as getting him into bed. After propping pillows behind his back, she placed the tray on his lap, then moved away and sat down near the footrail.

Amy waited for him to eat a few bites before beginning a conversation. "Tell me, why do you call this place Heartbreak Ranch? It's such a sad name."

"My ma named it. Said it broke her heart when Pa up and decided they should leave Philadelphia and go west."

"How long ago was that?"

He shrugged and shook his head. "Before the war. I remember we had a big, fancy house full of furniture I wasn't allowed to sit on, and servants to cook and clean."

"Why would your father give up all that...for this?" She gestured with a sweep of her hand.

"He'd worked in Gramps's dry-goods store since he was old enough to count, and hated it. Claimed he wasn't a salesman. He hankered to work outdoors."

Amy lifted her chin and looked up at the cloth-covered painting hanging behind Walker's head. Sam Heart had given up a beautiful home and a lucrative business to make his dreams come true. Then he destroyed her mother's dreams by betraying her.

"I know all about dreams," she told him. "When

my mother died, I vowed to make her dream of living on a ranch come true."

"And so, this is it?"

Amy nodded. "Your father must have been a better salesman than he thought to sell my mother a ranch she'd never seen," she jested lightly, knowing she was stretching the truth considerably to say that Sam sold the property, when he had most probably lost it to her mother at faro.

"We don't know that he sold it to her," Walker reminded her pointedly.

"No, we don't," Amy returned with all sincerity. In fact, she had no idea whether or not her mother had ever carried out her revenge. Changing the subject, she asked, "Were you and your father close?"

Walker appeared to consider the question before speaking. "We used to be...before Ma died."

When he didn't volunteer any more, Amy gently coaxed him into answering a few more questions but soon realized she'd made a mistake. She didn't want to know that Sam Heart had loved his wife or that he'd been a good father. She needed to think of him as the man who'd broken her mother's heart, the scoundrel who'd bet he could make a fool of Bella Duprey.

"After Ma died he just wasn't himself anymore. He started actin' funny—real restless-like. Nothin' I did—nothin' anyone did—satisfied him. Then he started takin' up with that woman." He shook his head in disgust.

Amy's heart leaped into her throat. "Woman? Wh-what woman?" To her dismay, her voice broke slightly.

"Jersey Lil. Runs the saloon in Havilah. I knew he was lonely, but I didn't figure he'd get himself involved with *that* kind of woman. A whore. When the business of the boundary dispute came up, I suggested he go to San Francisco and spend some extra time there. Just so's he'd be away from her."

From the tone of his voice, Amy knew Walker was feeling responsible for his father's apparent disappearance. She wanted to tell him he had nothing to do with what had happened between his father and her mother, but she couldn't. Not now. Maybe never.

LYING IN FRONT of the fire on her makeshift pallet of blankets, Amy stared into the low-burning flames. She'd turned from side to side so often in the past few hours that she felt like a well-roasted pig. She'd tried everything to fall asleep. Counted sheep. Counted the knotholes in the ceiling beams. Even tried to hypnotize herself by gazing at the sparks drifting up the chimney.

She couldn't stop thinking about Walker. Walker striding toward her in anger that first day. Walker holding her after she'd run blindly out of the smoke-filled house. Walker kissing her in the doorway. Walker's belt buckle. Walker lying in her bed, half-naked.

She put an arm around Toddy and nuzzled her chin into the curls atop his head. "What am I going to do, boy?" she asked in a troubled whisper. "I can't let

myself love him. There's too much between us. Too
many secrets. Too many lies.'' Even if the Pinkerton
man didn't discover the truth, *she* knew the truth—at
least most of it—and it was getting harder and harder
to keep it from Walker. Toddy cocked his head to the
side consideringly.

Guilt had been stabbing at her from opposite directions for several days. From Walker, because he
deserved to know what had become of his father. And
from her mother, because revealing what she knew to
Walker would be a betrayal.

A loud noise in the other room alerted Toddy. He
ran to investigate and started barking.

"Shut up, you miserable excuse for a dog," Walker said between his teeth. "Get out of here before
I—"

"What's going on?" Amy asked, staring at him
from the doorway. Walker lay on his side, his leg over
the edge of the bed and one foot on the floor. She
rushed over to him and started to help him back into
bed.

"No," he roared. "I have to get up."

"Don't be ridiculous. It's the middle of the night."

He grabbed both her arms and used them to bring
himself to a sitting position. "I don't care what time
it is. I have to go to the outhouse!"

Amy felt her face flame. "Oh, of course." She
thought about it a moment. "But you don't have to
go outside. The chamber pot is under the bed."

"No, thank you." Before she could offer him her
assistance, he rose to his feet.

"I'll go with you," she blurted, lifting his arm around her shoulder.

Walker took a step forward, then stopped. "This is one thing you can't help me with, all right?"

Suddenly realizing that she had actually offered to take him to the outhouse, she stepped back. That she felt foolish was a gross understatement. She didn't even want to imagine what he must be thinking.

It seemed like hours rather than minutes before he returned. He appeared none the worse for his late-night outing. In fact, he looked to be moving a little easier. She preceded him into the bedroom and waited for him at the edge of the bed.

"Walker, lie down." The dog command rolled too easily off her tongue. She was beginning to wish she'd never read her mother's journal.

"I wish you'd stop fussin' over me."

"I'm not fussing over you, for heaven's sake, I'm just trying to help," she said defensively, grabbing one of his arms. She positioned herself in front of him, a few inches right of his leg, and held on to him as he bent his knees and lowered himself toward the mattress. He was halfway there when she realized she didn't have sufficient strength to hold him.

"Walker! I can't hold—" His weight pulled her toward him.

In a tangle of arms and legs, they tumbled backward, falling onto the foot of the bed. It was a moment before she could recover enough to realize what had happened, and another before she could speak.

"Are you all right?" she asked. Walker lay directly beneath her, his eyes staring blankly at the ceiling.

He took a long time to answer. "I'm not sure yet." When she started to move off him, he groaned. "Don't!" He grabbed her upper arms and held her still. "You'll make it worse."

Afraid to move for fear she would hurt him more, Amy stayed where she was and waited for his cue.

After a moment she asked, "Are you sure I'm not hurting you more by lying on top of you like this? I could just sort of slide off and—"

"No." He pressed his hands to her lower back. "Stay where you are." Slowly his fingers traced up the ridge of her spine from her waist to her shoulders, relaxing her. Then, he slid his hands back down to her hips, his fingers pressing deep into her flesh, as he moved himself beneath her.

Only now, feeling the hard male swell against her abdomen, did Amy realize what was happening. "Walker, I—"

In a movement that took her by surprise, he gathered her in his arms and rolled them onto their sides. Before Amy could guess his intent, his mouth covered hers in a kiss that took her breath away. Ever since that first time he'd kissed her, she'd dreamed of him doing it again.

But unlike that first time, there was no gentleness in him now. His mouth was hard and demanding, almost bruising in its urgency to possess her. With a whimper of bewilderment, Amy held still. He parted her lips with his probing tongue. The shock of it thrusting inside her mouth—and of what those thrusts exemplified—sent her pulse racing and her senses spinning out of control.

"Walker, you mustn't—" she breathed into his heated mouth, even as she wrapped her arms around his neck. Though she'd never before even entertained the idea of making love to a man out of wedlock, though she knew she might be making the biggest mistake of her life and that the consequences could be devastating, she was helpless to stop him from doing whatever he wanted to. It was as if her body and mind were battling to take control of her will, and her body was winning.

A gentle breeze fluttered the blue-checkered tablecloth, reminding Amy of the painting that hung behind it and of her mother's desire that she not become a courtesan.

"Your back!" she said suddenly, her mind making one last attempt to gain control. She unwrapped her arms from around his neck. "You'll hurt yourself more—"

Instead of heeding her warning and releasing her, he kissed her into silence. If he was in pain, he didn't let on. He moved one hand to the back of her head and combed his fingers through her hair. He placed tiny, wet kisses down her cheek, then along the column of her throat.

Pleasure flowed through her veins like fine wine, intensifying a thousandfold when he untied the satin ribbon holding the neck of her nightgown together.

He spread the material wide and kissed the pillow of her breasts.

She moaned deep in her throat, her head pressed back against his arm. She arched her spine, bringing her already taut nipples closer to his lips. She waited impatiently to feel him put his mouth on her body and the moment he did she shuddered in reaction.

Wants and needs—only just acknowledged—overwhelmed her. Surprisingly, with everything she knew about lovemaking, neither her mother nor any of the girls had ever told Amy that a man could make a woman feel like this.

Scared and excited. Weak and strong. Her body alternately burned, then shivered.

A tingle of apprehension coursed through her when Walker slid her nightgown up her body, exposing one hip to the cool air. His fingers splayed over her skin, then moved lightly across her buttocks and down the back of her legs.

"I need you so much, Amy," he whispered against her mouth, his breath fanning the flames of her desire. "Let me love you."

Amy's heart swelled with joy. Was he telling her that he loved her? Or was he being a gentleman and asking her permission to take her? She couldn't be sure. And it didn't matter. Because, despite the moral rules she would be breaking, she had already decided that she wanted him.

Because she loved him.

The realization took her by surprise. And delighted her.

She loved him.

Emboldened by the depth of her feelings, she touched the corner of his mouth with the tip of her finger and whispered back, "Love me, Walker."

He looked deeply into her eyes for a moment, then spoke soberly. "Are you sure, I mean, really sure? I want to know for certain this is what you want."

His touching words only served to fuel her desire. "*You* are what I want."

He needed no further prompting. His hand moved between her thighs, nudging them apart, then closed over her like a white-hot brand.

"Amy. Amy." He groaned her name like a litany as his fingers explored the soft contours of her womanhood.

He groaned again, louder, and this time she heard the pain in his voice.

"Walker, what is it? What's wrong?"

He pushed himself away from her, rolling onto his back, a tortured expression on his face.

Amy rose on an elbow and leaned over him. "Your back?"

He nodded and moments later he laughed—a harsh, bitter laugh that translated his frustration.

Feeling cold and empty, Amy clamped her legs together. She supposed she should be grateful for the reprieve. But she wasn't.

"I'm sorry," he said, his voice raw with regret.

Amy brushed her lips against his mouth, then whispered, "I know. I'm sorry, too. But in a few days, you'll be good as new. Then, if you still want me…"

He guffawed. "*If I still want you?* Amy, I never wanted anything or anyone so much in all my life. I don't know what tricks you're usin', but you got me feelin' things I never felt before."

Tricks? Amy decided it would be prudent not to ask him what he meant.

He loved her. He still hadn't come out and said the words, but he'd said it in other ways, ways he probably hadn't even realized. Knowing that was enough…for now.

You can have it all, my darling daughter. The ranch. The man. And love. You can make both our dreams come true.

Amy looked back over her shoulder at the painting. It was still covered. Beneath her breath, she said, "*Oui,* Mama."

A BRISK BREEZE blew across the basin, ruffling the calico curtains hanging at the bedroom window. Walker had been awake for more than an hour, content to do nothing but think, and listen to the soft cadence of Amy's breathing.

He'd cursed himself a thousand times for falling off the roof. It was his own damn fault. He'd been prancing around like a stud horse showing off for a mare. Now he was paying for his carelessness, and so was Amy.

He nuzzled his lips into her hair, breathing in her scent. Lemon verbena. He was convinced now that his suspicions about her and how she'd gotten the deed to the ranch were unfounded. She'd told him the truth. He didn't need a Pinkerton man to confirm it. It amazed him that he could have ever doubted her. She was an open book—a picture book. There was nothing that couldn't be read right there on her face. Fear. Anger. Passion. Love.

He wondered if he was just as readable, because if he was, she'd know exactly how he felt about her.

He ran his fingers through his hair and watched the sunrise through the window. The breeze kicked up again, blowing the curtains and billowing the checkered tablecloth on the wall, giving him a brief glimpse of the painting beneath.

"What the—?" Carefully, he raised himself on one elbow and waited for the billowing tablecloth to give him another peek. He didn't have long to wait. The wind lifted the tablecloth, revealing what looked to be a woman's nude portrait like the one hanging over the bar at Jersey Lil's.

Amy stirred at his side, stretching like a lazy cat. "Walker? You awake?" Her voice was thick with sleep.

"Uh-huh."

"What are you doing?"

"Tryin' to get a better look at that painting. Looks like one I've seen before, but I can't imagine what you'd be doin' with it."

She stiffened. Then she raised herself up in front of him, blocking his line of vision.

"Lie down and roll over. I'll rub your back."

"No, I want to see it. It looked like—"

The moment she'd been dreading was finally here

and there was nothing she could do but face it. "It's a nude," she said, inching her way off the bed. "But unless you've been in San Francisco in the Cock O' The Walk, you've never seen it before."

She turned away from him and retied the ribbons on her nightgown. Then, taking a deep breath, she reached for the corner of the tablecloth and pulled it off.

Walker could only stare. It was a nude all right, a life-size nude of a woman reclining on a long red velvet settee. His eyes narrowed. His gaze moved over every inch of the woman's painted body—from her slender ankles, to her ruby red mouth, to her violet blue eyes. Incredible eyes.

Amy's eyes.

He pulled a long, hard breath, clenched his jaw, then slid an accusing look at her. "Was my pa as big a sucker as me?"

Even though she'd been expecting this, her eyes filled with tears. "I told you before, I never met your father." She'd thought he loved her, but love was unquestioning loyalty and trust. And he didn't trust her.

He reached across the bed and grabbed the quilt. "I gotta hand it to you, Amy. You fooled me good," he said with contempt.

"I know what you're thinking," she said, pointing to the painting. "That she's me, but you're wrong. I would never—" She stopped herself before saying something that would scorn her mother's memory.

"Come on, Amy," he cajoled, looking at her as if

she were ripe for the plucking. "Your secret is out. Now, how about tellin' me how you got the deed and where my pa is."

Disheartened by his behavior, Amy gathered her clothing from the nail behind the door and stood facing him. "The woman in the painting is my mother, Bella Duprey," she began, hoping her voice wouldn't crack. "She was something of a legend in San Francisco. The Queen of the Barbary Coast. She made the fatal mistake of falling in love with your father, and when he tried to make a fool of her, she cheated him out of the deed to Heartbreak Ranch, then had him shanghaied." She glanced at Walker, who was staring at her openmouthed. "At least that was her plan," she continued. "I don't know for certain, since she died that same night in a fire that destroyed the Cock O' The Walk. It's all written down in her journal. There, in the trunk," she finished, pointing to it beside the bed.

She didn't wait to find out if he had any questions. As far as she was concerned there was nothing more to say.

It was over.

Sick and shaking, she left the bedroom and slammed the door shut behind her. Toddy sat waiting for her by the kitchen table. She kept her gaze trained on his while she changed into her clothes. She understood now how much Toddy had meant to her mother. He was the most loyal and trusting friend a woman could have.

"Let's go for a walk." She fastened his leash and

went outside, no particular destination in mind. Allowed to take the lead, Toddy began an investigation of all the trees in the area. By the time Amy thought about how many trees he'd visited, they had walked a mile or more, all the way to the top of the hill.

A strong breeze blew over the mountains from the west, whipping Amy's skirt about her legs. Shading her eyes against the sun, she looked out over a vast, fertile basin, dotted with grazing cattle and live oak trees. A good distance from where she stood, there was a large white house, surrounded by a white, three-rail fence and a half dozen outbuildings and corrals.

Amy stared at the house in confusion. Walker had told her there weren't any neighbors. Had she misunderstood him? Or had he lied?

Her questions demanded immediate answers. And there was only one way to find out.

Amy marched resolutely down the other side of the hill. The closer she got to the house, the more impressive it was. There were neat green lawns, well-maintained outbuildings, newly whitewashed fences and corrals teeming with animals.

Slightly winded, she approached the arched gateway and squinted at the wooden sign hanging overhead. She recognized the brand burned into the wood.

A broken heart.

Just like the one on her front door.

This was Heartbreak Ranch.

Amy stood staring at the sign while her mind raced for any explanation other than the obvious one.

Walker had lied to her. All this time he'd let her

believe that her tumbledown shack was the only house on Heartbreak Ranch. She looked up at the big white house still a quarter of a mile away and remembered wondering where Walker and his men lived, where he had disappeared to the night Toddy chased him over the hill, and where he had gone all the nights since.

Now she knew, knew why Walker didn't want her taking his horse to find his men. Knew why he wouldn't give up the ranch without a fight.

Holding Toddy on a shortened leash to keep him close to her side, Amy walked toward the house, thinking that at any moment someone would see her and alert the ranch hands to her presence. But no one seemed to notice, except a pair of gray burros that galloped up to the fence and brayed at them.

Toddy yipped and ran behind Amy, winding his leash around her legs.

"Toddy, for heaven's sake," she said, trying to get untangled. "They aren't going to hurt you, you big baby."

"Something I can do for you, ma'am?" a deep voice asked, taking her by surprise.

Amy twisted to see a man standing behind her.

"Yes. Matter of fact there is. You need to hitch up a wagon and get your boss. He fell off my roof and hurt his back."

"Walker fell off a roof?" The ranch hand scratched his head as if he couldn't believe it.

Amy nodded, then agreed to wait while he brought the wagon around.

RAGE HAD DONE wonders for Walker's back. Even before Amy left with Toddy, he was out of bed, on his feet and looking in the trunk for the journal she'd mentioned. A red velvet gown and a faro dealing box confirmed what he suspected. Amy was a—courtesan was the word she'd used. Just a fancy name for a whore. The bottles in the trunk were of no interest, nor was the jeweled dog collar he'd come across.

He picked up the leather-bound book fully expecting to see a list of clients, but was surprised instead to discover it really was a journal.

A couple of hours later, Walker was dressed and sitting on the front porch brooding as he reread the last entry.

What Amy said was true. Her mother had had his father shanghaied. She'd drugged him, cheated him out of the deed, lured him up to her bedroom, then ordered the crimps to take him away.

Or had her plan gone up in smoke along with the rest of the Cock O' The Walk? Maybe his father had died in the fire.

His father shanghaied or dead, Walker had to face that his pa was gone for good. He sat stunned by the finality of it for a few moments, letting it sink in. He shook his head. As much as he loved his father and would miss him, Walker didn't approve of him trying to make a fool out of Bella Duprey. He'd witnessed his father's downward spiral since his mother's death and Walker recognized that this kind of disastrous conclusion had been inevitable. Bella Duprey was only marginally to blame. And Amy, he knew, wasn't to blame at all.

He looked up when he heard the rattle of a wagon coming down the hill. His foreman was driving and Amy and Toddy were sitting beside him.

Walker struggled out of the chair and waited for the wagon. When it came to a halt, he handed Amy down in spite of her attempt to push him away.

Looking confused, the foreman said, ''The little lady said you fell off the roof and needed me to fetch you home.''

''Fetch?'' Walker stared pointedly at Amy, then glanced at Toddy. ''Figures.''

''What?'' asked the foreman.

''Nothin'.''

''Well, are you coming or not?''

''No. I'm stayin' right here for the next couple of days—to recuperate. Go back and tell the boys to get to gatherin' up those mamas and their spring calves.'' Walker turned around and started to walk away when the foreman called him back.

''Hey, I almost forgot. One of the boys picked up your wire when he was in town.'' He handed Walker a folded piece of paper.

''Thanks.'' Walker read it, then stood staring at the missive long after his foreman had gone. He'd hoped it would say his father was alive and well, but instead it more or less repeated what Amy had told him. It ended with a statement that the last anyone saw of Sam Heart, he'd been heading up the stairs of the Cock O' The Walk with Bella Duprey.

When Walker looked up, he saw that he was alone. Amy and Toddy must have gone into the shack. His first thought was that he and Amy needed to talk, to sort things out. He would admit that he'd been wrong to keep the truth hidden from her if she'd admit that she should have told him what she knew about his father's misadventures. They were both wrong, but they both had dreams to protect. It occurred to Walker then that he and Amy actually shared the *same* dream. Heartbreak Ranch.

Taking long, purposeful strides toward the shack, Walker flung the door open wide and stepped inside. Only Toddy was there to greet him.

"Where is she?"

Toddy barked once, then walked over to the bedroom door and scratched his paw against the frame.

"Good Toddy. Good dog," he said, patting Toddy's head. Walker pushed against the half-open door and saw that Amy was busy packing her belongings.

"What do you think your ma would say if she knew you were giving up her dream?"

"She should have thought about that when she cheated your father out of his deed."

Walker looked down at his boots, then back up at Amy. "From what I can tell, my pa did a little cheatin' of his own."

She glanced up, her gaze meeting his. "You read the journal?"

"Yep." He picked the book up off the end of the bed and handed it to her.

Amy stopped packing and took it from him, her

fingers caressing the cover. Then she laid it in the trunk on top of her clothes.

The realization that she was preparing to leave sent a surge of panic through him. "Dammit, Amy. You're not leavin' till we've talked this out."

Amy slammed the lid of the trunk shut and turned to face him. "Don't you 'dammit, Amy' me, Walker Heart. You lied to me!"

"And *you* withheld what you knew from *me*."

Amy turned to look at the painting and put her hand to her mouth. Walker saw that she was on the verge of tears and chastised himself for being so rough. "Look," he said, taking a step toward her. "Let's call it a draw and split the pot."

He waited for her to make a move, but she didn't.

"I've been thinkin'," he said, his heart in his throat, "that there's one way to solve everything." He took a deep breath. "You could marry me."

Amy whirled around and stared at him, her eyes shining with tears.

"Marry you? You want me to *marry* you?" Her voice conveyed utter confusion.

He swallowed the lump in his throat and looked down at Toddy, who was sitting on the floor beside her.

"I just thought—" He broke off, wondering what to say next. He didn't want to beg, but neither did he want his proposal to come off like a goodwill gesture. "Ah, hell, Amy. I'm not very good at sayin' what's in my heart, but the truth is that I love you. I'd be right proud if you'd be my wife."

At his words, her sobs lessened and a small smile began to form on her face. "Oh, Walker. You're sure? Because I love you, too."

Grinning, Walker held out his hand to her. "Come here and see if you can teach this old dog some new tricks."

Amy gave a surprised laugh and ran into his arms. He held her close and breathed in the scent of her. He suddenly thought, this would be the moment they would tell their children and grandchildren about. It was a pleasant thought.

Behind them a woman's accented voice whispered, *"You can have it all, mes chers—the ranch, each other and the dream."*

A movement, so slight it was almost imperceptible, pulled Walker's gaze toward the painting over the bed. "Did you see that?" he asked, staring at the painting with narrowed eyes.

"See what?"

"Maybe I'm goin' crazy here, but I could've sworn Bella Duprey just winked at me."

Amy turned her gaze to the painting of her beloved mother and smiled.

JOSIE'S STORY
Jill Marie Landis

CHAPTER ONE

Heartbreak Ranch
Spring 1890

WILLIAM HEART REINED IN atop the hill and let his gaze drift over the wide basin below. Rich grazing land, cut by fences, stretched like a patchwork quilt from a creekbed that fringed the hills to the surrounding mountains cloaked in haze. A huge barn and outbuildings along with corrals and holding pens stood at the base of the hill. Across from them, where the land began a gentle rise, a white frame house presided over the landscape. The place was well tended and newly whitewashed. The windows of the house sparkled in the spring sunshine.

Heartbreak Ranch. Will would have known the place anywhere, for the house was exactly the way his father, Sam Heart, had always described it. The journey to this place high in the Tehachapis had been long, but no longer than one would expect when coming all the way from the slopes of Mauna Kea on the Big Island of Hawaii.

As he gazed down at the old house, his heart swelled with anticipation, for in a few minutes, perhaps less than a quarter of an hour, he would be standing face-to-face with Sam Heart's *haole* son Walker, the American half brother he had never known.

Will nudged the horse with his knees and the animal responded immediately. He was proud of the red roan Andalusian stallion he had purchased in Bakersfield, anxious to get the horse back to Hawaii and breed it with his rugged Hawaiian stock. He couldn't wait to see his younger brothers' faces when they saw the animal's huge size and its color, the same as the island's iron-rich soil. But before he could leave California, Will wanted to put a face to the name he had heard his father mention so often.

He let the horse negotiate the steep, rocky hillside and in no time reached the base of the hill. Crossing the quiet road, Will glanced over at the outbuildings. They seemed to be deserted. He had passed an occasional line rider in the hills and had seen a few men working the far edge of the basin, but no ranch hands appeared to be in the corral this afternoon. He headed directly toward the house.

He passed by the front door, aiming to tie up at a hitching post, which he knew from his father's detailed accounts to be around back. As he skirted the side of the house, he drew up short when he suddenly heard the sound of voices carried on the breeze. By the time he realized he had ridden straight into an elegant garden party, it was already too late to turn back.

At least six tables with eight guests each were assembled beneath the leafy oaks and maples in the yard. The tables were covered with starched white linens, floral china and gleaming silver. Sunlight glinted off the stemware; copious bouquets of spring roses filled cut-glass vases on each table. A footed glass cake plate crowded with petits fours made his mouth water.

All eyes turned in his direction and conversation ceased as he dismounted. William was suddenly very aware of his trail-weary duster and battered black felt hat with its unusual hatband made of a dried flower lei.

With a cursory search, he tried to locate Walker Heart amid the well-dressed men and women gathered at the tables. He froze the second his gaze fell upon the most beautiful young woman he had ever seen in his life. Her bearing was as regal as that of a member of Hawaiian royalty, the *ali'i*. She sat with her shoulders straight, her head erect. Thick, rich, amber hair the color of dark honey was piled atop her head in the latest style. Tendrils escaped to tease her ears and cheeks. Even from where he stood across the grassy yard, Will's hands itched to loop one of those strategically placed locks behind her ear. He became even more mesmerized when he realized she was staring back at him.

"Can I help you?"

A deep voice near his elbow jerked William out of his trance. He turned and blinked, startled to discover standing beside him a tall thin man with neatly oiled, carefully parted blond hair and faded blue eyes. The gentleman had separated himself from the gathering and was waiting expectantly for an answer. So too, it seemed, was the rest of the group. One woman had even paused with her teacup halfway to her lips.

Will reached up and straightened his hat. He cleared his throat. "I'm here to see Walker Heart."

A hushed murmur rippled through the crowd. Women put their heads together and whispered as they continued to stare up at him. A few of the men shook their heads with a look of disgust.

The dandified gent beside him had long, tapered, ink-stained fingers and addressed William with his voice discreetly lowered.

"If you're here about a job, you can wait for the foreman, Clay Henderson, up at his old shack." He pointed behind them.

Here on the mainland, with his light brown skin and slightly Polynesian features, Will was used to being mistaken for an Indian. In most cases he had been treated as nothing better than dirt. After three months of travel along the Pacific coast, he had still not grown used to such treatment—nor did he intend to. Standing a good half a head taller than the gentleman beside him, knowing full well that centuries of royal blood flowed through his veins, Will drew himself up to his full height.

"I'm not here about a job. My name is William Ipo," he said, quickly substituting the Hawaiian word for sweetheart. He was not willing to explain his own relationship to this place in front of all these strangers. As he stared at the beauty across the yard, *ipo* was the first word that came to him.

"I've come all the way from Hawaii to see Walker Heart on a very private matter," he added.

Another round of speculation passed through the crowd. William stood his ground, but the man beside him shifted uncomfortably. Then, to Will's surprise, the amber-haired goddess at the head table stood, very carefully swept past the gaping guests and made her way over to him.

JOSIE HEART felt the blush of embarrassment rise from the lace edge of her high collar and race to her hairline. She could not take her eyes off the dark-eyed stranger who had interrupted her carefully planned, perfectly executed garden party.

The huge man stood there looming over poor Julius, who did little but shift nervously from foot to foot.

Josie sighed. Julian was a gifted poet, a first-quality writer, a well-read, well-educated man, but strength and assertiveness were not his strong suits. She stopped beside Julian and found she had to crane her neck to look up at the bronzed stranger.

"I'm Josephina Heart," she began politely, "and this is Julian Fairchild. I heard you ask for my father, Mr.—?"

"Ipo. I need to speak to Walker Heart in private." His dark eyes quickly scanned the faces in the crowd and then found hers again.

Josie was instantly lost in the big man's exotic, deep brown eyes. So lost that she found it hard to concentrate on what William Ipo had just said. To think he was from Hawaii, the tropical paradise she had read about, the enchanted land somewhere in the South Pacific, filled her with curiosity. Finally she came to her senses and found her voice.

"I'm afraid it's too late for that, Mr. Ipo," she whispered.

Josie took a deep breath and steeled herself to utter the phrase she had been pressed into using for two years, the phrase that still caused her dark memories and great sorrow.

"You see, Mr. Ipo, I lost my father and mother to yellow fever in '87, so whatever business you have to discuss with them, you'll have to address to me. I'm in charge here."

She carefully smoothed down the skirt of her muslin gown, uncomfortable in the blinding white fabric after having worn mourning black for nearly two years.

The imposing stranger seemed momentarily stunned as he glanced over at the assembly again. "I won't bother you now, miss. I'll just wait until you are free, maybe this evening..."

Josie could almost hear her mother's voice in her ear. A lady would never turn a traveler away. She knew propriety dictated that she should send this handsome man to the bunkhouse, but on impulse, either because of something she read in his eyes or her own surprising reaction to him, Josie blurted, "You're welcome to join us for tea, Mr. Ipo."

She felt Julian make a furtive movement beside her. The newcomer immediately shook his head.

"I don't want to intrude on your luau, ma'am," Ipo said, his words laced with a melodic accent.

"Then tie up your horse by the back door and go on into the house. Magdalena will show you to a spare room where you can wash up. Then she'll get you anything you'd like to eat."

He touched two fingers to his hat brim, nodded and said, "*Mahalo*. Thank you, Miss Heart." Then he smiled, adding with a slight shrug, "You will have to forgive me. Some of the words of my island home are so much a part of me that I don't even realize I'm using them."

"Of course, you are forgiven, Mr. Ipo." She was certain a man with that smile would be forgiven anything. Josie watched as William Ipo led the roan in the direction of the back door.

Julian took her arm and, as he escorted her back to her place at the head table, he leaned close and whispered in her ear. "Do you think that was wise, Josie, inviting a perfect stranger into your home like that? What will people think?"

What will people think? It had been one of her mother's constant concerns—one Josie usually heeded—until this afternoon, until she laid eyes on William Ipo.

"People will have to think what they want to think. Right now, we should get back to our guests." She let Julian escort her back to the head table and was amazed to find herself trembling as she took her seat.

Ada Fairchild, Julian's mother, leaned close, her

lips pursed, her frown deepening. Permanent lines were etched between her brows.

"What in the world did that man want, Josie, dear? And *why* is he going into the house?" Ada whispered.

"Because I sent him in. He seems to be a gentleman. He's come all the way from Hawaii, the Sandwich Islands, to see my father about some business." Josie glanced at the back door, but William Ipo had already gone inside.

"Well, it's too bad he had to interrupt the party like that. After all you've done to make certain everything would be just perfect for this special day. Such a shame—"

Josie looked at the woman on her left, the woman who would soon be her mother-in-law. Then she turned her gaze to Julian on her right. Finally, Josie looked down at the Spode china with the delicate cherry-blossom pattern that she had inherited from her mother and sighed.

She had never, ever in her life believed in love at first sight. Not until today, not until a few moments ago when she first laid eyes on William Ipo. Now, as she sat with her fingers locked together in her lap, aware of the sweat on her palms, she knew without a doubt that such an incredible phenomenon existed— for Cupid's arrow had just hit her hard.

Right in the middle of her engagement party.

CHAPTER TWO

AFTER WHAT SEEMED to Josie like hours of smiling and making small talk, the last guests departed. Ada Fairchild left with friends, insisting Julian see that Josie tended to her unexpected visitor and then sent the man on his way.

Josie felt her heart beating triple time as she gave last-minute instructions to ranch hands who were dismantling the party tables and storing them in the barn.

Ada Fairchild had insisted on holding the affair at the ranch, convinced that an outdoor setting would be far more romantic, not to mention more comfortable than trying to cramp all of her guests into the dining room of her home in Tehachapi.

Julian hovered beside her as she moved quickly toward the house. She paused outside the screen door and took a deep breath in a weak attempt to calm herself, then opened the door and stepped into the kitchen.

Magdalena, Josie's maid, was standing in the center of the busy room overseeing the women Mrs. Fairchild had hired to help her with the multitude of party dishes, silver, glassware and linens that needed to be washed and put away. The soft hum of Spanish filled the air as the women chatted companionably while they worked.

"The *señor* is in the parlor, Josephina. I offered him food but he wanted only coffee," Magdalena said, as Josie glanced up at Julian, then hurried through the kitchen toward the front of the house.

"Thanks, Magdalena," Josie called over her shoulder. She passed through the narrow pantry, then the hallway that connected the older section of the house with the kitchen that her mother, Amy, had added not five years earlier.

She halted on the threshold between the hallway and the parlor, arrested by the sight of the tall, broad-shouldered stranger who stood beside the window. Lost in concentration as he stared out at the stockyard, William Ipo obviously had not heard them come in. Julian lingered behind her, silent as a shadow.

Josie Heart, who at the age of eighteen had found herself in charge of a huge cattle ranch, a girl who had never been at a loss for words in her life, suddenly discovered she was speechless. Afraid Julian would somehow break the spell before she had William Ipo's attention, she cleared her throat and stepped into the room.

The man from Hawaii made a half turn in her direction, and when his eyes met hers across the room, Josie's step faltered. She nearly tripped over the pastel hooked rug in front of the settee. Julian grabbed her elbow and helped her quickly right herself. Josie tried to will away the blush that stained her cheeks as she crossed the room.

"Your home is beautiful," William said in a lilting cadence that made her pulse jump a notch faster.

"My mother took great pride in this house." She glanced around the room, so familiar, so welcoming with its sunny yellow wall coverings and vases of wildflowers mixed with her mother's roses. Amy Heart had made certain that she achieved the style of the times, filling the room with color and a collection of items near and dear to her. Josie had not changed a thing.

"I am truly sorry to hear you have lost both your parents, Miss Heart."

"You said you had something to tell my father, something private. I'm in charge of Heartbreak Ranch now, Mr. Ipo—"

"Call me Will, please," he interjected and seemed to shift uncomfortably.

She nodded. "Feel free to discuss any business matter you might have had with my father. But first, let me introduce you two," she said, turning to Julian. "This is my fiancé, Julian Fairchild. He has my trust and confidence. Anything you say here will go no farther."

As she watched William move with an easy grace and contained power, Josie felt herself flush again. She quickly turned around and headed for the settee, wondering how, in the name of heaven, this man could possibly have such a disturbing effect on her. She avoided looking at Julian for fear he would notice her intense discomfort. She felt breathless and found it hard to believe the men couldn't hear her heart pounding.

Will studied the *haole* man with skin the color of a shark's underbelly. Julian Fairchild walked around the settee to stand behind Josie Heart. Every inch a gentleman in his dress and demeanor, Fairchild was everything Will wasn't. Fair, slender, refined and no doubt well educated, this whey-faced man, who said nothing but stood watching so closely, had somehow managed to win the heart of the most captivating woman Will had ever seen on either side of the Pacific.

"Please sit down, Will." She nodded at an overstuffed chair upholstered in shining gold fabric.

Will felt himself move like a sleepwalker, unable to take his eyes off Josie. Once he had settled in the deep, comfortable chair, he sighed and began to "talk-story," as his mother, Nani, liked to say.

"I came here to tell your father that *his* father, your grandfather, Sam Heart, passed on six months ago. He died peacefully, in his sleep, on the Big Island of Hawaii after attending luau for his wife's second cousin's youngest child. We thought maybe he ate too much."

He watched Josie's stunning, blue-violet eyes darken in confusion. "My grandfather, Sam Heart?"

Will nodded. Surely she knew of so close a relation. Surely her parents had told her about Sam Heart?

"He was Walker Heart's father and the man who founded this ranch."

"But—" Josie was about to ask for an explanation when Julian cut in.

"I believe Amy and Walker chose not to subject Josie to the sordid details of Sam Heart's past. But I've learned some things here and there about the man. I'm quite sure I was told that Sam Heart disappeared around 1869, Mr. Ipo. He was quite the gambler, I've heard, and it is believed he was too ashamed to return to the basin after a trip to San Francisco where he lost the ranch. No one ever heard from him again."

"If he lost the ranch, then how did it stay in Heart hands?" Reeling with shock, Josie had to know.

"Your mother arrived with the deed. Walker married her and the ranch belonged to a Heart again."

"I can't remember Mother ever mentioning Sam Heart." Josie sat frowning, aware of how little her mother had told her of the past.

"Sam Heart was shanghaied while on that trip to San Francisco," Will said. "He sailed around the world twice before he jumped ship, met a beautiful *wahini* and lived out the rest of his life in Hawaii."

"A va-hini?" Josie asked, mimicking his pronunciation.

Will nodded. "A woman. He married her."

"He met a Hawaiian woman and never came back to California? How could he turn his back on his only son?" Josie wondered aloud. "Did you know him well?"

The concern in her voice made Will hesitate. He glanced once at the man standing protectively behind

Josie Heart and admitted nothing more than, "Yes, I knew him well."

"You say he married this woman. Did he have other children? Did my father have any half brothers or sisters?"

"Nine."

"Nine!"

She paled and her hand flew to her throat. Will watched Josie's long, tapered fingers toy with the lace edging the collar of her gown. Her gaze met his and in her eyes he read her anxiety.

"Oh, my God. Do they intend to lay claim to Heartbreak Ranch? Are you representing them?" Her tone was strained; her perfect complexion had gone ghostly pale.

"Now, Josie—" Julian laid his hand on her shoulder.

"Do they?" she demanded of Will again.

Josie was fighting so hard to stay composed that, rather than cause her any more worry, Will quickly shook his head and smiled, trying to reassure her.

"They don't want any part of your Heartbreak Ranch. Sam Heart had a golden touch. He was able to buy up plenty of land on the Big Island. His Hawaiian *keiki,* his children, have no desire to live here on the mainland."

Josie felt her fear slowly subside, but not entirely disappear. William Ipo seemed sincere enough. Desperately, she wanted to believe him. Still, hearing such shocking news—that her grandfather had abandoned his only son to settle in Hawaii and father a whole other family—was unsettling.

"What was he like, this Sam Heart? My parents never told me anything about him." Josie feared Will Ipo would leave now that his message had been delivered. She watched Will casually lean back in the chair once more. His eyes took on a faraway look.

"He was handsome, even in old age. Dark hair sprinkled with gray and snapping black eyes. He was a hard man in many ways, but he claimed the years at sea did that to him. He and your father never got along. Sam always said Walker was more like his mother, more sensible. Sam liked to tease, loved to gamble. He was forever spending too much money on newfangled inventions that showed up on the island carried over on the merchant ships.

"My...his wife, Nani, still has all the kitchen gadgets Sam bought her stuffed in boxes and drawers. Every time he brought home another, she would tell him that even if she knew what the thing was for, she couldn't use it. She likes to do things the old way." Will laughed. "One of the last items he purchased was a box for saving soap slivers."

Listening to him, Josie slowly relaxed enough to smile. She suddenly felt the warmth of Julian's hand on her shoulder and was reminded of his presence.

"Please, sit down, Julian. I'll have Magdalena bring in some coffee for you, and more for you, Will," she said when she noticed the Hawaiian's empty cup.

"Actually, I should be leaving. I have work to do,"

Julian said, clearing his throat and throwing a meaningful glance at William Ipo.

Josie was ashamed of the wave of relief that poured through her. She was appalled at herself for actually wishing her fiancé would leave her alone with William Ipo. She was off the settee before Julian had a chance to change his mind, walking around to take his arm and lead him to the front door.

"I'm so sorry for keeping you this long," Josie said, smiling up at him. "I entirely forgot that you said you were working on that new piece for the *Summit Sun*."

Julian glanced at William again and then back at Josie. "I really shouldn't leave you two alone like this," he said in a voice barely above a whisper. "My mother wouldn't approve, and neither would yours if she were still here."

She whispered back. "But you've seen for yourself that Mr. Ipo is a perfect gentleman. Besides, Magdalena's here. I have to invite him to dinner—the poor man rode all the way into the basin on his errand. The least I can do is be polite. Besides, remember how intrigued I was when I read Miss Isabella Bird's *Six Months in the Sandwich Islands?* There's absolutely no harm in chatting with him over dinner and then sending him on his way." She tried to reassure Julian with a discreet pat on the arm. "You go along and get your story done for the *Sun*."

Julian sighed and carefully smoothed down his hair with both hands. "I suppose you're right."

"You know I am." She smiled up at him.

When he took her hand, his palm felt slick with hair oil. He hovered, staring down at her, obviously still uncertain. "Mother would object."

"She doesn't have to know everything, does she? Now go, and don't forget your hat," she reminded him. "It's in the kitchen."

"I'll get it." Still showing signs of concern, he kissed the back of her hand with much ceremony and propriety. The slight show of affection was all she had ever allowed, not that he'd ever dared attempt anything more. They had been friends since childhood, both of them raised according to a strict moral code. A true lady did not allow a man to take liberties before marriage, nor did a true gentleman press himself upon a lady.

As soon as he walked out of the room, Josie closed the door and leaned against it, hard-pressed to hide a smile as an unexpected rush of delight surged through her. At last she had the exotically handsome, dark-eyed, soft-spoken and incredibly massive William Ipo all to herself.

CHAPTER THREE

WILL FELT HIMSELF becoming mired deeper and deeper into quicksand of his own making. Josie smiled down the length of the table from him, prettily presiding as hostess across a sea of crocheted ecru lace, shimmering water goblets, sparkling cutlery and china bowls heaped with steaming mashed potatoes, a boatful of gravy and a platter of Heartbreak Ranch's prime sliced beef.

He had been captivated since the moment he laid eyes on her, and now that he had complicated the situation by not telling her outright that his name translated to William Heart, he couldn't find a way to tell her the truth. She was flirting so openly and smiling at him so trustingly as she hung on every word he said that Will couldn't bear to see her shining eyes fill with embarrassment when he confessed that he was not merely a close friend of Sam Heart's, but his first son by Sam's Hawaiian wife, Nani.

He felt things had passed the point where he could tell her that he was her half uncle. If he did, she would not only feel that she'd made a fool of herself, but at the very least, she would become suspicious of him, certain he had come to take over the ranch. After admitting the truth, he doubted he could convince her that he intended nothing of the sort.

So Will sat there and listened as she chatted on about what she had read of his islands and felt himself sink into shame at both his deception and his disturbing and forbidden attraction to her.

"Will? Mr. Ipo?"

He started, nearly dropping the heavy, hollow-handled knife against the rim of the floral china. "What?"

"I was asking if it's true the ancient Hawaiians practiced human sacrifice? I once read an article written by a former missionary who had spent years in the Sandwich Islands, and he reported many such practices had once existed."

Will couldn't help but notice the slight shiver that swept her when she broached such an unsavory subject. He watched, mesmerized, as she carefully blotted the tempting corners of her lips with a linen napkin. It wasn't until she'd returned the napkin to her lap that he could answer.

"Before the coming of the *haoles,* the white strangers, the Hawaiians did practice human sacrifice. *Kanaka kapu,* the tabooed men, were sacrificed as part of our original religious customs—before the island's gods were replaced by the missionaries." Will pulled the bowl of mashed potatoes over to his plate and began dishing up another generous helping.

When he looked down the dining table again, Josie was studying him closely. "Did you make the voyage here just to bring word of Sam Heart's death?"

He paused with a forkful of potatoes halfway to his lips and lowered it to his plate. "I was in the Pacific Northwest visiting some transplanted cousins before I came to California to buy several stallions. I've already shipped all of them, except for the roan I rode in on, back to Hawaii. I plan to breed them with Hawaiian stock."

"So, you have a ranch, too? Is that how you came to know the Hearts?"

Will dropped his gaze to his plate. "Yes. I have a ranch." He met her eyes again, cursing fate, cursing Sam Heart and cursing himself for having to suffer the knowledge that he had fallen head over heels in love for the first time and the object of his affection was his own niece.

"I have to admit that I love Heartbreak Ranch more than anything else, but at times the responsibilities are overwhelming," Josie admitted with a sigh.

"You have some help, don't you? What about Julian?"

"Julian?" Josie laughed and Will's hand clenched around his napkin.

She had not once mentioned her fiancé during the meal, but after the way she had been staring at Will as if he were a ripe mango hanging on a low branch, he had all but forgotten Julian Fairchild himself.

"Julian hardly knows one end of a horse from the other—"

"That might not bode well for you on your wedding night," he said without thinking and watched the color in her already rosy cheeks deepen considerably.

"Mr. Ipo," she said, trying to sound offended but failing when she could not hide her smile, "I don't think what Julian knows about horses will matter in the least when…when…oh, never mind."

"I'm sorry if I offended you. I've noticed I have a bawdier sense of humor than mainlanders. Not to mention, I may be a bit out of practice with my manners. I don't often have an opportunity to share dinner with a lovely lady like yourself."

He drank her in with his eyes, knowing it was time he took his leave, but it gave him heartache to know he would never have the chance to see her again, to hear her sweet voice or look into the depths of her bewitching eyes.

"Dinner was wonderful," he said, laying his napkin alongside his plate. "I have to go now if I'm to arrive at the Golden Gate Hotel in Havilah at a decent hour."

"Havilah?"

He nodded. "I was told there's a Doc Jamison there who is an expert on horse breeding and care. I want to talk to him before I head back to Los Angeles. I'm sailing home next week."

Josie felt a swift jolt of panic hit her harder than a mule's kick when she realized William Ipo was planning to leave. She tried to ignore that he had set his napkin aside and was waiting for her to acknowledge what he had just said. Frantically she searched for any excuse to keep him there. She felt like a shameless hussy, but she couldn't help herself.

Everything had been planned. Before William Ipo

rode into her life, everything had been in perfect order. She was engaged to Julian, her dear, dear lifelong friend, so there was really no excuse for what she was feeling for the man seated opposite her. There was no excuse for the way he made her blush with just a look. There was certainly no excuse for the warm, melting sensation she experienced in an unmentionable part of her body. All she knew was that Julian had never dared to look at her the way Will Ipo was looking at her right now, nor had she ever before felt so very sensual, feminine or alive.

And not since her parents died had she experienced such a sinking sense of loss.

With a heavy heart she stood, ever the perfect hostess, to signal that he could take his leave. "Be careful on the trail," she warned, knowing full well she could not invite him to stay the night, at least not in the house. Quickly she added, "If you'd like to sleep in the bunkhouse with the men—"

"Thank you, but I must go."

They stood, sharing an awkward, lingering silence while the tall clock in one corner of the dining room chimed the quarter hour. Josie bowed her head wondering what he might do if she showed up in Havilah before he left. At least then she could accompany him on his ride through the basin and down the road to Caliente. Surely there could be no harm in that, nothing for anyone to gossip about, just a few friendly hours passed with a close friend of her grandfather's—

"*Mahalo,* Josie. Thank you. I'll see myself out."

To her dismay, when she looked up she realized that he was already standing in the doorway. If she didn't pull herself together, Will would be gone before she even had a chance to walk him to the door.

"Wait!"

Just as she shoved back her chair with such force it nearly toppled over behind her, the door behind Will burst open and Clay Henderson, ranch foreman, burst into the room. Past fifty, he had a head of gray hair and lines around his eyes that the sun had carved there over the years. Clay gave Will a cursory glance and turned his attention to Josie.

"Damian's got the colic," he said. Before Josie could respond, Clay stared up at Will. "You the Hawaiian that rode in today?"

"I am. Damian is a horse?"

"Best damn piece of horseflesh we've had on this ranch for a while. He's got the colic bad." Clay turned to Josie. "Been walkin' him for two hours and I didn't want to disturb you, but I thought you'd want to know, seein' as how he means so much to you."

Josie fought back tears as she listened to Clay talk about the stallion, one of her father's last major stock purchases. The horse was a coal-black Arabian that they hadn't really been able to afford at the time, but Walker Heart couldn't pass up the opportunity to add it to his extensive string of horses. She looked down at her perfect white gown and made a decision.

"I'll go up and change and meet you out at the barn." Then she turned to Will. "Is there an old Hawaiian remedy you know of that might help?"

Will shook his head. "We tried one once with turpentine, laudanum and warm water, but I hate to tell you what happened. Now we just keep 'em walking and hope for the best."

Josie turned to Clay. "You look exhausted. I'll change and take over for you since you have to be up before dawn."

"I'll go out until you are ready," Will said.

"Oh, would you?" She sounded more than pleased.

There was no way Will could refuse with Josie staring up at him with such admiration in her eyes. Feeling part coward, part thief, he looked away. Since he had gained her trust and admiration under false circumstances, the very least he could do was stay a little longer and try to help out.

THEY WERE ALONE, just the two of them, she and Will. It was everything Josie had longed for during dinner as she came to know him better. Now they shared soft lamplight from the lantern hung beside the barn door, the sweet scent of wildflowers perfuming the night air and a counterpane of stars hanging above the basin. The Tehachapi Mountains stood like silent chaperons, waiting and watching.

For the past three hours, side by side, they had trudged through mud and manure as they walked Damian around the corral. Will had never once complained. Instead, he had kept her mind off worrying about the stallion by telling her tales of Sam Heart's home in Hawaii. She knew all about Nani, her grandfather's Hawaiian wife, a woman Will described as tall and robustly plump, and about the children Sam had fathered before he died.

She learned about Will's *ohana*, his extended family of cousins and second cousins, aunts and uncles, the luau feasts held to celebrate weddings and birthdays, anniversaries and homecomings. His descriptions of the azure sea and the pounding surf, the trade winds and the tropical flowers were so clear she could almost feel the sea mist and smell the fragrant plumeria on the air.

"What are you thinking?" His voice came to her through the semidarkness. She glanced up at him, a silhouette against the darker mountain shadows.

"I was just thinking of how much you must love your home," she said with a sigh. "I can hear it in your voice, hear it when you speak in Hawaiian." She decided he would probably never leave the islands, not even for love.

"I do love it," Will said softly. "As much as you love your Heartbreak Ranch."

"Sometimes I wonder what will become of this place."

"Surely your own *keiki* will stay on here. You'll teach them to love the land as you do."

Her step faltered. He reached for her elbow, and when his hand cupped her arm, Josie felt an electrifying jolt of longing sear through her. She had never, ever reacted to Julian this way, never waited breathlessly for his touch. Something mysterious was happening to her, something she couldn't fathom. She wished her mother were alive so that she could pour her heart out to her. Perhaps then the secret of what William Ipo did to her might be explained.

"Julian doesn't want children," she said softly.

"What?" Will stopped in midstride.

Between them, Damian tossed his head and tried to bite himself in the side. They quickly started walking again.

Josie sighed. "Julian is a writer, a very gifted and talented writer, who is highly sensitive. He thrives in a tranquil setting and feels that children would only intrude upon his work."

"Hawaiians love children," Will said, staring off at the outline of the mountains.

Josie remained silent and continued to prod Damian along.

Will found it hard to believe there was a man alive who would not want a houseful of children by her. He knew the disturbing thoughts that followed that line of thinking should not have been entertained by one so closely related to Josephina Heart.

Finally, Damian began to settle down as the colic passed. The danger over, they led the Arabian to his stall in the barn. When they both reached for the latch at once, Will's hand touched Josie's wrist and lingered too long. His fingers slipped up to hers and he enveloped her hand in a firm but gentle hold. Near enough to catch an elusive scent of roses as he leaned closer, he could feel her warmth. She was staring up at him expectantly, too expectantly.

She was tempting, forbidden fruit. She was his niece. His own half brother's child.

And he wanted her more than he'd ever wanted anything in his life.

With a shudder, he let go and stepped away, but the tension continued to throb between them, lingering on the air like the alluring scent of roses that wafted around her.

He had to leave. Had to get away from Josie and the unfulfilled longing in her eyes. Will watched her step back. She was uneasy with his silent rejection. Her eyes quickly became shadowed with self-doubt and apology. He cursed himself as the source of her embarrassment.

"It looks like the horse will be all right. I'd best be heading to Havilah." Fighting to ignore the shadowed questions in her eyes, Will turned his attention to Damian.

"It's very late. You don't know the trail," she said softly. "There's a small settlement of Kawaiisu Indians over the hill who are very peaceful. If you run into any trouble, ask for James Panau." She paused momentarily and blushed. "He may be drunk, but he'd not be that far gone yet and might still be able to help you. He is raising his son, Ben, alone."

"I'll be all right." Will moved quickly, afraid the caress in her tone might persuade him to stay. He didn't pause until he was at the open barn door. Finally, he turned and then, feeling he'd put safe enough distance between them, looked back.

She was standing where he left her, blinking furiously, the color of her wide eyes reflected indigo in the lamplight.

"You'll have to pass by here on your way to Caliente to catch the train—"

"I really don't have much time."

"Perhaps you can just stop and say goodbye." She was holding her fingers locked together at her waist. Her gaze dropped to her hands, then shot back up to him.

There was no way he could deny her, or himself.

"I'll try." He nodded in her direction, feeling a complete coward as he said, "Aloha."

CHAPTER FOUR

TWO SECONDS after Will stepped outside and was swallowed up by the darkness, Josie dropped to her knees in the straw that littered the barn floor. She covered her burning cheeks with her palms. How could she have been so brazen? Where had she gotten the courage to be so bold as to throw herself at Will Ipo like that? Was it any wonder the poor man had wanted to get away from her so badly that he practically *ran* out of the barn?

When he had held her hand she'd gone weak in the knees. She had even been on the verge of asking him to kiss her. She prayed the longing had not shown on her face, but something in the way he had reacted told her differently. His expression had gone beyond shock. He had been downright appalled.

"You'll have to pass by here on your way to Caliente to catch the train..."

Josie groaned aloud and leaned against the door to Damian's stall. When the horse started to nibble on her hair, she stood away from the door, ran her hands down the front of her split skirt and then reached up to smooth her hair into place. Taking a deep breath, she was determined to put the disturbing thoughts of Will Ipo out of her mind. What she had done had been unthinkable. She had nearly kissed a man who had no intention of returning her unwarranted, unsolicited affection.

Her mother had taught her far better than this. Josie prayed Amy Duprey Heart had better things to do in heaven tonight than to look down upon her wayward daughter. Mama had attended one of the best Eastern girls' schools and had done her best to pass along all the rules of propriety. Josie had learned a woman was never to take a man's arm unless he offered it, just as she knew she should never have been so forward and begged Will to visit Heartbreak Ranch again before he left for Los Angeles.

In two months she and Julian were to be married. As she crossed the dark stable yard, Josie decided that she'd best forget Will Ipo and set her mind on the wedding plans. The bawling of the yearling calves newly separated from their mothers and penned in the nearby stockyard was such a familiar racket that she barely acknowledged it as she hurried toward the house.

Without taking great care to be quiet, she let herself in the back door. Magdalena snored like a steam engine and slept like the dead in her small room off the kitchen. Josie hurried through the darkened house and then up the stairs to the room that had been her parents'. The housekeeper had left a light burning for her on the bedside table. Exhausted but still too keyed up to sleep, Josie pulled off her blouse and skirt and then, standing in the shadows in her chemise, poured water into the large basin on the washstand and began to wash her hands and face.

An hour and a half later she was bored with the sound of her bare feet hitting the floorboards as she paced the room in her long, white cotton nightgown. She was a fool, a fickle female, practically a fallen woman. Even more appalling was the notion that she didn't really care if she ever laid eyes on Julian again. She had convinced herself that if she didn't see Will Ipo once more before he left that she would certainly perish of a withered heart.

Pacing over to the window, she held the drapery aside and looked out at the night sky. From the second-floor vantage point she could see across the dark basin and the foothills beyond. William was out there somewhere, hopefully in Havilah or very near it by now. She pictured the tall, handsome Hawaiian with smiling eyes walking into the Golden Gate Hotel, summoning the clerk, settling into his room.

Was he thinking of her?

She groaned. How could he not when she had all but thrown herself at him? The thought of what might have happened if he had been a bit more receptive sent a chill down her spine. Alternately cold and then hot, she pressed her cheek against the cool windowpane and sighed.

"Oh, Mama," she whispered into the darkness. "What in the world am I going to do?" Josie closed her eyes and tried to think of what her mother might advise and she recalled the day her mother lay dying. Walker Heart had already passed on and Amy, although not yet fifty, had lost the will to go on without him.

Josie's own bout of yellow fever had been slight and, afterward, she and Magdalena had nursed both Walker and Amy. Near the end of her mother's life, Josie had hovered at Amy's bedside all day, refusing to leave. The trees had cast long afternoon shadows across the lawn when Amy awoke and said in a thready voice barely above a whisper, "I've taught you all I know, Josie, honey. You're more than capable of running Heartbreak Ranch. That's why I don't mind leaving it in your hands."

"But, Mama," she had protested as tears streamed down her face, "you can't give up. You're young yet. I need you—"

Amy slowly moved her head from side to side on the pillow. "You have Clay and the others. And there's Julian. He's such a gentleman."

Her mother had always wanted a gentleman for Josie. Someone with an impeccable background and social standing. Josie didn't know why it was so important to her mother that she marry well, especially when her papa openly admitted he didn't care a whit about gentlemen. All he had ever wanted to be was a rancher, and he hoped Amy would never throw him off the place. Every time he said it, they would laugh and share a secret smile.

Now, as Josie stood in their room staring out at the night, she could almost hear her mother's dying words. "God forbid you should ever reach a point where your life looks bleak, Josie, but if you're in need, dire need, darling, look through the old trunk up in the attic. It's your Grandma Bella's legacy to us. It will help you find the strength to face anything.''

Josie figured that if a withering heart didn't constitute dire need, then she didn't know what might. She couldn't understand why this overwhelming desire for Will Ipo possessed her so. Perhaps there was some hidden flaw in her, some explanation for this obsession.

She picked up the lamp and hurried down the hallway to the door that led to the attic stairs. Holding the lamp aloft in one hand and gathering the material of her gown in the other, she carefully walked up the narrow stairway.

The attic was cold and drafty and smelled musty. When she dropped the long skirt of her nightgown and the flounce grazed the floor, it sent up a puff of dust that made her sneeze. She looked around until she spied an old leather trunk shoved up against one wall.

"This is a wild-goose chase, Josie Heart." She chided herself in a whisper as she crossed the dusty, creaking floorboards and bent down, holding the lamp closer to the trunk. Propped up behind it was a large, rectangular object covered with a yellowed sheet. Curious, Josie carefully set down the lamp at a safe distance and went back to tug at the fabric. The sheet fell aside, partially exposing a gilt-framed portrait of a woman who looked startlingly like her mother. Because the trunk sat in front of the huge frame, only the woman's hauntingly familiar face with violet eyes and one bare shoulder were visible.

Josie grabbed a leather handle and pulled the trunk aside. Her eyes went wide and she gasped when the artwork was revealed in all its startling glory. There, reclining on her side on a velvet chaise, naked as the day she was born, lay her mother. Too stunned to move, Josie stood for a moment and stared as jumbled thoughts raced through her mind.

Amy Duprey Heart—the woman who had always insisted on good manners and a show of good breeding, her *mother,* a paragon of virtue—posing nude on a chaise longue? It was unfathomable. Unthinkable.

Still in shock, Josie sank to her knees and alternately stared at the portrait and then the trunk, as if the latter were Pandora's Box. Had it not been for her mother's last words, she would have been afraid to open it for fear of what dark secrets lay inside.

"Look through the old trunk up in the attic.... Grandma Bella's legacy...help you find the strength to face anything..."

The trunk was unlocked. She reached out and tugged on the latch. The long unused hinges creaked as she slowly lifted the lid, peering curiously into the dark recesses of the old trunk. Instead of the musty smell she expected, a heady, unrecognizable herbal scent that reminded her a bit of lemons wafted out of the interior of the trunk.

Some kind of heavy fabric lay on top, hiding whatever was beneath it. She lifted the material, realizing that it was a garment of rich, red velvet. She raised the piece in her hands and watched as it unwound to reveal a scarlet gown with a deep, plunging neckline.

"Oh, good heavens!" she whispered, and let the dress fall into her lap. Reaching into the trunk she lifted out an intriguing wooden box. An intricate painting of a tiger decorated the shining, varnished lid. In the lamplight, the tiger's twin emerald eyes appeared to be winking up at her. She fiddled with the lid and found yellowed playing cards inside. With a shrug, she set the box on the floor.

How much time had passed she didn't know, but she was aware that she didn't have much of it to waste. Will Ipo would be on his way to Los Angeles tomorrow and if he stopped by to say goodbye, she wanted one more chance with him. Desperate for something that would give her hope, Josie fished around inside the trunk and pulled out a jeweled dog collar.

Grimacing, she rolled her eyes. Toddy. The collar could only have belonged to Toddy, the disgusting dog that her mother had inherited from Bella Duprey. From the day she was born, Toddy had always treated her as an intruder, so Josie had stayed away from the hateful creature and had only vague memories of the huge poodle. Her mother dearly loved the old thing, even when the dog had been obnoxious enough to up and die of a heart attack right in the middle of Josie's fourth birthday party.

The creature's untimely death had sent Amy into hysterics, which in turn had frightened Josie and her young guests half to death. It had taken all of Walker's and Clay's patience and perseverance to calm the children, but the party was beyond salvaging. Her mother had the men build a small stone mausoleum to mark the dog's grave site. Toddy's final resting place overlooked the ranch from the hillside across from the house.

Josie snorted and tossed the glittering collar back into the trunk.

Then she saw it: a leather journal lying in the bottom of the trunk next to a collection of bottles and vials, some still half-filled with liquid. She took out the journal, careful not to disturb any of the mysterious vials.

Leafing through the book, she could tell immediately that the many copiously filled pages had not been penned in her mother's hand. The front piece explained that the journal was that of Bella Duprey. It contained sections, one on something called "Captivating Your Man," one entitled, "Toddy's Tricks and Commands." Another section was "My Life—Bella Duprey," followed by "Recipes for Romance and Other Concoctions."

Josie's gaze flew back to the portrait. The eyes of the reclining nude seemed to be staring directly into her own. She found it hard to look away. When she shifted closer to the light, the journal dropped atop the gown that was still lying in her lap. A loose page fell out and fluttered to the floor beside her. Josie lifted the folded page, opened it and recognized her mother's handwriting.

Josie dearest,

If you are reading this, then it is because I am not with you and you have turned to your grandmother for help. Although you never knew her, Bella Duprey was an incomparable woman with quite a reputation, one I kept hidden from you for reasons that will become obvious once you read through this journal.

I was never ashamed of my mother or of what she did, for without her I would never have met your father or come to Heartbreak Ranch, but I intended to keep her history from you, until you were old enough to understand. As you read, you will realize what a strong-willed woman Bella was and I hope you will draw on the same strength to overcome whatever difficulties you are now facing. Mother left this journal for me and all of her descendants, struggled to pen it in English so that future generations could read it and use her knowledge.

There is a portrait of Bella that used to hang over our bed until you were born. Your father and I decided that it should be stored. Perhaps you will be able to locate that in the attic, too.

Dear Josie, I wish I could be there for you, but as I am not, I hope you will find the answers you need in the pages of this book.

> Always remember me,
> Your loving mother

The hours sped by as Josie sat on the dusty floor with the journal open in her lap. As she scanned the with the journal open in her lap. As she scanned the pages of the book in the dim lamplight, she would occasionally glance over at the portrait of the woman whose life had been so colorfully chronicled by her own hand. For a second she thought the portrait of Bella was smiling at her, but dismissed the feeling as the result of lack of sleep.

No one could have slept through the adventures of Bella Duprey. From life on the streets of France to fame on the Barbary Coast, Bella tamed men and made a name for herself, leaving her every triumph and discovery carefully noted for her descendants.

Immersed in skimming through the compelling material, ever mindful that her time was running out, Josie nearly gave up hope of ever finding a way to win Will Ipo's heart. That is, until she discovered a passage in "The Art of Fascination" headed "Things to Do with Champagne."

As she read the unbelievable sexual acts suggested, she was alternately scandalized and then convinced she must have inherited more from Bella than a trunk and violet eyes. Obviously she was cursed with the same hot, harlot's blood—for as she perused the detailed instructions for making love with a partner under the influence of an elixir mixed with champagne, she easily imagined herself in the role of a wild temptress beguiling Will Ipo. Not once did thoughts of Julian Fairchild interrupt her fantasy.

Poor Julian. No matter what the outcome of tomorrow's meeting with Will—if there was another encounter with the Hawaiian at all—she was bound and determined to call the wedding off. She could never marry Julian now, not after knowing what real, soul-shattering love felt like.

As the lamp oil burned low, a new aura of sensuality came over her. She felt bold and daring, challenged rather than stymied. No longer desperate, but determined, Josie slammed the journal closed. She put the tiger box inside the trunk and gathered up the journal with the red velvet dress and the vial she needed, then closed the trunk lid. She carried the items to the bottom of the stairs and then returned for the portrait. Bella deserved to be ensconced in her rightful place over the bed. Perhaps her grandmother's painting would bring her luck.

In the kitchen, she moved with the stealth of a thief as she flew down the steps to the cold cellar below the pantry and found the two remaining bottles of champagne in her parents' meager collection of wine.

She raced to her room, dropped the supplies on the bed and hung up the dress. She sneaked back to the cellar to chip ice from the blocks stored in a straw-filled oak box and hurried up to her room to chill the champagne.

Then, too excited to sleep, she curled up with the journal again and read until just before dawn. When she could no longer hold her eyes open, she slipped Bella's journal beneath her pillow and fell asleep.

Her dreams were full of vignettes in a Barbary Coast bordello, where she and Will Ipo cavorted on satin sheets beneath the portrait of Bella Duprey.

CHAPTER FIVE

WILL WAS FULLY convinced he was an idiot. He wasn't asking for trouble, he was begging for it as he stood sheltered from the spring rain on the front porch of the Heartbreak Ranch house, knocking at the door. When no one answered immediately, he quickly turned to leave, but before he took a step, the door swung open behind him.

"Will?"

The sound of her voice pierced his heart. When he turned around, Josie was standing in the doorway smiling back at him. But something was different— no longer was her heart in her eyes. In fact, the change in her was so dramatic, all he could do was stare.

Slowly she sized him up as if he were an *ahi* caught in a net. Her confident smile—so different from the hopeful, pleading expression she'd worn last night— was so bold, so intriguing, that he was speechless.

"I'm so glad you took the time to stop by again," she said lightly. "Come in. No need to stand out there in the rain."

"I can't stay long," he finally managed as he whipped off his hat and stepped over the threshold. He followed her into the now familiar parlor with its arrangement of settees, tables covered with bric-a-brac and books, the piano draped with a fringed shawl.

"Surely you have time for a cup of tea." She shook out his wet duster and hung it on a nearby hall tree alongside his hat.

"Just one," he said, wishing he felt happier that she had obviously gotten over her infatuation. He wished he could say the same for himself.

"I'll get the tea," she said, heading for the kitchen. "I've already got the water boiling."

He started to follow her out of the parlor. "Where's your cook?"

She halted abruptly in the narrow hall and slowly smiled. "I gave Lena two days off. She's been wanting to go into Caliente to visit with her sister and see her nieces and nephews. After she worked so hard with Mrs. Fairchild to put the engagement party together, I thought she could use the rest."

Knowing they were alone together in the house made Will uneasy. True, it was broad daylight outside, still early afternoon, but they were unmarried and without chaperons. He told himself his discomfort stemmed from the fact that he had found it hard to sleep for thinking of Josie. His wayward thoughts were leftover from his state of mind last night.

"I suppose Julian and his mother will be here to keep you company for dinner," he said, trying to make conversation and purposely calling her fiancé to mind.

"They've gone to Bakersfield for three days." Her voice echoed in the hall.

She would be alone tonight. Will sighed, determined to cut his stay even shorter.

He paced the confines of the parlor until she returned with the tea tray. It was impossible not to notice the way her hips swayed provocatively as she crossed the room and bent to set the tray on the tea table in front of the fireplace. A low fire burned behind the grate, taking the chill and dampness out of the room.

Will moved to stand in front of the fireplace and held his hands out to the warmth. Although the Californians were proclaiming it spring and shedding their winter clothes, he had never been so cold.

Josie straightened. He watched her reach up with both hands as she tucked a loose strand of dark amber hair into the bun on the crown of her head. The movement caused her breasts to thrust upward. What was a man to do, but stare?

"One lump or two?"

Will nearly choked. "What?"

"In your tea. One lump of sugar, or two?"

"Three," he finally managed, indulging his sweet tooth.

She smiled up at him as she used delicate silver tongs to drop three cubes of sugar into a cup of steaming brew. As she handed him the delicate cup and saucer, which were almost too small to hold in his big hands, Josie looked directly at his mouth.

"It's a special recipe of my grandmother's. It might

take a sip or two for you to get used to the taste,'' she said.

Will pursed his lips and blew on the steaming liquid.

Josie appeared content to watch.

"Aren't you having any?" he asked her, blowing over the rim of the cup again.

"Mine's cooling." She pointed to a cup of tea already poured and resting on the tray. "Why don't we sit down?"

He sat. Will continued to stare at her over the rim of the teacup. Perched uncomfortably on the edge of the settee, he felt like an awkward giant caught up in the spell of a dainty, beautiful enchantress.

He took a sip of tea, looked up and found Josie smiling at him with satisfaction.

"Tastes like almonds," he said.

"It's mostly herbs. Very relaxing."

"I shouldn't get too relaxed. I want to get to Caliente before sundown." He thought he saw a flash of panic in her eyes, but after studying her carefully, he decided he was mistaken. She appeared as calm and collected as when she opened the door to greet him.

They shared tea and ginger cakes and all the while Will felt himself grow more uncomfortable, unable to concentrate on the conversation. After two and a half cups of tea he had let himself become lulled by the cheery warmth of the room, so much so that he didn't feel like moving, even though he knew he had to leave.

Josie's smiles were far too tempting. He wanted to

drink in her essence, to commit her every smile, every movement to memory. Then when he returned to Hawaii he would have the images of this last afternoon with her to remember.

JOSIE WATCHED Will sink into the lethargy described in the section of Bella's journal entitled "Recipes for Romance and Other Concoctions." It was all she could do to keep from leaping off the settee and putting the rest of her plan for the evening into action, but she forced herself to follow Bella's instructions to the letter, to savor each and every moment and let the elixir take effect.

She had deviated from the instructions a bit, mixing some of the brew into his tea so that she might get to the next step—offering him champagne. According to Bella's notes, once William had taken the prescribed amount, his will would become as pliable as artist's clay, but his sexual prowess would be enhanced, not diminished. After imbibing the elixir mixed with champagne, he would become the most consummate of lovers. And then, at least for tonight, if not forever, he would be hers.

She was throwing more than caution to the winds. She was throwing away her future with Julian, setting herself up for humiliation and censure if—when Will came out of his stupor—he held this night's folly against her. But she was willing to take that risk to win his love, willing to do anything to make Will realize that they belonged together. She couldn't let him ride out of her life as suddenly as he had appeared, not even if it meant staking her untarnished reputation on it. Losing her virginity was a small price to pay to win his love.

Still, there were no guarantees. Her grandmother had written as much in one section of her memoirs. Even the best-laid plans went awry, but even if Will should hate her for what she was about to do, she would still have this one night with him to remember; perhaps she would even have his child. The idea should have terrified her, but it did not. An inner strength and resolve drove her. She would savor tonight and face the outcome, no matter what the cost. She would lock away every detail in her heart. It would be the one dark secret of her life.

One night of passion with Will Ipo meant she would give up what she now realized would have been a staid, passionless life of respectability with Julian. If Will rejected her, she would still have Heartbreak Ranch.

Will sat across from her, smiling a lopsided smile that made her heart jump. She couldn't help but notice that he never took his eyes off her. His unfocused gaze kept straying to her lips, her breasts, her waist. She could almost feel her skin burn where his dark, chocolate-eyed gaze touched her.

Josie shivered and felt a blush stain her cheeks when she thought of what she had discovered in "The Art of Fascination." The book was on the bedside table, the pages marked so that she could follow Bella's instructions to the letter once she got William into her bed.

"Josie?" His speech had slowed, but his eyes were still focused on her. "I'm going to tell the...the Hearts all about you when I get back to...Hawaii. Everything about you...and Heartbreak Ranch. And...don't you worry. No one will be coming to try to...to take this place. You have my word."

"Thank you. That will put my mind at ease."

She wanted to tell him that come morning, if everything went according to plan, he would be so enamored with her that he would never entertain the thought of leaving Heartbreak Ranch again. And even if he did, he would insist she be at his side.

"There's...s...something else I have to tell you, Josie. Something important. I don't want you to think...less of me because...because I didn't tell you this before but..."

He paused abruptly and reached up to rub his fingers across his forehead.

"What is it, Will?"

"I...forget." He looked befuddled, as if the answer was within his grasp but he couldn't quite put the words and the thought together.

Josie almost leaped off the couch and shouted with joy. It was working. Bella's potion was really working. She had feared the ingredients in the strange vial with English and Chinese markings were too old, that they had lost their effect, but she could see that Will was slowly slipping into a trancelike state.

He sat back against the settee and simply smiled at her.

She got to her feet and took the teacup from his

hands. He seemed almost surprised to discover he had been holding it at all. Setting the cup and saucer on the tea table, she reached down and took his hand. He made no protest, nor did he shy away. His fingers closed over hers as he sat there staring up into her eyes.

"I'm going to go slip into something comfortable. You look like you could use a rest."

"But…I have to…leave," he mumbled.

She leaned down and pressed the tip of her finger to his lips. "I'll be right back," she whispered, tracing her finger along the seam of his mouth, across his cheek and then around his ear.

Will shivered and closed his eyes. Josie's hand shook as she straightened. She fought back a wave of shame. So far everything was going just as Bella's notes said it would. Will was falling under the spell of the elixer, unable to think on his own. He was hers to command, hers to enjoy, hers to captivate.

He didn't seem to notice when she backed out of the room and left him sitting on the settee.

CHAPTER SIX

THE PARLOR was awash in candlelight. Without any desire to do more, Will surveyed the room from the settee. How long he sat there, he didn't know, but he had no desire to move. Somehow, that fact didn't bother him as it should have. Instead, he watched the fire behind the grate melt into glowing embers as the sun disappeared behind the mountain outside and the sky faded into dusk.

He heard men's voices in the corral and knew that the ranch hands were going through the motions of the end of a long day riding herd over stubborn cattle. Half-expecting Clay to show up at the house to report to Josie, Will wondered if he would be able to answer if the foreman addressed him. But Clay never appeared and Will didn't move, except to close his eyes.

He heard the soft rustle of fabric and knew that Josie was in the room again even before he opened his eyes. When he saw her, he thought for a moment he might be dreaming. Her hair was no longer upswept in its usual style, but hanging long, a few tempting tendrils artfully arranged to appear as if they had just strayed over her bare shoulder. Her lips were cherry red, pouting as if they needed to be kissed. Her cheeks blushed subtle rose. Will would have squirmed in his seat if he could have, but instead he merely sat and stared up at the beautiful innocent who had somehow transformed herself into the most beguiling, most deliciously tempting woman he had ever laid eyes on.

Curves and satin skin were well displayed against the rich, velvety fabric of her blood-red gown. She wore no fancy jewels, no pearls or diamonds to complement the garment. She needed none. She was perfection itself, temptation personified. She was all he ever wanted, all any man could want as she stood there smiling down at him, her violet eyes shining with age-old secrets and something else, something he did not wish to acknowledge.

She reached out for him, extended her hand and willed him to take it. "Stand up, Will darling, and come with me."

He didn't think he could move, not without any feeling in his arms and legs, but his heart was still beating, he was well aware of that, and his senses were working overtime.

Surprised that he could move after all, he took her hand and felt her warm, smooth fingers curl around his.

"Where are we going?" His voice sounded strange, faraway, as if it belonged to someone else.

Josie licked her lips, slowly, provocatively. "Does it matter?"

He shook his head. It didn't matter. If she led him over a cliff, in front of a train or through the fires of hell right now, it didn't matter one single bit.

His legs still worked, although five minutes ago he wouldn't have put money on it. She led him down the hall to the stairway and gave his hand a gentle tug. It was all the encouragement he needed to begin the ascent to the second floor. Her hips swayed from side to side, mesmerizing him as he followed her up the stairs. At the landing she paused until he was beside her, then looped his arm through hers as she turned toward the room at the end of the hall.

"It's dark here," he mumbled.

"Do you mind?"

"No."

"Here we are," she whispered as she opened a door. "Welcome, Will Ipo. Welcome to my room, my heart, my life." She stepped back, stood in the center of the room and motioned him in with a dramatic wave of her arm.

Somewhere in the back of his mind, in a place where caution and morality dwelt, came a sharp pang of warning. Will halted on the threshold, straining to think, to remember what that warning might mean, but all the time he was trying to recall he was staring at Josie, at the way the velvet gown caressed her, at the ivory skin showing above the very low, very indiscreet neckline.

He stepped into the room, crossed the space that separated them. Propelled by something beyond reason, he did the only thing his befuddled mind could think of—he took her in his arms.

IT'S WORKING!

Josie clung to Will, nestled her cheek against the

hard wall of his chest and listened to the erratic beat of his heart. Her plan was working. The elixir had taken effect, and she had Grandma Bella and her own mother to thank. Earlier in the parlor when she had found Will sitting stock-still where she had left him, Josie had felt a pang of guilt for having gone to such lengths, but now with Will's strong arms around her, all of her doubts fled.

Tonight. Tonight. She kept repeating the thought as she led him to a table set for two in one corner of the room. She had used the best china and crystal. Candles shed the only light. The champagne was chilled. She had opened one bottle before she went downstairs to fetch him.

Tonight I'll finally know what it means to be a woman.

Tonight I'll make him mine.

She refused to think beyond tonight. The consequences of what she was about to do were too many to dwell upon. Thinking about all the repercussions might cause her courage to falter.

"I thought we would have a light supper first," she said softly as she led him to the table and pulled out a chair for him.

He stood there stiffly, as if uncertain as to what he should do.

"Sit," she commanded in a honeyed tone.

Will sat. Josie leaned over and kissed him full on the lips. Her head began spinning so fast she was afraid she might swoon, so she closed her eyes and concentrated on the warmth of his mouth. Tempted to take more, to try one of the daring tongue-in-mouth kisses she had read about in Bella's journal, she pulled away and forced herself to take the seat opposite Will.

"It's nothing fancy, just a cold supper," she said.

She had been too afraid to light the oven and make much of a fuss in the kitchen. She had told Clay before he rode out with the men that morning that the engagement party had taken more out of her than she realized and that she was exhausted. She told him she had decided to send Lena to her daughter's and she intended to rest quietly in the house for the next couple of days. She emphasized that she didn't want to be disturbed. After hiding Will's horse in the lean-to behind Magdalena's herb garden, she was certain there was nothing to draw attention to the house.

When she took a bite of cold potato salad, she expected Will to follow suit, but he only sat there staring at her in a most disturbing way.

"Aren't you hungry?"

"What?" He blinked.

"Eat, Will."

Will picked up his fork and scooped up a healthy portion of potato salad. Josie smiled as she leaned over the table and gave him a pat on the cheek. She had palmed the small vial and added a few drops to his glass before she poured his champagne.

Supper, she decided a quarter of an hour later, was a bad idea. Perhaps if she had given Will the first dose of elixir with dinner instead of in his tea, things might have gone better, but she had to get him up to the suite—the only room where they would not be seen by any of the men who happened by the house.

Now Will couldn't do anything but sit and stare. He ate when she told him to and drank on command, but other than that, he simply watched her with a vacant look in his eyes.

"Would you excuse me?" She waited for him to nod, quickly gave up and pushed away from the table. The old velvet dress was so tight around the midriff that she could barely breathe. Bella Duprey had either possessed an hourglass figure or the world's most reliable corset.

While Will sat staring into the candlelight, she hurried to the side of the huge tester bed her parents had shared. Above the headboard hung Bella's portrait. Her grandmother lay in all of her nude glory, smiling down over the bed. Josie reached for Bella's journal on the bedside table and then, sitting on the edge of the bed, she quickly leafed through it until she found the page where the instructions for use of the elixir were recorded.

She scanned them quickly, gasped and covered her mouth with her hand. The book lay forgotten on her lap when she realized she had used twice the amount of drops called for. No wonder Will was in such a stupor.

She had wanted him pliable, not mindless.

"The Art of Fascination" detailed "Things to Do with Champagne." Bella's colorful subtitles included "A Mouthful of Champagne and More," and "A Little Bite Better Than Chocolate.'' They had all intrigued Josie. She had very deliberately studied "Instructions for Virgins…or Popping the Cork.''

As she glanced across the room at the man sitting stock-still at the table, she realized that she might have read the notes of an expert on lovemaking, but there was no way she could take the initiative and force Will through each and every step of lovemaking.

When she picked up the journal again, it fell open to a page in the copious section entitled, "Toddy's Tricks and Commands." In bold letters, Bella had written, "When issuing commands, always be specific and very, very explicit. Speak clearly and distinctly, but softly, in a tone as sweet as the purest honey.''

Although Josie thought the instructions were meant for dog training, she was desperate for clear, direct advice—and this was as good as she was going to get. She left the journal propped open on the table. Then she stilled her shaking hands, smoothed her skirt and took a deep breath. She crossed the room and stood at Will's shoulder. Reaching down, she straightened his collar, smoothed his long, dark hair where it curled against the black serge and then cupped his chin and turned his face so that he was looking up at her again.

She took another deep breath and let it out,

"Will, I love you," she said boldly. "I want you to make love to me tonight. It's my first time and I want it to be memorable. I want to know what it is like to have a man inside me, to thrill to his touch. I want to feel your lips on my body. I want you to take your fill. I want to remember this night for the rest of my life. I want that more than anything. Please, Will. Make love to me. Now.''

The invitation was about as specific and explicit as she could get. She closed her eyes and waited to see if he could do as she asked, knowing there would be no pleasure in having to command his every move, even with the instruction manual at hand.

She heard the chair hit the floor and when she opened her eyes again, Will was looming over her. He slipped his arm beneath her knees and scooped her up against his chest. The velvet skirt draped over his arm. Josie threw back her head and looked at him in awe as she looped one arm around his neck. When he turned with her, heading for the bed, she reached out and snagged the open bottle of champagne with her free hand.

''Wait,'' she said as he gently laid her on the spread. ''Put this on the table, please.'' She handed him the champagne.

He set it aside and then took her in his arms. His big hands were surprisingly agile as he reached around behind her and began working the long row of buttons that ran down the back of the gown. When they were free, he slipped the narrow fabric strips off her shoulders and pushed the gown to her waist in one swift move.

Josie blushed and tried to look away, but he held

her chin in his hands and made her look up into his eyes.

"You want to remember this night for the rest of your life," he said, repeating her directive. "You have to watch."

She shuddered, sighed and let him pull the dress all the way off her. Slowly, purposefully, surely, he stripped her of her underthings, her stockings, her shoes. When she lay shivering in anticipation, trying to cover herself with her hands, he leaned over her and began to kiss her with such intimacy that she forgot everything but Will, forgot that she had resorted to drugging him, forgot the propriety and modesty her mother had taught her.

She moaned into his mouth when his tongue slid between her teeth and explored. As he pressed closer and cupped her breast in his hand, she reached out and clutched his shoulders and drew him down upon her. His wool jacket felt rough and erotic against her nipples, driving her to yet another level of arousal.

"Now, Will. Please. Take me now."

"No," he whispered. She thought that he was going to refuse, to walk out of the room and leave her there, then realized he had only pulled away so that he could strip off his clothes.

She watched and waited with every nerve tingling. He was glorious, huge, his skin rich and golden brown all over. She imagined him on his island splashing in the sea in all his long, lean, naked glory. Embarrassment kept her from meeting his eyes, curiosity forced her gaze to roam down his chest, to his navel and below. He was fully aroused. She closed her eyes and bit her lip, willing herself not to think of the pain that would surely come when he deflowered her.

"You afraid?"

His voice sounded hoarse, as if he had to strain to speak.

"What?"

"Are you afraid?" The words came slowly.

"No," she whispered the lie. But she *was* afraid. She felt fear, longing, need, curiosity. But abandon outweighed them all. She raised her arms in invitation.

The bed springs creaked when he knelt over her and braced his hands on either side of her head. He leaned down and took her lips in a soul-searing kiss. As he lingered over her and toyed with her lips, their mouths were the only place they touched.

Josie moaned again and laid her hands at his trim waist. She ran her fingertips up and down his ribs, reveling in the smoothness and contours and felt herself melting inside. Her body wept for him, ached for release.

"Please, Will," she begged. "Please take me now."

PLEASE, WILL.... Please take me now...

The sound of her voice came to him from far, far away. There was no way he could resist, not now, not ever. As he lowered his head and took her nipple in his lips, something stirred in the back of his mind, a warning he was powerless to heed. He pushed the thought aside and slid his hand over her hip to the inside of her thighs. She was warm and wet and waiting.

Waiting for him to make them one.

Take your fill.

He whispered Hawaiian love words in her ear and gently tugged on her earlobe with his teeth as he slipped his fingers into her to make certain she was ready for him. He lowered himself over her, eased his way into her hot, honeyed recesses, slowly edging in and withdrawing when he reached resistance.

She wrapped her legs around his waist to keep him from leaving her. It was a blatant, silent invitation that sent him over the edge. He drove into her, sheathed himself in her and then held himself rigidly still until he felt her settle against him and begin to move again.

I want to remember this night forever.

He gave her what she wanted, brought her to fulfillment again and yet again before he reached his own climax. His head was beginning to pound as he pulled out of her and drew her up against him. From somewhere far off, a woman was weeping, fitfully whispering words of love even as she begged forgiveness for some deception.

Fully satiated, Will held Josie tight and closed his eyes against the throbbing pain in his head and the heaviness around his heart.

CHAPTER SEVEN

EARLY-MORNING SUNLIGHT sneaked through the edges of the draperies, slashing across the carpet, glinting off the champagne bottle's green glass. Josie wanted to run and hide from the sun and the reality of what she had done last night, but she was afraid to move and disturb the man who had held her all night long.

Her mind in turmoil, her soul racked with guilt, she had not had a moment's sleep. Instead, she had lain there imprisoned in Will's arms, listening to the slow, even cadence of his breathing, pondering on the exquisite joys of lovemaking. And wondering how Will was going to react.

Daring to tip her head back on the pillow, she was able to stare up at Bella Duprey. Much to her chagrin, the portrait appeared to be smiling even more than she recalled.

Go ahead and laugh, Josie thought in answer to Bella's smug expression. *You got me into this.*

When she settled back against the pillow and glanced over at Will again, her eyes widened in shock and fear. He was awake. Confusion marred his brow as he lay there frowning at her. He shook his head and blinked, as if trying to clear his vision.

Josie managed a weak smile.

Will let go of her and shot out of the bed, then stood there stark naked, staring down at her. When he realized he didn't have a stitch on, he jerked the spread off the bed, whipped it around his waist and knotted it. He looked for all the world exactly like an etching of a Polynesian warrior she'd seen in a copy of *Oddities of the World's Geographical Outposts*.

"I can explain everything—"

He cut her off without warning. "Oh, no, you can't. There's no explanation for this…this…"

"Transgression?"

"Outrage!" Will shot his fingers through his hair.

"I was only trying to—"

"You have *no* idea what you've done!" His complexion had darkened with his fury. "What in the hell did you give me last night?"

Reaching up, he pressed his hands against his temples and began to massage them. His dark-eyed gaze shot around the room, stopping briefly on the table littered with the remains of their dinner and then on the bedside table and the empty champagne bottle.

She was shaking now, trembling like a newborn filly. He looked mad enough to kill her.

"I only did it because I love you, Will. I couldn't let you ride out of my life without even trying to make you realize that you love me, too."

"Jesus, Josie." He sat down heavily on the edge of the bed, his back to her, his shoulders slumped as he propped his elbows on his knees and continued to massage his temples.

She got to her knees, drew the corner of the sheet over her body and scooted across the bed until she was kneeling directly behind him. When she reached out in a tentative attempt to touch him, he shrugged her away. Cut to the quick and burning with embarrassment, she dropped her hand.

He peered over his shoulder, still eyeing her suspiciously.

"I should have kept going. You haven't known me long enough to love me, Josie. How can you say you love me when you know nothing about me? You're infatuated, you're curious...but love?"

"Deny there was something between us from the moment you rode into the yard—"

"Oh, there's something between us all right."

"Before last night, before we made love...there was magic. Until I saw you, I didn't know what love is. With Julian—"

"Ah, yes. Julian. What about Julian?"

"That's over now, of course. No matter what you think of me, no matter what happens, I'll never marry Julian. I knew that the minute I decided—"

"To lure me up here? What in the hell did you give me? I've never felt this bad, even after drinking too much *okolehao*."

She pointed to the journal on the table. "Just an old elixir of my grandmother's. I found her journal in a trunk full of her old things. I think maybe the ingredients might have gone bad."

"Your grandmother? I'm glad I never ran into

her.'' He laughed, but the sound was full of bitterness, not mirth.

He had stopped railing at her and was silent for so long Josie began to hope he had finally calmed down enough to think things through. There was still a chance.

''Can you ever forgive me, Will? I'm so ashamed.'' She sat back on her heels and buried her face in her hands.

Will shifted onto his hip and half turned so that he could face her. It was the morning after her first time and she should have been happy, should have been with a husband who would cosset her and tempt her into making love again. She should have been a bride on her honeymoon with her whole married life ahead of her. Instead she was trembling, on the verge of tears, her spirit broken.

He almost reached out to take her in his arms, and would have, if the act would not have compounded the problem. She was everything a man could ever want in a lover and a wife. Josie was intelligent and beautiful, capable of running a huge ranch on her own. Only a cruel twist of fate kept them apart. He silently cursed himself for ever leaving Hawaii. He should have stayed on his side of the Pacific.

''Josie, this whole debacle is more my fault than yours.''

She shook her head. ''No. No, it was that horrible old trunk of Bella's, the journal, the elixir.''

''I should have been completely honest the day I met you, but when I told you about the Hearts, you were so very terrified of losing this place, there was such fear and worry in your eyes that I held back.''

Will knew he wasn't making much sense, knew he would have to go slowly, to explain carefully. There was no softening the truth.

"What do you mean? What did you hold back?''

"My name isn't Will Ipo. It's Will Heart.''

"Heart?'' Her hand went to her throat and she swallowed. "What do you mean, *Heart?*''

"Sam Heart was my father. I'm the oldest of his Hawaiian children.''

"So you're my...*uncle?* You can't be.'' Josie was staring at him as if he had just told her he was a cold-blooded murderer.

He ran his hands over his face. "Half uncle. And I wish to God I wasn't.''

Josie's mind was spinning. She had seduced her own uncle. Her father's half brother. This exotic, erotic man was her blood kin and had failed to tell her that until now, when it was too late...too late.

What had she done? Her one night of glorious passion, her attempt to win Will's love had ruined her life.

He was up now. With swift but efficient movements, Will was getting dressed, preparing to leave her.

How could she blame him for running out?

"You're leaving,'' she whispered, clutching the sheet against her breasts, unable to keep her voice from shaking. She realized she sounded like a lost waif but couldn't help it. Her life was over, ruined, all because she'd had no power to deny her need for Will Heart.

He paused with his hands on the top button of his shirt, dropped them to his sides and went to her. For a moment she thought that he was going to reach out and touch her, but he halted a good arm's length away and stood staring down at her, his brow furrowed in thought. Then he turned away. As he went after his boots he said, "In Hawaii, not two generations ago, this would not have been frowned upon. Among the *ali'i,* royal families intermarried to keep bloodlines pure. Brothers even married sisters."

"Too bad this isn't Hawaii," she said glumly.

Will sat on the chair he had occupied at the table last night and began to shove his foot into a boot. "That's why we must put this night behind us. I'm riding out of your life forever. You're young. You still have Julian. Maybe that little book of your grandmother's will tell you how to hide that you are no longer a virgin from him. What's done is done. We have to forget—"

He paused as he put on his second boot and stood up.

"And forgive? Can you forgive me, Will?" She would have given anything to take it all back. Anything.

"I forgive you, Josie. After all, it's as much my fault that this happened. I can't honestly say I didn't want you from the moment I laid eyes on you, but I never thought.... I should have told you the truth." He smiled, a slow, sad smile.

He picked up his jacket, settled his hat on his head. She thought he was going to leave without a word, but then he paused on the threshold and stared at the nude in the painting above the bed.

"That's my grandmother, Bella Duprey." Josie couldn't even bear to look at the portrait.

Will leaned against the door frame. "Your *grandmother*? Bella Duprey is the woman who bilked my father out of this ranch in a card game."

Josie shook her head. "No...that's impossible. My mother was her daughter. How could my father have ended up married to the daughter of the very woman who stole his ranch?"

"How did I end up in bed with you?"

"Oh, my God," she mumbled.

"The Heart men must all be cursed as soon as they meet a woman with Bella Duprey's blood."

Josie watched him push away from the doorframe and run his fingers around the brim of his hat. She had a hard time meeting his eyes.

"Where's my horse?"

"Out behind the house, in the old shed behind the herb garden. The men will be out working cattle by now. You shouldn't have any problem getting out to the road before you run into anyone."

"I hate to leave you like this, Josie. If there was anything I could do, anything at all, to change things."

There was nothing he could say to make things any different, to make things right. Even "I love you" was out of the question now and she knew it.

"Just go. Please." She couldn't bear the bitter-sweet torture any longer.

"Goodbye, Josie," he mumbled as he turned and walked away.

"Goodbye," she whispered, holding on until she heard his footsteps on the stairs. She gave him time to exit the house and then buried her face in her hands and began to sob.

CHAPTER EIGHT

WHEN JOSIE TOLD Julian the engagement was off, he reacted in his usual composed, collected manner. Deep down, she suspected he had never really wanted to be married at all. Ada Fairchild was a different story. She alternately railed at Josie and then tried to play on her conscience. What would people *think?* She had *always* thought of Josie as her daughter. Julian *needed* her, needed a good wife since, God knows, she, Ada, wouldn't be around much longer.

Finally, after an exhausting interview with both of them, Josie was alone in the big, silent house. Slowly, she walked upstairs and went straight to the bedroom, climbed onto the bed and took down Bella's portrait. Despite the weight of the painting, she wrestled it up the attic stairs and rested it against the wall. She took one last look at Bella reclining there so smugly before she threw the sheet over it. Then she carefully replaced Bella's journal, gown and the vial and slammed the trunk lid shut. The secrets of Bella Duprey would not be passed on to any more of her descendants, for Josie knew that since she could not have Will, she would never marry.

Straightening, she brushed the dust off her skirt, stiffened her spine and walked out of the attic. Josie pulled the door shut behind her, turning her back on the past, determined to face a long, bleak future alone.

EVEN THE SIGHT of a rainbow shimmering against Mauna Kea and the velvet air of the gentle trade winds could not cheer Will Heart when his ship reached the harbor at Kawaihae on the Big Island. He could see his family gathered at the water's edge eagerly awaiting the unloading of the ship that remained anchored offshore. He removed his hat and waved it over his head as he stood there at the rail, staring across the emerald water that separated him from everyone in the world he held dear. Everyone but Josie.

Since the day he had left her, he had not thought of anything else. Her eyes, her smile. More and more of his memories of the night they made love came back to him over the days and nights of the voyage, as if the elixir Josie had given him had buried the details in the corners of his mind. Time seemed to draw them out.

He waited to be on the last dinghy to take passengers ashore, unwilling to disembark until he was certain it was almost time for the big roan to be swung over the side and lowered into the sea. The animal would be forced to swim to shore like the other livestock. Thankfully there had been no shark sightings that day. He would have hated to bring the prime horse so far only to lose him now.

When he stepped ashore, his mother, Nani, greeted

him with a flower lei and open arms, nearly crushing him in her enthusiastic embrace. His brothers shouted aloha as they gathered to help escort the frightened horses and cattle swimming up to the shore.

"You not going mainland again. No moah." Nani admonished him sternly in heavy pidgin English as she shook a plump finger in his face.

"You miss me, Mama?"

Her face broke out in a wide, sparkling smile. "I miss you, Wiliama. Too much. No moah mainland for you. I like keep all my boys Hawaii."

Unable to keep the heaviness out of his tone, he shook his head. "No more mainland for me, Mama. I'm staying right here." His eyes followed the sloping land that led up to the gentle mountainside.

"What's dis I see? Why you so sad, Wiliama?"

His mother always read him like a book. "It's nothing," Will lied as he threw his arm over her broad shoulders. Nani was nearly as tall as he, her once lithe body now heavy, her hair showing few signs of gray. She always wore plumeria blossoms pinned in her hair and her dark eyes always sparkled with merriment. But right now she was watching him with deep concern, just as she would have done any of her nine children if they were hurting.

"I make *lau lau* for you, Wiliama. You eat, you come happy, you see." She reached up to pat his cheek as they stood side by side at the shoreline, watching the men lead the terrified animals across the beach.

Will was looking at his brothers and the others

without really seeing them. All he could think of was Josie and how he had left her. She would break her engagement, just as she said she would. But where would that leave her? After what she had done, he truly doubted she would ever seek out a husband. She was soiled goods. She had ruined herself because she had to have him. Although he did not admit as much to her, the same mysterious, compelling need had drawn him to her from the moment he laid eyes on her. There was definitely something more than mere attraction between them, some twisted reason fate had played itself out the way it had.

The thought of his mother's assurance that a bit of *lau lau* would make him happy brought a lifeless smile to his face. Will wondered if he could ever be truly happy again.

"WAIT HERE, Clay," Josie commanded as she kicked her horse and headed off through the scrub oak on the hillside. It was the third time that morning she had left the men staring after her without any explanation.

After she suffered through another bout of dry heaves, having emptied the contents of her stomach earlier, she mounted and rode back to the spot where she had left the others. Only Clay was there, waiting for her with a look of concern.

"What'd you eat for breakfast?"

"The bacon must have been bad," she said offhandedly as their mounts wove their way over the dry hillside. The summer grass had long since turned from rich emerald to gold. In late August, even mornings were too hot to bear.

"Seems to me if a body was eatin' bad bacon, she wouldn't have it every day." He reined in sharply, pinning her with a steely, blue-eyed gaze. "Let's have the truth, Josie. Ain't no one but me here to look after you now, me and Lena, and you've always been able to twist her around your little finger."

Josie took a deep breath and tightened her hands on the reins. She looked across the land. She wasn't rich by any means, not when all she had was tied up in cattle and land and both were subject to disease and the weather. But she had more than most, much more—even if she didn't have the one thing she wanted, the one person in the world who was forbidden to her, even now, when she needed him the most.

"I'm having a baby, Clay—"

Before she could say more, the foreman exploded. "Goddamn that mama's boy Julian Fairchild. I should'a knowed when the wedding was called off that he'd turned tail for some reason."

"I broke off the engagement, just like I told you."

She took a deep breath, knowing full well that she had Clay's trust. He had been her father's foreman and was as loyal as the day was long. The day he signed on at Heartbreak Ranch he swore he was done traveling and that they would be stuck with him until he died.

"I don't care what kind of fool notion you got in your head, young lady. Walker Heart left me to look after you and I'm gonna do what he'd do if he was here. I'm gonna ride into town and bring that damn Julian back at the end of a shotgun barrel.''

"The baby's not Julian's."

"I don't care if he hollers like a stuck pig, he's gonna do right by... What'd you just say?"

"The baby isn't Julian's, Clay, and I don't want to hear any more about bringing anyone back at the end of a shotgun barrel. I'm having this baby and I'm not ever marrying the father, or anyone else for that matter. If you're too ashamed to work for me, then you can leave. I won't hold you to any promises you made my father."

Her declaration left him stunned speechless, which for Clay Henderson was a new experience. He opened his mouth to speak, shut it, then whipped off his hat and ran a soiled kerchief over his forehead before he shoved his hat on again. When he glanced over at her, his brow was furrowed.

"It had to be that goddamn Hi-waiian," he mumbled, thinking aloud. "Wasn't it? You slept with that big handsome Hi-waiian that rode through here last spring."

"It doesn't matter who—"

"If I ever see him again, I'll kill him on sight."

"You won't either, you old buffalo. Besides, we'll never see him again. He's gone back to Hawaii and he won't ever be back." She was amazed at how time and fear of what was to come had dulled her senses, if not the pain.

Unable to hide his fury, Clay rode on ahead. She knew he would eventually come to respect her wishes, but he would have to work through his anger and disappointment in her. As Josie watched Clay skirt a rock formation jutting out of the hillside, she thought of Will and of the lonely days and nights, the challenges ahead. Standing alone on the hillside, Josie whispered to no one.

"No, he won't be coming back."

"Mebbe today you finally tell me whats'a mattah, Wiliama."

Will stared up at Nani, who stood over him, with her fists planted on her hips, the flounce of her *muu-muu* still swaying from her rapid charge across the wide lawn in front of their hillside home.

"What do you mean, Ma?"

"You know what. Tree months now you been home. Tree months long I gotta look dis sad face. You no moah happy and I like know why."

Will sighed. "I fell in love on the mainland. I fell hard."

Her frown deepened. "You love one *haole* girl? One mainland girl?" She shook her head, her lips pursed.

"I'm half *haole*, Ma, or did you forget?"

"You not going back mainland." Fear of losing him was behind her disapproval.

"I'm not going back."

"Mebbe I let you go one time moah, bring dis *haole* girl back Hawaii. You be happy den."

Life was simple for Nani. It always had been. He wished like hell it could be simple for him.

"I can't, Ma. I can't ever have her."

"So. She tink she too good for my boy?"

He could see her anger rise and tried to head off the eruption. No one slighted any of Nani Heart's children. Not ever.

"She loves me, too. At least she did when I left her."

"Den whats'a mattah? Go get her. I get tired you do nothing but look da sky all-a-time."

Will shook his head and then leaned back against a coconut palm and watched the trades blow the passing clouds across the sky. Without telling Nani everything, he knew he had to give some explanation as to why a future with Josie Heart was impossible. Otherwise his mother would never leave him alone.

"Ma, when I was in California, I went to see the ranch Papa talked about all the time. I saw the place he came from. His son, Walker, had passed away, so I was too late to meet my half brother, but I did meet his daughter, Josie."

How could he explain, how could he convince his mother that he had fallen hopelessly in love in less time than it took to ride around the Big Island?

Nani hiked up her skirt, gingerly lowered her bulky figure to the ground beside him and smoothed out the material of her *holoku*, the Mother–Hubbard style gown the missionaries had introduced to the island women. When only her bare feet and ankles were visible, she was satisfied. She leaned toward Will and brushed his hair back off his forehead. With a sad smile she said, "Dis Heart girl, she da one?"

"I'm afraid so, Mama. I fell in love with my own brother's *keiki*."

She took his hand and held it gently, sharing his pain as together they looked out over the mist-covered mountain, listening to the breeze that rustled the palm fronds and the cardinals calling out to one another in the trees.

Finally, Nani sighed. The sound seemed to come from the bottom of her toes. "Wiliama," she began, "I need talk-story. You listen. Long time ago, I was young girl. Pretty girl with no sense. I very wild. Very *lolo*."

"I can't imagine you acting crazy, Ma."

"I did when I sure I love one married *haole* man. But it no work. Pretty soon later, I meet Sam Heart. Sam plenty sick. Plenty tired from working on boat all-a-time. Sometin' make me love him. He loves Nani, too. Plenty. When Sam Heart ask me marry him, my heart go broke. I gotta tell him da truth. I already have one *keiki* in belly, *keiki* from the *lolo* time I lose my head over married *haole* man."

Will tried to comprehend where his mother's story was headed and then realized with shock that she was sharing a deep dark secret she had kept from him for his whole life.

"You were already pregnant when you married Papa?" He shoved away from the palm and took her upper arms in his grasp. Nani tried to look away but he forced her to meet his eyes.

"You were already pregnant, with me, when you married Sam Heart?"

"You make me shame," she whispered.

"No, Mama. No shame." There could be no shame when he felt like sunshine had just burst into his heart. "No more shame." Overwhelmed by the news, he had to ask, "So, I'm really not Sam Heart's son?"

She took his face between her hands and gently cradled it. "In all ways, Sam Heart is your faddah. All ways but blood, Wiliama. Sam always love you as his firstborn *keiki*. I nevah want tell you, but today I see the sadness in your eye and know I gotta tell you da truth. You and dat *haole* girl on da mainland not got same kine blood."

Will shook his head, then began to laugh as he pulled Nani into his arms and hugged her tenderly. They rocked back and forth, locked in an embrace until she shoved away from him. Her frown was intense, meant to be threatening, but Will only chuckled.

"What's wrong, Ma?"

"Now you going mainland, yeah? Mebbe you not come back home." Her voice trailed off and she would not meet his eyes.

Will pushed off the ground and braced himself, reached down and pulled Nani up beside him.

"Mama, you've just given me the one thing in the world I want most, but don't think I'll turn my back on you. Josie might not want to give up Heartbreak Ranch enough to move here, but you can bet we'll be back as often as we can manage. I love you, Ma. Besides, I want to find out as much as you can tell me about my real father. And, most of all, I want you to get to know Josie.'' He took her arm and started off across the lawn toward the clapboard cottage nestled against in the hillside.

"So you going back, den, to dat *haole* girl, for sure?"

"For sure, Ma. I just hope she'll still have me."

CHAPTER NINE

IT HAD TAKEN Will longer to make arrangements to leave the island than he had expected. Nearly a month and a half after his mother's revelation he finally found himself standing in the dark at the ranch house door again, feeling the bite of a crisp, late October night. He'd skirted the bunkhouse and outbuildings and ridden straight to the front door, hoping to find Josie at home, wishing he could have arrived before sunset.

Lamps were burning in the house, but the curtains were shut tight. As he raised his hand to knock, he hoped she was home, then prayed she was alone and had not married Julian after all.

At first, no one answered, then finally he heard footsteps on the other side of the door. The lock clicked and the door opened. She didn't react, didn't move, but simply stood there staring as if she were seeing a ghost.

"Josie?"

She was thin and pale. Violet shadows stained the translucent skin beneath her eyes. He stepped over the threshold unmindful of propriety and took her in his arms.

"Josie, what's wrong? Are you ill?"

She stood so stiff and cold in his arms that his heart pounded with anxiety. What in the world had happened to her since he had been gone? Five months had taken their toll and he could only blame himself.

Josie finally found the strength to stir in his arms. She'd had one of the greatest shocks of her life when she opened the door and found Will standing there looking gloriously sun-kissed, tall and proud and vibrant with life. If he hadn't grabbed her and held her close, she would have fainted dead away at his feet.

She took a moment more to compose herself and revel in the feel of his embrace before she planted her hands against the front of his heavy, sheepskin-lined duster and leaned back to look up into his eyes.

"Will," she whispered. It was all she could say.

The sound of heavy footsteps echoed in the hall. Will glanced up over Josie's head and watched as Clay Henderson pounded toward them with an old shotgun in his hands.

"Step away from her, mister, so's I can blow you to kingdom come." Clay's face was crimson, his jowls quivering with rage.

"Clay, no—" Josie whirled around, shielding Will as she stared down her foreman. "Put that old thing away. You'll wind up blowing yourself to bits."

"You've got a lot of nerve coming back here, mister." Clay ignored Josie's warning and kept the gun trained on Will.

Will had intended to move Josie out of harm's way, but Clay's words made him freeze, his hands gripping her arms. Somehow the foreman had learned what had happened between them. Somehow word was out and Josie was suffering for it.

"You told him?" Will said in disbelief.

"Told me? Hell, the whole damn basin had to know eventually, Ipo. Now, set her aside and face this like a man, though knowing what a coward you are, I can see why you'd hide behind a woman's skirts."

Will gently but firmly tried to coax Josie away. She clung like *opihi* clings to rocks in a tide pool. Reasoning quickly, Will realized Henderson had called him Ipo, which meant Josie hadn't confessed everything—but how had the whole basin come to know?

"Listen, I'm sure we can sit down and talk this out," Will began.

"Ain't nothing to talk out—"

"Clay, please, don't." Josie raised her hand, imploring Clay to stop.

"Hell, it ain't right not to know why I'm gonna kill him, is it?"

"Know what?" Will glanced down at the crown of Josie's head and then flashed his gaze back to Clay Henderson.

"You rode out of here and left Josie's good name in ruins and I ain't takin' that lightly. If her pa was here, he'd be doing just what I'm about to do."

"Stop it, Clay!" Josie pulled away from Will and took a step toward the foreman.

"Josie, get away now, step out of range."

"Clay, put that gun down or you're fired," she cried.

Will stayed where he was, frozen to the spot, terrified he'd lose Josie now that he had a right to lay claim to her. He didn't breathe until Clay slowly lowered the gun. Hurt emanated from the older man's eyes.

"Is that the way it is, then? You're choosin' this no-good, low-down stranger, takin' his side after he left you to go through everything all alone?"

"I love you, Clay," Josie said, her voice breaking, "but you don't know the whole story. If you'll just calm down…" She reached back for Will's hand and then out for Clay's. As she stood between them, clinging to each of their hands, she finished. "If you'll just let us explain, we'll tell you why we can't ever be together."

"We'll tell him why we *thought* we could never be together," Will corrected. "Then I'll tell you both why we *can* and why I've come back to make you my wife, Josie Heart. If you'll still have me."

His fingers tightened on hers as Josie stared up at him with tears shimmering in her eyes.

"What are you saying?" she whispered.

Will reached up and pulled off his hat. As he slipped his arm around her shoulders and drew her near again, he looked over at Clay and said, "Would you come in the parlor and hear me out?"

Once they were settled, Clay peppered them with questions and, despite her embarrassment, Josie quickly gave him most of the answers. She outlined the events of the night she seduced Will, as much as she dared, and then told him it wasn't until the next morning when the elixir wore off that Will told her he was Sam Heart's son.

Will had not let go of her hand throughout the telling, even though Clay had spent the entire time glowering at him with blood lust in his eyes.

"Now it's my turn to talk-story," Will began. "I was like a walking dead man when I got home," he began. "I had convinced my mind that I would never see you again, Josie, but my heart was dead inside. My mother could see my unhappiness. Although she knew it would shame her to tell the truth and she would probably lose me to you, she told me of my true heritage and freed me to marry you."

Josie reached out for his other hand and clasped them both to her heart. "What are you saying?"

"It seems Sam Heart wasn't my father, although he raised me as his son. My mother was already carrying me when she married him. She told Sam the truth but he wanted her enough to claim me as his own."

"Are you saying we're not related at all?" Josie slowly let the truth of his words sink in.

"Not by so much as a single drop of blood."

"That don't 'scuse you of anything in my book, boy," Clay growled. "The deed was already done, so to speak, when you rode outta here. This little gal here broke off with Julian, which had folks talkin', but then, when she was breedin' and started showin' and was still trying to work the ranch—"

"What are you saying?" Will went cold, his gaze roaming over Josie, taking in her pale cast, the dark shadows beneath her eyes. The deep sadness that lingered there. He let go of her hand and fingered the black cuff of her equally black gown.

"You were *pregnant?*" He couldn't seem to keep his hands from shaking. It was a possibility he hadn't even let himself consider.

She bit her lips and closed her eyes. He watched a tear leak from beneath her lashes and trail down her cheek.

"She miscarried a boy a little over two weeks ago," Clay said, never taking his eyes off Will.

Now Will could well understand the hatred he saw in Clay's ice-blue eyes.

"Oh, God, Josie, I'm so sorry. What can I say? What can I do to make this up to you?"

He hated himself for abandoning her when she had needed him the most. He had left her alone to suffer the loss of their son. His son. A boy he would never be able to hold in his arms.

Without a word, Josie went into the circle of his embrace and laid her head against his shirtfront. He could feel the moist warmth of her tears through the fabric.

Clay stood up and left them without a word, but the look he shot Will from the doorway spoke volumes. Will knew it would take time, if not years, before the two of them could become friends, but he promised Clay Henderson with a single nod that he would make things right for Josie. He meant to be there for her for the rest of their lives.

"I feel so helpless." He knew he still could not

possibly feel the loss as much as she, who had carried their child beneath her heart for more than five months.

"Just love me, Will," she said, pulling back to look up into his eyes.

"That's too easy. I've loved you since the moment I laid eyes on you." He brushed her hair back off her face and looped a long, thick strand behind her ear.

Josie tipped her face up to his and without a word, offered him her lips, her love, her life. Will leaned close, kissed the tears from her cheeks.

"I vow I'll never give you cause to shed one more tear, Josie Heart, if you'll marry me."

"Of course," she said on a sigh. "I can't think of anything I want more."

As he kissed her full on the mouth, Will felt her arms slip around his waist. When he lifted his head, she looked up at him and said with a tremulous smile, "You know, if I had never dabbled with Bella's elixir and taken a chance, you might have gone away thinking we were too closely related to be together. We would never have known the truth."

"Josie?" he whispered as he nuzzled her ear.

"Hmm?"

"Make me a promise."

"Anything."

"Don't ever, ever dig into that trunk of Bella Duprey's again. I have a feeling there's nothing but trouble stored inside."

"I promise I'll leave it alone."

"Maybe we ought to get rid of it." He smoothed

his hand over her hair, rubbed a strand between his fingers as he kissed the crown of her head.

Josie's frown was hidden against his chest. She would keep the promise not to open the trunk again, but she knew she would never be able to bring herself to get rid of it, not when there was every possibility that one day they might have a daughter, another strong-willed, hot blooded descendant of Bella Duprey.

"Josie?"

"What?"

"I said maybe we ought to get rid of that trunk."

Her mind made up, Josie leaned back so that she could smile into Will's eyes.

"What a good idea, darling, but don't you worry a bit about it. You just forget about that old thing." She kissed him full on the mouth to reassure him.

Humoring her, Will kissed Josie back, knowing as sure as the sun would rise tomorrow that Bella's trunk wasn't going anyplace.

HARMONY'S STORY

Dorsey Kelley

CHAPTER ONE

Heartbreak Ranch
Early Summer 1917

TOPPING THE KNOLL overlooking Heartbreak Ranch, Ben Panau abruptly reined in. The familiar stab of anger and loneliness knifed through him at the sight of the young woman below.

As always, Harmony Heart consumed his senses. Dawn cast morning sunlight over the mountain behind the house, and it seemed to Ben as if the brilliant rays caressed her ripe woman's body, burnished her hip-length mane to a shining, dark gold.

Oblivious to him, she stood beside her brown and white paint horse in front of the big old barn. He watched as she rinsed out a bandanna in the watering trough and rubbed it over her delicate nape. Ben's eyes narrowed. The rising sun backlit her slender legs through her split riding skirt. Her slim waist was cinched by a wide leather belt and her breasts thrust against a prim white blouse.

He forced himself to draw a long, slow breath. She had a body fashioned by the devil himself—tempting a man beyond endurance. And Ben Panau was definitely a hot-blooded man. How many times had he imagined those slender limbs clamped around his hips as beneath him she bucked and writhed in ecstasy?

Despite the sexuality Harmony's lush body exuded, he knew she was untouched. He knew of her many suitors and how she'd rejected them all. Although her body was the work of Lucifer, everything else about her personified all things innocent and good. She symbolized everything he lacked, but everything he craved: purity, privilege, respect...and she was so unattainable.

Harmony was the product of her prosperous parentage: everyone in the valley knew the Heart lineage sank deep roots into the last century. She was descended from a bold mix of exotic foreigners, adventurers, ranchers and even, it was whispered, a Barbary Coast madam. Tales about the madam were so vague and murky, he didn't give them much credence. Not that it mattered. Ben wouldn't have cared whether Harmony was delivered of royalty or whelped from a brothel.

With an effort, he turned his head away from the vision below. God, what a fool he was. As if a dirt-poor half-breed who came from a family of drunkards and rustlers would ever have a chance at the daughter of the valley's most prestigious and powerful cattle rancher.

Unfortunately, though the Kawaiisu Indians were generally peaceful, many were poor. What chances did they get to make themselves better? Precious few.

His hard eyes swept the majestic ranch house with its spacious veranda. A profusion of suncups and poppies embraced the ground floor walls. William had built the grand home for his wife, Josie, the year Harmony was born. A brand was burned into the front door—a broken-heart brand. The wide porch had been designed for sipping minted iced tea on lazy afternoons while dirty peasants like himself rode rank horses and ate dust chasing cantankerous cattle.

Carefully tended climbing roses ascended the stately white pillars and invited the admiration of callers. Their vines possessively hugged the wide front steps. Velvety blooms in yellow, crimson and soft coral welcomed those who were accepted into the hallowed doors of Heartbreak Ranch. The pillars rose to hold an equally impressive second story and announce to all that in this dynasty, there was *money*.

Ben's callused hands fisted on the pommel. Even though when they were children and he'd rescued Harmony from one reckless scrape after another, in all his life he'd never been invited inside the big house.

Along with the anger came a surge of frustration and bitter resentment. How he hated the bigoted whites who for years had sneered at him, who'd casually tossed disparaging taunts about his heritage. How he hated the judgmental, holier-than-thou attitudes of the valley people. It was a trap from which he feared he'd never escape.

Forcing back resentment, he urged his horse forward to pick its way down to the corrals. Clearing the debris from the water hole he'd been sent to had proved a task easily accomplished, but there was more work to be done, six new horses to break. And he knew he wasn't being entirely charitable to William Heart. A hard but fair man, William had never treated him with disrespect, or behaved as if he didn't value Ben's work breaking and training the ranch horses. No, William had treated him well, if impersonally.

But it wasn't enough. Secretly, Ben hungered for more. Forever lonely, ashamed of his mixed blood when logic told him he shouldn't be, he was angry and empty inside. He wanted to change the course of his life. At twenty-seven, he was a man, and a man needed a woman—someone to do for, to sit beside in front of a warm fire. He wanted a woman who rode out before dawn so she could let down her long hair and kick her paint pony into a wild headlong gallop over the meadow floor.

He wanted Harmony.

She thought her rides were private. She thought no one knew of her need to escape the strictures of society, escape the restraints she had to accept as the only daughter of William and Josie Heart. He understood what motivated Harmony, what made the blood flow through her veins. In a way, she was as limited by her position as he was by his.

He knew she even thought her private baths at the creek were unseen. She was wrong.

Harmony didn't notice as he approached her now.

If he let out a screeching war whoop, would she even raise her head? She rarely noticed him, and if she did, it was merely to smile or wave. Ben couldn't admit to himself that he lived for those brief, casual smiles. That the easy curve of her lips or a stray, tantalizing breath of her sweet fragrance had the power to halt his breathing. But it did, God help him.

Things couldn't go on this way. Not one to let matters lie, he was restless to effect change, to force others to respect him as an equal. He vowed to make Harmony aware of him as a man. For so long he'd been feeling the building pressure inside him to act. He'd make something happen, and soon, to shake up the complaisant rancher's daughter.

Somehow he'd prove himself.

HARMONY GATHERED her thick hair and pinned it back into the staid chignon she always wore around ranch headquarters. As an only child, she was acutely aware that she was being groomed to someday take over management of the ranch. There had been no son born to William, and yet she'd never sensed any regret on his part that she was female. In fact, only a single daughter was born to each generation for over fifty years.

All her life Harmony had basked in nothing but William's encouragement, and she strove to be worthy of that pride.

To go out riding alone, to gallop wildly and heedlessly across the land, bent low over her pony's neck, letting her hair tangle with her horse's mane, then, at the end of such an unseemly ride to strip and cool her overheated body in the softly swirling pool that formed at the bend of the creek—it was scandalous.

Yet these secret dawn and dusk rides were what made it possible for her to return, to bind her hair tightly to her head and again assume the manner of a gently reared young lady. Thank God no one knew of her escapes; she didn't know what she'd do if she were forced to abandon them.

"Miz Harmony?"

The voice behind her made her whirl in surprise.

"I didn't know anyone was there." When she saw who it was, she relaxed and her gaze fell away. She'd grown up with Ben and had never taken much heed of him simply because he said so little. He was quiet and intense, but safe.

"You didn't notice me." The faint hint of accusation in his tone confused her.

She shrugged. "I was...thinking."

He secured his horse to the corral fence and stripped the saddle from its back. "About your ride?"

She glanced at him sharply.

He was looking at her with a strange intensity and immediately she wondered if he could know where she went and what she did on her morning treks. She felt the first faint stirrings of alarm.

"Where have you been?" she asked, turning to him. When he merely smiled enigmatically, her alarm began to build.

"Don't worry, Miss Harmony, I won't tell anybody about your private little rides."

She went still. "You followed me?"

Dropping the saddle to the ground, he bent and untied a spade and a sharp-toothed saw from the latigo strings behind the seat. Straightening, he held them up. "Today? I had to clear out that spring after the last rain. Wasn't anywhere near you."

"But how would you know where I was?" she demanded.

"Today?" he repeated.

"Of course I mean today." She put her hands on her hips, more concerned by the moment. She'd shrivel up and blow away like a dandelion gone to seed if she thought any man had observed her private ablutions.

Without answering, he lifted the heavy saddle with one hand and headed for the tack room. She followed hard on his heels into the dim interior, which smelled of ancient leather and fresh horse. "Well?"

Lifting the saddle onto a peg alongside dozens of others, he laid an arm across the cantle and tilted back his hat to regard her. "Don't know exactly where you went today, ma'am," he drawled. He removed his hat and studied the single feather that decorated the band. "Could be you felt like riding around the rimrock, like you did last Thursday."

Chagrin tinged her cheeks a hot pink. But more than the mortification, she felt a rising fury. "You— you've *spied* on me."

He shrugged his large shoulders. "I think of it as seeing you don't come to any harm, get into trouble."

"I don't need a nursemaid," she stormed. "I've grown up on this ranch—just like you. I'm as capable of taking care of myself as you are."

He moved his shoulders again. "Maybe, maybe

not." Collecting a halter, he strode back into the sunshine and headed for his waiting horse. She chased him out, incensed by his nonchalance. Light glinted off the blue-black highlights in his hair before he resettled his hat.

"Ben Panau, I don't believe you were watching out for me. I think you were—were following to peep at me. Why, I could have my father horsewhip you off this ranch! How dare you?"

Abruptly he swung around to face her. She stumbled back a step, realizing at that moment how his shoulders stretched the faded old chambray shirt that clung to him. Why, she couldn't even see past their width to the house. He propped his hand on his hip. Even more alarming, his obsidian eyes glittered down at her. "How dare I take what you offer? You've got tubs up in that fancy house your daddy built, don't you? You don't have to go down to the creek."

Never had the almost silent Ben Panau spoken to her so brazenly. What on earth had gotten into him? She drew herself up. "Simply because I occasionally enjoy bathing out of doors doesn't give you permission to sneak around peeking at me. If you were a gentleman—"

His sudden laughter startled her. "A *gentleman?*" Throwing back his head, he guffawed heartily, his white teeth flashing against the darkness of his skin.

As his laughter trailed off, he regarded her with scorn. "I am what I am, Miss Harmony. A half-breed. A horse wrangler. A man." With this last, he appeared to loom closer though she did not see him move.

He reached out a hand then, and at odds with his aggressive manner, did a startling thing—with the tips of his brown fingers, he tenderly touched her cheek. She was so surprised at the abrupt gentleness, she couldn't move. He'd inherited his father's handsome features, his height, black hair and bronze skin, while his mother's white blood softened the sharp facial angles of his Indian legacy. Suddenly he filled the parameters of her vision, and all she could do was stare into the fiery depths of his eyes.

In them she read so many things she'd never seen before—a surfeit of emotion she'd had no idea he'd kept hidden. She saw incisive intelligence, fierce banked anger and desire. She could not ignore it when his gaze swept down her body like a heavy hand.

She shivered and her own fury abated. Powerful feminine awareness shot through her as she took in the deepness of his chest, the power of his muscular arms, the waiting intensity of his expression. A stray current of air brought an elusive wisp of his scent— like horses and clean earth and high mountain breezes. Without thinking she breathed him in. Who was this potent, forceful man? She'd known him all her life, yet how had she ever thought this untamed, dangerous creature *safe?*

"Harmony!" A deep masculine voice called from behind her.

"Yes, Papa," she answered with a relief she couldn't explain, and whirled to face her father as he descended the stairs of the big house. Ben stepped back.

The fiftyish, graying man walked with a regal bearing that befitted his station as owner of the biggest ranch in the valley, as well as pride in his Hawaiian heritage. He wore fine linen trousers, a white shirt and a straw hat with his trademark dried flower hatband. Beneath the brim his expression was solemn.

He took her hands. "Your mother and I have just received news from Hawaii that your grandmother is very sick."

"Grandma Nani?" Harmony cried, instantly recalling images of a plump Polynesian woman with a soft, comfortable chest and an ever-present smile. "What's wrong with her?"

"I don't know." In his hands William crushed a bit of white paper Harmony hadn't noticed before. "The note was quite terse. Your mother and I must go to her immediately."

"Of course," Harmony murmured. Despite William's startling announcement, she was acutely aware of Ben Panau, still standing behind her. He remained silent, but she could feel his dark eyes scorching her back. He listened to every word; she knew it.

"You know what this means, don't you, daughter?" William asked, holding her by the shoulders now.

Bewildered, she shook her head. "What, Papa?"

He drew a breath and looked deep into her eyes. "It means you must manage the ranch. You will have full authority. Full control. Since you were a tiny *kei-*

ke, I've trained you in these matters. Your mother and I will be gone several months. Do you think you are ready?''

Harmony felt her eyes widen, her heart rate accelerate. All her life she had diligently tried to learn each aspect of ranch life and its management. For this land of her forebears, this rich, producing, beautiful land, she knew a deep abiding connection that infused her very soul. She was a proud woman—perhaps even possessing a touch of arrogance—and she knew it. But she had so much to be prideful of. How could she help it?

And now, though the position would not be permanent, to be temporarily responsible for the property would provide a testing ground.

It was something for which she'd waited years.

Swallowing convulsively, she nodded. ''I'll take care of everything, Papa. Just see to Grandma Nani. You can count on me.''

For a long moment William searched her eyes. Apparently he found what he wanted in them, because he seemed to sigh in acceptance. ''Remember one thing—even though your heroine in Washington is trying to get the politicians to give women the vote and property ownership, it isn't law yet.'' He gave her a stern look. ''So, at least in public, you'll have to defer to Old Clay. You understand? And Magdalena will be here, of course.'' Magdalena was the grandly corpulent housekeeper, whose warm cookies and warm hugs seemed to solve all problems.

''Yes, Papa,'' she said with wildly uncharacteristic

meekness. She knew when to keep her mouth shut. William was a forward-thinking man. He respected women's intelligence, agreed they should have the legal rights so long denied them. But he was still a man.

For the first time William noticed the Kawaiisu still quietly observing them. Surprising Harmony, her father said, "You'll help her all you can, won't you, Ben?"

Ben Panau straightened, drew himself up. His gaze strayed to Harmony and his eyes briefly glowed. "Yes, sir. Whatever she asks of me, I'll do."

Satisfied, William started back for the house. "Josie is packing now. We leave within the hour. The steamship leaves San Diego harbor in two days. It'll take five just to sail to Honolulu."

A slim woman, who wore her blond hair coiled about her head, appeared in the great doorway. Her striking violet eyes, which Harmony had inherited, were darkened with worry. "We're all packed, William. We can go now."

"All right, Josie," William said. "I'll have a wagon hitched and brought around."

Josie came down the steps to lay her hand on William's arm. "No. We'll ride together."

William smiled into her eyes.

As Harmony watched, something passed between the two, an exchange she'd witnessed often between her parents. A meeting of minds. An understanding. Great love and communication she'd never seen enjoyed by any other couple.

Although Harmony savored their unconditional

love, she also understood that the force of emotion shared by them was an invisible but powerful circle in which she could not be included.

Only in recent years had she begun to long for the same incredible bonding for herself. Was there a man in the world who could engender in her an equal devotion—a love that would bind her to him for life? And did a man exist who could give such love in return?

"GO, GO!" BOOMED Old Clay Henderson. "Have a good trip. Don't worry about a thing." When hired for the position of foreman many years ago, Old Clay had already had a mane of gray hair, stooped posture and tortoise-rough wrinkles furrowing his sun-browned skin. The man was ageless. But he had proved an adept foreman for Heartbreak Ranch, and his loyalty was unquestioned.

He stood beside a nervous Harmony while Ben saddled the horses William and Josie would ride to the railway station in Caliente.

Two geldings were brought out, both hip-marked with the ranch's signature broken-heart brand, and bags were tied to latigo strings behind the saddles. Ben held the reins while William helped his wife mount. William directed a constant stream of reminders and directions at his daughter.

"And if we're not back for fall roundup, just go ahead as we always have. Remember to cull those old cows from over at the cow camp. Old Clay will help you. Rely on him."

"Yes, Papa," Harmony said. For some reason she was having difficulty saying goodbye. Suddenly she was apprehensive about being left alone, even though she was a full twenty-one years old. Doubts assailed her. What if she made damaging decisions, brought disgrace upon Heartbreak Ranch?

She stood beside the stirrup of her mother's horse and felt a moment of panic. As if guessing her doubts, Josie leaned down and hugged her. When the older woman settled in her saddle, she gasped and her hand went to her throat.

"Oh goodness," Josie exclaimed. "William, I forgot all about the Wilkersons' visit. We won't be here."

With natural ease, William mounted. "It's lucky they're coming now, Josie. They'll help keep Harmony company. She can entertain them. They'll only be here a few weeks, and then they'll go back East." He smiled and his almond-shaped eyes crinkled wickedly. "I know how sorry you'll be to miss your cousin's visit."

Josie laughed self-consciously.

"You don't like the Wilkersons, Mother?" Josie asked curiously. She'd never met her mother's distant cousins from Boston.

"It's not that," Josie said hurriedly. "Edna and Randolf are just a bit…stiff. That's all. I'm sure you'll have a wonderful visit with them. Give them my regrets, won't you?"

"Of course, Mother. Don't worry about a thing. Go and take care of Grandma." Harmony squared her shoulders and stepped back. She'd been trained for this moment. She would do her parents proud. After all, she had Old Clay as an adviser and there was none better. The grizzled cowhand had forgotten more about cattle ranching than she ever hoped to learn.

This thought buoying her, she waved her parents off and pivoted toward the barn. Ben was still there.

He stood with one long muscular leg propped behind him on the corral fence and his arms draped along the top rung. Everything about him shouted lazy nonchalance. Everything except his eyes; they glittered.

His mouth twisted in a shrewdly knowing grin, and she had the abrupt and uncomfortable notion that he sensed her underlying uncertainty. She wondered if he could know of her desperate desire to do her parents proud and run the ranch well.

Under his regard, she flushed. *Damn.* She found herself hoping that tomorrow when she woke this new Ben would magically return to the reserved, quiet man with whom she'd grown up. She certainly didn't know how to cope with the sharp-eyed, plain-speaking, *disturbing* male who now confronted her.

Without her parents as a buffer, she'd have to handle Ben on her own.

HARMONY'S FIRST TRIAL came less than four days later when she was confronted by a disaster guaranteed to strike fear into the heart of any self-respecting rancher.

Magdalena shook her awake in the middle of the

night. "Harmony, dear, you must get up. There's a terrible fire."

As Harmony dressed and rushed downstairs, every lamp blazed unnatural illumination into the dead of night, but it couldn't blot out the ominous shimmer of fire on the horizon. Beside the foreman, Ben stood tensely, along with four hastily dressed cowhands whose shirttails hung loose outside their jeans.

Without preamble, Old Clay spit orders. "Ben, you, me, Roberts and Julio will head for the Beyers'. We can help them clear land before the flames get to their barn. Get two buckboards hitched and find the shovels."

Three wagonloads of neighboring men careened into the yard. She wasn't surprised. As the largest ranch in the valley, her home had always become disaster headquarters.

She gathered her skirts. "The neighbors are coming, Clay. I'll organize a water brigade. We'll get barrels filled at the creek and send the men after hoses and buckets. Cook can prepare sandwiches."

The raging inferno swept through the valley, damaging two small ranches, decimating others. The flames roared through a good half of the alfalfa William had planted for winter feed, ate up at least a third of the natural cattle forage. Thank God it hadn't come near Harmony's beloved meadow.

No one knew what started it.

Through some miracle, human lives were spared, although some livestock was lost.

Then Clay, who was helping dig a final trench for

a last backfire, slipped as he was shoveling dirt and
fell into the ditch.

Ben leaped down and hauled him out. Old Clay
was still alive, but his leg and several ribs were broken.

While Magdalena splinted Clay's leg and tightly
wrapped his ribs, Harmony arranged to send him
down the mountain to a good doctor in Caliente. She
had Ben lay the foreman into the back of a buckboard
and tucked a blanket under Clay's chin.

"You'll be all right," she assured him, wiping his
grimy face with a damp rag. "Doc Scranton will fix
you up and you'll be back in no time."

He smiled weakly, and Harmony had to hide her
concern over his sunken features.

"Ben will help you run the ranch, Missy," Old
Clay wheezed out. "He's a good boy—got a solid
head on his shoulders. He'll be your foreman till I'm
back on my feet."

She stared after the wagon until it disappeared, ex-
haustion weighing down her limbs. Surely Old Clay
hadn't meant Ben Panau?

But, tiredly, she thought of the world events happening outside her valley. With the growing public
demands for action overseas, President Wilson had
declared war just months ago. Harmony sighed. The
War to End All Wars was robbing the area of able-
bodied men, young men, capable men. Even though
the ranch was prosperous, it was running on a cowhand staff of stove-up old-timers and youths shaving
peach fuzz.

She recalled images of Ben as a youngster, trotting after Old Clay, and later as an adult, aiding the patient foreman. Though nobody said much about it, Clay had taken the Indian youth under his wing, taught him, encouraged him.

And now it became apparent that Old Clay fully expected young Ben to step into his boots.

Harmony would have to see Ben every day, instead of just occasionally. She would need to confer with him, ask his opinion, rely on his judgment. They were being thrown together by circumstance, bad luck and, she thought ruefully, some wicked demon's idea of a good joke.

Ben Panau had suddenly become very important to her, and integral to the success of Heartbreak Ranch. Harmony wiped a hand over her eyes. In spite of his altered status and what it might mean in the long run, all she could think of was one thing.

Ben Panau had seen her naked.

CHAPTER TWO

A THIN FILM of smoke hung in the air, filtering the dawn's sunrise through otherworldly colors of melon and coral. Falling soot and ash covered the buildings, the ground and even the backs of the cattle. Harmony tasted the stale odor on her tongue and grimaced.

Though she'd finally gotten several hours of sleep, she still felt tired. However, it was her duty to supervise the return of the many water wagons, to thank her neighbors for their quick response to the fire and to see that they were all fed breakfast before going back to their own ranches.

When the last wagon rumbled down the rock-lined drive, she spied Ben near the corrals. He was giving orders to two men. She approached and waited for him to finish. When he turned and settled his dark eyes on her, she felt edgy, nervous.

"Good morning." She tried to greet him lightly. "How does it feel? Your new position, I mean."

He tipped his hat, still studying her. "It's a good fit, I think. I've assigned Roberts and Julio to the horses since I won't have time for them now."

"It takes two to do your old job?" she asked, then, watching the men head for the horse pasture, answered her own question. "You have always done the work of two men, haven't you?"

Ben shrugged and allowed himself a small smile. "If you say so, ma'am," he drawled.

Harmony laughed briefly, then glanced out over the blackened hills. Self-consciously, she folded her arms beneath her breasts. Out of the corner of her eye she studied him. He stood solidly on run-down boots. Wear-faded jeans clung to him. Open at the neck, sleeves rolled to his elbows, the worn, blue chambray shirt couldn't hide his swell of biceps, honed by hard ranch labor. A black Stetson was pulled low over his eyes.

For just the briefest moment, Harmony's breath caught.

To distract herself, she turned her gaze to the charred hills and her mood turned somber. "I hope you've listened well to Old Clay, because we've got rough times ahead." She faced him apprehensively. "I've got to get the ranch in order before my parents come back in three months. I can't have them return to—to this." She gestured to the burned grasslands and knew he understood.

He studied the hills, gaze narrowed. "When we can, we'll reseed. It's not too late in the year to grow more feed. I've got to spend a week or so riding out with the men to take a tally, see exactly how much stock was lost—what we've got left. Meanwhile we'll be moving cattle to unburned pastures. Thank God none of the buildings went up."

"Yes," Harmony agreed, his composure reassuring her. "I suppose we should be thankful for that."

On the basis of their childhood friendship, Harmony liked and respected Ben. Back when they were kids, it seemed he was forever rescuing her from scrapes. When she was nine and an inveterate tree climber, she'd gotten herself up so high in the old oak in the meadow that she'd been too frightened to get down. She'd cried for an hour until eleven-year-old Ben scaled the tree, then patiently and kindly talked her down.

Later, he hadn't allowed the other ranch children to tease her about it.

Other such occasions flitted through her mind. She guessed she'd taken him for granted, assumed he would extricate her from whatever predicament her rash impulses propelled her into. He was simply always there—like the great immovable mountain at the foot of which Heartbreak Ranch was built.

Despite her misgivings, she was glad to have his knowledge at her disposal now.

Her gaze slid over his high chiseled cheekbones. He had a generous mouth and even teeth, which in his rare smiles flashed brilliantly against his tanned skin. Night-dark brows winged over his eyes, his most arresting feature. He glanced down at her now, a question in their inky depths.

Quickly she averted her gaze, embarrassed to be caught staring. "Uh, I'll just go get a bottle for that leppy calf. It's been hard on the little guy with his mother lost in the fire."

Before she could hurry away, Ben placed a deliberate hand on her slender shoulder. "I won't let you down, Harmony. Together, you and I will set the ranch to rights."

Vital, strong, his hand covered her shoulder like a burning brand. Streaks of heat lightning shot up her spine. She managed a weak nod before turning away. She didn't like the feelings coursing through her whenever she and Ben met. It was as if a new, dynamic man had appeared in her life, but a man she already knew. How could that make sense?

TO SUPPOSE THAT Ben was pleased to be promoted to foreman was to predict that the sun might come up in the morning. Of course it would. And of course he was.

While saddened about Old Clay's injuries and concerned about lost forage and stock, Ben knew that these circumstances were temporary.

The dearth of fit men caused by the war, combined with the valley's terrible fire and Old Clay's incapacity—all had created this opportunity for Ben. It was a boon he would not squander.

With hard work, he'd try to overcome the stigma of his ne'er-do-well family, his whisky-sot father. As he always had tried.

James Panau had long been Caliente's town drunk. While Ben hated what James had become, he couldn't bring himself to hate his father. How could he—his own flesh and blood? The good memories were pitifully few, but Ben treasured them. No, he couldn't hate James.

But he could distance himself. And so, since adolescence, when Old Clay had decided there was something worthwhile about young Ben, he'd done everything he could to be different from James Panau. Ben never drank, he kept his manner reserved, and when it was time to work he made sure none could say he was lacking. By the age of sixteen Ben had moved into the ranch bunkhouse, where he still lived.

Now, watching Harmony hasten off to get the leppy calf's bottle, he knew a deep satisfaction. At last she was becoming aware of him, whether she wanted to or not. Sensitive to every nuance of her mood, he knew she was beginning to look at him as a man.

Soon, he vowed she would look at him as a lover.

THE DAY CAME when the Wilkersons were scheduled to arrive, and Harmony took special care with her appearance. Before her bedroom mirror she checked her high-necked white blouse, decorated with miniature buttons to the throat. The blouse tucked into a neatly fitted sienna brown skirt of light muslin. On her feet she wore sensible soft half boots. She gathered her thick hair into a modest chignon and pinned it tightly to her nape.

Satisfied she looked like a grown woman capable of running a cattle ranch, she headed for the kitchen to instruct Cook on the week's menus, as well as refreshments to be served upon the Wilkersons' arrival.

That accomplished, she collected a large mug of black coffee and a warm bun slathered with freshly churned butter. On the spacious veranda, she sank her teeth into the fragrant bun and scanned the road on which the Wilkersons would arrive. Yesterday she'd sent her father's best surrey—a black carriage of four large wheels and fringed top—to the railroad station in Caliente to collect her mother's cousins.

William had purchased a modern Mitchell automobile but, woefully, the road to town was not yet in good enough shape for regular travel in the horseless carriage.

Though she'd never met Randolf and Edna, Harmony was determined to be a gracious hostess. Word of her behavior would certainly get back to Josie and William, and Harmony would make sure the Wilkersons had every reason to heap praise upon her. She considered this another small test she must pass on the path to proving her worth as manager.

Perhaps when William returned, he would be so thrilled with her work, he would consent to let her continue—at Old Clay's side, of course. Never would she wish to push the foreman out of a job, but someday he would retire....

The clatter of the black surrey came from the dirt road leading to the house. Rushing out, she hesitated at the top step, shading her eyes against the sun. Working at an outdoor table pushed up against the outside of the barn, Ben was repairing a broken plow. Parts and tools were spread out on the table in a jumble. At the surrey's approach, Harmony saw him glance up. Wiping his hands, he strode forward.

Hurrying down the steps, she met the couple as the man pulled the horse to a halt and set the brake. Ben reached the carriage at the same moment.

"Welcome to Heartbreak Ranch," Harmony sang out, and was chagrined to hear so much of her natural exuberance invading her carefully modulated tones. At all times her mother was serene, calm, in control. Harmony was determined to emulate her. She cleared her throat. "Um, please, come in and rest yourselves," she said, her voice now satisfyingly amenable. "You must be very tired."

"Indeed," the woman replied tartly. "All that bumping and jostling—why, it's a wonder my poor head hasn't rattled clear off my shoulders!"

Solicitously Ben reached up, and without looking at him, the woman placed a gloved hand delicately in his and gathered her skirts. Edna Wilkerson was a handsome woman who'd aged rather well into her late forties. Her hair, still a rich brown with only a few silvered streaks, was evenly plaited and pinned into a crown atop her head. A tiny bird-box hat was perched on top, with an even tinier sparrow nestled among silk leaves and berries.

Her Gibson Tuck blouse was high-necked with a hand-embroidered floral motif on the front panel. It tucked neatly into a belted navy serge skirt. Her smartly fashioned shoes were glacé kid with a Paris toe. A delicate lace parasol lay over one shoulder. Harmony eyed the entire ensemble with envy. Her own brown muslin skirt and simple blouse made her feel plainer than the sparrow decorating Edna Wilkerson's hat.

Somewhat daunted, Harmony fell back on her rehearsed speech. "Uh, I hope you'll enjoy your stay here. I'm Harmony, William and Josie's daughter. Unfortunately, my parents were called away to Hawaii on urgent family matters—"

"What's that?" the man barked, speaking for the first time. "William's not here?" He was tall and thin, with long furrows beside his mouth that gave him a dour appearance. He wore unrelieved black, and a wide, flat-brimmed hat. For no reason at all, Harmony thought of an oversize buzzard.

"I'm terribly sorry. They wish me to convey their regards and deepest apologies. If you would—"

"Goodness, Randolf," Edna burst out. She released Ben's hand and sank back heavily onto the carriage seat. She faced her husband with alarm. "We've come all this way and they're not *here*. This is unconscionable!"

Randolf made no effort to disagree, merely sat in the surrey scowling at Harmony as if she were entirely responsible. One part of her wondered if they would ever make it out of the conveyance, or would simply turn it around and head back to the railroad.

Harmony wrung her hands. Matters were not getting off to a good start, not at all. "It's my grandmother—she's very ill. They had to go, you understand."

"I understand one thing, missy," Randolf boomed.

"Your parents invited us out here for a nice long visit, and when we arrive, they're not even here to receive us."

"Yes." Edna fairly quivered with indignation. Her little bird quivered, too.

"I'm so sorry. Please. Cook has prepared a wonderful meal in your honor—roast duck and baked apples and fresh string beans. Won't you come in?"

Randolf continued to eye her balefully, but Edna heaved a sigh of resignation. "Well, I could force down a bite. Do you know it's all of sixteen miles from town?" she demanded, as if Harmony had no knowledge of the surrounding area.

Again she placed her hand in Ben's open palm, but this time she actually looked at him.

Suddenly she gave a little yelp and snatched her hand back, tucking it beneath her chin. She stared at him wide-eyed. Weakly, she mewed, "Randolf?"

"Stand back," Randolf commanded Ben. "I'll hand my wife down."

Harmony gasped at the cut. Her gaze flew to Ben's face. His brows lowered and his skin darkened, but he retreated several paces. Silently, he watched the man help his wife to the ground.

Edna murmured anxiously, lowering her voice but not so much that both Harmony and Ben couldn't hear. "Is that an *Indian*, Randolf? Why, I can't believe..."

"Don't let him bother you, my dear," Wilkerson reassured his wife. "Won't let the dirty savage near you."

At a loss, Harmony sighed inaudibly. Dismayed by the Wilkersons' attitude, she knew that, unfortunately, such bias still bit deeply into many white minds—even now, long after most tribes had been herded onto reservations.

The Kawaiisu were a peaceful people and had co-existed amiably with the white valley ranchers for many years. But the Wilkersons couldn't know that, Harmony reasoned.

Ben glared daggers at Harmony, his dark eyes snapping condemnation, his mouth drawn tight and hard. Fierce anger emanated from every line of his stiff frame. She blinked. What did he expect her to do?

About to make a protest, Harmony saw Randolf flip the horse's reins to Ben. Then suddenly she had her hands full ushering the chattering, complaining woman and the grim man up the steps and into the house. Inside, she belatedly realized she'd forgotten to thank Ben.

TWO INTERMINABLE DAYS passed while Harmony entertained the Wilkersons—*inside* the house. Nothing she could do would persuade them to tour the property, take the air or even recline on the veranda.

She was forced to allow Ben to manage things on his own, but she didn't worry much. She had complete confidence in his ability—she simply wanted to be helping.

She served the guests tea and scones Cook had specially baked. She saw to it baths were drawn. She played the piano—Bach and Mozart. But mostly she listened to Edna talk…and talk…and talk. Randolf occupied himself with a careful reading of a year-old issue of *National Geographic*.

In the late afternoon of the second day, Harmony wearily sipped her fourth cup of tea and politely nodded at the proper times. They were seated in the parlor, a small room decorated with thick area rugs, several striped settees and oaken sideboards. A comfortable room, though seldom used, Harmony had always liked it. Until now. Today it felt stuffy and claustrophobic. Outside, she could tell it was a real scorcher. But there would be the ever-present breeze soughing through the valley. She gazed longingly out the window at the sunlit meadow.

Edna had serious and set views on the proper upbringing of young ladies. Having no children of her own, she considered her childless state a uniquely wonderful platform from which to objectively judge how others should raise them. Now, she reached over and patted Harmony's knee, bringing her back to the room with a jolt.

"Of course it's obvious that Josie has done an exemplary job of teaching you beautiful manners. What a lovely young lady you've turned out to be—not at all like those rather *fast* girls you see now in society—with their modern ideas."

"Well," Harmony answered awkwardly. "Thank you."

"So circumspect and genteel," Edna continued approvingly. "I'm certain you'll catch the eye of a nice young man in your valley here."

Harmony murmured agreement, feeling it prudent not to mention she'd already received—and rejected—offers from most of the affluent ranchers' sons in the area.

"Of course you're so removed—here in the country—from sophisticated city life. Why, you can't have heard about the doings of that horrid Alice Paul and those silly suffragettes." Edna shuddered delicately. "Marching on Washington, indeed! Can you imagine what poor President Wilson must think? It's no wonder he continues to reject their appeals. Women voting," she scoffed. "Owning property."

Harmony frowned at the mention of her idol, Alice Paul. She squeezed her eyes shut and prayed for forbearance; she knew that all people were not so modernistic in their views about women's rights.

"Stupid, empty-headed notions," Randolf agreed with his wife, not looking up from his close perusal of a pair of half-naked African women staring at him from the pages of the magazine.

"I don't know what I'd do without my Randolf," she went on, dreamy-eyed. "Why, he takes care of everything. A woman shouldn't have to worry about business and money and such. Isn't that right, dear?"

"Yes, dear," Randolf replied without removing his attention from the magazine. Suddenly he glanced up. "Say, who's running the ranch while William's gone?"

"A very good foreman," Harmony replied. In light

of Edna's comments she refrained from mentioning *she* was actually managing the ranch.

"Point him out to me," Randolf demanded, tossing aside the magazine and rising. He hitched his pants up over his gaunt frame importantly. "Best make sure the man's doing his work and not slacking off. William would want me checking up, I'm sure."

"Oh!" Harmony cried, "That won't be necessary. Ben is a fine, extremely competent foreman. Don't let it concern you." A picture of Randolf discovering that the ranch manager was the "dirty savage" burst into her mind.

"I'm sure he's competent," Randolf agreed. "I'll just keep him on his toes." He patted her shoulder and clumped determinedly out the front door.

Harmony sat frozen, unable to think of a way to stop him. After he'd left, she endured yet more of Edna's moralizing. Grimly she waited for the explosion.

When ten interminable minutes passed and her nails had dug furrows into her palms, Randolf returned. "Asked around—a cowboy said this Ben was out checking stock." He rubbed his lean chin. "I suppose that's good."

"He's very thorough," Harmony said, glad of the reprieve. She seized a nearby plate of baked goods. "Can I interest you in another of Cook's ginger snaps?"

Disaster averted, if only temporarily, Harmony watched with sinking heart as Randolf resumed his seat and magazine and Edna launched into yet another lecture on the evils of "fast" young women and the merits of good schooling, demure manners and ladylike behavior.

After being shut in for forty-eight hours, Harmony could bear it no longer. Abruptly she stood, startling the woman, for once, into silence. "I'm sorry, but I've enjoyed your conversation so much that I completely forgot a very important duty my father assigned me. I must...um...check the hay supply."

"What's that?" Randolf interjected. "Hay supply?"

"Oh, I mean the...uh, reseeding for the burned fields. Our foreman is having several pastures cleared. I'll just be an hour or so. Please rest and refresh yourselves. I'll look forward to seeing you both at supper. Cook is preparing a delicious meal of garden vegetables and chicken stew."

With that, she escaped to her room, pulled on her split skirt and crept down the back stairs. Glorious sunshine spilled over her face and Harmony relished it. But it *was* hot. At the barn, no one was around save a saddled horse standing three-legged at the hitch rail. It was Ben's big bay gelding. Eyes half-closed, the bay swished away flies with a languid black tail. Ignoring it, Harmony caught up her paint pony and heaved a saddle onto its back.

"Come on, Apache," she whispered into the mare's alert ear, "We're going to escape—at least for a while." With that, she mounted and headed along the meadow trail at a circumspect trot.

Once out of view of the house, she tore the pins

from her hair and kicked her pony into a headlong gallop. After her confinement inside the house, it felt marvelous and wonderfully unconstrained. The wind blew through her hair, which streamed behind her like a banner. White-blossomed buckeye trees flew past. Scents of spicy sage mingled with the pleasant odor of sun-heated earth. The acrid smoke was almost gone. She laughed with sheer joy.

After a mile, she drew up and let Apache blow. With one hand, she loosened the tiny pearlized buttons at her throat and held the edges of her blouse open to let the breeze cool her. For the first time in two days she felt as if she could draw a deep breath. The clarity of the mountain air filled her lungs and she sighed, at last relaxing.

Sun beat upon her uncovered head, but she didn't mind. Already the shadows were lengthening and the afternoon winds were dying down. Within an hour or so it would cool.

It took only twenty minutes of riding to reach her favorite bend in the creek. Willows swayed gracefully over the clear gurgling water. It splashed onto a rich emerald profusion of lilies, reeds and lupine. Groupings of boulders framed the alcovelike area and, as she slid off her mount, Harmony smiled.

Now, more than ever, she needed these private jaunts. Enduring Edna Wilkerson's endless monologues would try a saint. Harmony wondered if, after several weeks of Edna's company, she would maintain her sanity. To prevent herself from running screaming into the night she promised herself frequent rides.

A good horsewoman, she waited until it was safe for her mare to drink—so that she wouldn't colic—then led the horse forward. After Apache drank, Harmony took a stake rope from her saddle and picketed the mare on a patch of grass. Knowing what was expected of her, the mare began happily cropping.

Harmony sank down on the bank and removed her half boots and stockings. She dipped her toes into the cold water and wriggled them like tiny fish. Water gently rushed over her ankles.

Head back, she lay on the grass and breathed slowly. The only sounds were the rustle of willows and the chatter of squirrels. After a few minutes the sun became uncomfortable. She stood and stripped down to her drawers. Glancing around, she resolved to keep an eye on Apache for signs of anyone approaching.

Nude to her waist, she felt deliciously wicked and free. At the center, the slow-moving creek's depth was perhaps only four feet. Harmony sank up to her shoulders and sighed in pleasure. Nothing could be more luxurious than the rush of cool water gliding over sun-warmed skin.

She closed her eyes and savored the sensation.

When she opened them again, not ten feet away at water's edge, Ben Panau reclined. Next to her clothes.

Harmony gasped.

Ben grinned.

Solicitously he tipped his hat. "Afternoon."

"What are you doing here?" Beneath the water she crossed her arms over her breasts. The sting of embarrassment brought a furious flush rushing to her face. "Go away. Now."

"Naw," he said lazily, leaning back. "We're gonna have us a little talk." Reaching out, he fingered the pearlized buttons of her blouse, neatly folded on the grass beside him.

She swallowed at the implied threat. He would not allow her her clothing until she complied. His callused hands looked alien and rough touching her feminine things. "What do you want?" she demanded.

"I want an explanation," he said, his grin fading. "I want to know why you're catering to those people."

"The Wilkersons are my mother's cousins," she spat. "As hostess in her absence, I have to entertain them. Now, go away."

He eyed her, his gaze going over the tops of her gleaming shoulders—all that was visible above the water. "Uh-huh. Well, was I you, I'd throw 'em right out."

"Of course you would," she replied in withering tones. "You don't know anything about social customs."

When his face darkened, she wished the words back. Now was not the time to insult him. Nor did she wish to hurt his feelings. He'd always been good to her. It wasn't his fault he'd had no cultural education.

"You never used to be so prissy," he observed.

"Nor so concerned about what others thought. Why, when we were kids—"

"We were just that, Ben, *kids*. Now, we both have adult responsibilities—"

"Do you think I'm a dirty savage?" he cut in.

Startled, she frowned. "Of course not."

"Then why didn't you dispute it?"

She let out a frustrated breath. "People are entitled to their own opinions, Ben. Whether you think they're right or wrong."

"Sure, and if you don't speak up, pretty soon it starts looking like you agree with them." Idly, he picked at a slim reed and began to chew it. "You like those folks, Harmony?"

Again, she was surprised. She groped for an answer. "I have no opinion one way or another. They're family, and they deserve to be treated with respect."

She saw her mistake the moment she made it.

He jumped on her statement. "Don't I deserve respect?"

"You do," she agreed. "Haven't I always given it to you?"

Slowly, he nodded. "It's something I've always liked about you." His gaze lowered, and she could tell he was searching beneath the water's cover for a glimpse of her nudity. She sank lower, tightened her hands on her bare breasts. As long as she stayed submerged, he wouldn't be able to see a thing, she assured herself. But the sun was beginning to sink behind the mountains. Surrounded by their height, the land would quickly fall into dusk and darkness. And it could get very cool in those shadows.

Under her palms, Harmony felt her nipples pucker. The water was already beginning to chill her.

"Ben," she enunciated clearly, "please go away. I'm getting cold."

He made no move. "Not yet. We've got more to talk about."

"Certainly," she placated. "And we will." Fixing him with her most imperious daughter-of-the-powerful-rancher stare—the one that never failed to gain results—she informed him, "Right now, I need to get dressed, *if* you don't mind."

"I mind," he replied, and his casual disregard of her glare told her that the man who sat so relaxed before her might not be so easy to manage.

A current of cooler water eddied about her legs and she shivered. Ben Panau was behaving in a ridiculous, embarrassing, thoroughly outrageous fashion. And it was terribly unsettling.

By holding her hostage beneath the safety of the water, Ben had complete command over her.

Never had she experienced such loss of control; no man had ever dared what Ben Panau dared.

Perhaps it was the cold seeping into her veins. Maybe it was the sheer outlandishness of the situation. But her brain wouldn't function properly. For one of the few times in her life, she couldn't imagine what to do.

"You ever think about me, Harmony?" Ben asked softly. "You ever...notice me...watch me?"

Harmony swallowed. "What—what do you mean?"

His gaze roamed her face. "I notice you. Watch you. You're not the kid I used to rescue all the time, are you? You're all grown up now. A woman."

"Yes," she agreed cautiously.

"A man marks such changes in a female. For a long time now, I've noticed such in you." Again his gaze dipped to search the water beneath her shoulders.

Harmony drew a breath. "You're not going to let me get out, are you? You're going to humiliate me— make me get my clothes while you watch, because I didn't defend you in front of the Wilkersons." The notion so mortified her that tears sprang to her eyes. She'd never revealed her body to any man. At least not intentionally.

Something in his eyes flickered. He shifted position and spit out the reed. In an instant, she knew she'd hit upon his intention.

"Damn you, Ben!" The rush of anger dried her tears. Proudly she lifted her chin. "I won't get out. I'll stay here until dark. You won't see a thing."

He shrugged and squinted into the sky at the faint circle of moon already visible. "Full moon tonight."

She blinked. A full moon was almost as good as a lantern. He would see everything.

She began to curse, using epithets she'd heard out of the toughest cowhands, the scruffiest laborers. Having grown up on a ranch, she'd been exposed to much of the earthier side of men.

Instead of being insulted, Ben began to smile. His amusement fueled her anger. She stepped up the curses until he was grinning broadly, then howling with mirth.

"Miz Harmony," he drawled when his guffaws finally wound down, "I surely do admire a woman who can curse."

"Get out!" she screeched. "Go away."

"Maybe I will. If you apologize."

Her breath coming in furious gasps now, she felt murderous. She'd have liked to hang him from the highest cottonwood. She'd have liked to see him bound and dragged over barbed wire. She'd have liked to shoot him through the eyes. "*Apologize?* For what? I've done nothing to you."

"I would defend you, Harmony, from any breath of an insult. I'd never let anyone speak against you."

She didn't know how to react to his statement. The sun sank lower still, hesitating at its perch on the horizon, until Harmony felt the temperature drop further. She began to shudder with cold…and guilt. She saw now that this was a battle of wills—a war from which would emerge one victor, and one vanquished.

She tamped down the guilt she didn't want to feel. *She* would conquer.

On the bank, Ben negligently crossed his long legs. He lifted her blouse and then did a strange thing. He brought the garment to his face and inhaled.

His dark lashes drifting closed, Harmony could see him savoring the scent—her scent—as if it were the most fragrant delicacy, the most heavenly treasure.

His gesture stunned and bewildered her. Some of her anger faded and a new shudder passed through her. She was honest enough to admit that it had nothing to do with the cold. "Don't," she whispered.

"Don't?" he echoed. He lowered her blouse, and his gaze sharpened, sliced into the deepest part of her. "How? How can I stop smelling your sweet scent, stop listening to your voice, stop looking at your body?" He shook his head, not expecting her to answer.

"Please," she whispered, not knowing why. Her body was racked with great shudders now, the blood freezing in her veins. Soon, she knew, she would faint from the cold. The will to win the battle waned by degrees as the temperature dropped. "Won't you allow me some dignity?"

Ben got to his feet. He stood at the water's edge, arms loose at his sides. "I'll turn my back, Harmony. You can get out. But first let me see you—"

Before he was finished she was shaking her head side to side, wet strands of her long hair violently slapping her cheek.

"Just...some of you," he amended, and she heard an odd note of yearning in his voice. "Just—" his voice dropped to a husky murmur "—just your breasts. For a moment only."

"No," she gasped. "No. No."

"I'll never get to have you, Harmony. A poor Ka-waiisu. A half-breed. I'm not good enough for you. I know that. Someday you'll marry a rich rancher's son. You'll fall in love and have his babies—not mine." His voice had taken on an unexpected gentle tone she'd never heard from him before. She stared at him, wide-eyed, somehow touched in spite of herself.

"I want only a memory," he went on in that same lulling tone. "Something to carry with me into the long years ahead when I'll have to watch you take another. Have you ever wanted anything so badly you'd sell your soul to get it? Have you ever longed and pined and dreamed for something?"

She tried to answer, but whether because of the cold or the odd, stirring emotions he was eliciting in her, she couldn't speak.

"Well, for me," he murmured huskily, "it's you. It's always been you."

At the end of his speech he stood silent, hands open and empty. Beneath the brim of his black hat, his dark eyes were luminous in the waning light. Inside her cold breast, Harmony felt the warmth of his glowing eyes.

Something inside her responded to him, something she had no understanding of, no base of reference. The world fell away and all that was left was the cool, swirling current of the creek, the golden ribbons of light flowing on its surface. And Ben.

On the ranch, Harmony understood herself simply to be part of the whole; each animal, each building, each person had a purpose, a place, a role to be played. The rhythms of night and day, work and weather, all comprised the entity that was Heartbreak Ranch.

Although pampered, admired, loved, Harmony knew she was merely one cog in the wheel.

No man, however assiduously he'd courted her, had ever made her feel her life and breath were imperative to him. No man had ever looked at her with such stark need. The realization shook her to the core.

Proud, strong, silent Ben Panau had given her a precious gift: a glimpse into the vulnerability of his soul.

She made him vulnerable, she realized, and her wonder grew.

Was his request, asked for so eloquently, too much to grant?

A crazy impulse gripped her. Then she, who'd never felt the intimate touch of a man's gaze, slowly began to rise from the water.

"Damn your eyes, Ben Panau," she breathed, shocked at herself even as first her shoulders, then her torso rose until she stood with the golden water pooling around her hips.

With her hands still covering her breasts, she drew a deep, deep breath. Eyes downcast, shaking uncontrollably, she lowered her arms.

Total silence greeted her.

For a long, timeless moment she withstood the agonizing quiet. Finally, she raised her eyes and looked at Ben. His hands, which before had hung loose at his sides, were now clenched into tense fists. His shoulders were stiff and set, his stance rigid.

But it was his face that arrested her.

Even in the murky light she could see the stain of

bronze color that spread over his high cheekbones. The skin of his face had gone taut, his nostrils flared, his jaw clenched. His eyes glittered with myriad jet sparkles, engulfing her in their intensity. She felt consumed.

Her cold nipples puckered even tighter. Her breasts grew heavy, weighted. Below the water, beneath her sodden drawers, a curious warmth formed in her abdomen and spread thick, honeyed rivers down... down.

A gust of wind blew strands of her hair against her cheek, partially obstructing her vision. But through the veil, the impressive, frightening bulge in his jeans caught her attention. She gasped.

The sound shook him. Suddenly he jerked around, turning his back. "Get dressed," he gritted out.

CHAPTER THREE

CATTLE WERE DISAPPEARING from the ranch.

A month had passed since the incident at the creek, and much to Harmony's dismay, the Wilkersons had chosen to extend their visit. They'd decided that Harmony's parents would appreciate their watching over their daughter while they were away.

As the days crept by and Ben said nothing offensive, Harmony's outrage cooled to a simmer. She vowed never to put herself in such a position again, and around him she was stiff and formal. Now that she had more important things to worry about, she resolved to try and forget.

Old Clay was recovering slowly after a short hospital stay. He encouraged Ben and Harmony to follow their instincts in the running of the property.

But now cattle were missing. When valuable stock disappeared from a cattle ranch, something had to be done. But every time Ben came into her field of vision, memory of his expression when he'd seen her body gripped her all over again. Even now, thinking of it, her breasts tingled.

"Five more head gone today," Ben reported to her grimly. He took off his hat and swiped the sweat off his forehead before resettling it. The midsummer afternoon was hot and still, with none of the normal breezes to cool off the ranch. At the corrals where Harmony took Ben's report, dust hung suspended in the air.

"At first I thought it might be just a couple of hungry families," Harmony said, forcing her mind to business. "When it's only a cow or two my father usually turns a blind eye."

"I know." Ben looked at her inscrutably. Unspoken between them was the knowledge that occasionally the poor folk living in shacks on the other side of the mountain—most often Indian families—"borrowed" a fat steer. Never had the Hearts begrudged hungry people food for their table. Briefly Harmony wondered if any of Ben's rapscallion relatives had availed themselves of free beef. Everyone knew about Ben's drunken father, shady cousins and reprobate uncles. Not that it mattered.

"Want to post a few outriders?" Ben suggested.

"How many head have disappeared altogether?" she asked thoughtfully. She didn't wish to draw the few men they had from their regular duties if it wasn't necessary.

"Twenty-five," he replied. "And Julio had to put out another fire."

"*What!*" she cried in alarm. "Another fire? But the first was started by lightning, wasn't it? We haven't had any summer storms lately. That leaves an accident, or…deliberate arson."

Ben shrugged, obviously reluctant to make assumptions. "Julio happened to be riding over by the cow camp. We don't normally go down there this time of year, but he was looking for missing calves. He found where someone camped, not a day ago. But the fire began at least fifty feet away. Julio thinks a burning branch was carried to a patch of dry brush.''

"The cow camp?'' She let out a tense breath. "It'd be a logical place for rustlers to start a fire. A big blaze over there would draw all the men—leaving the herds unattended.''

He nodded reluctantly. "Easy pickin's.''

"Send two riders out each morning,'' she decided, no longer in doubt. "Have them watch for anything different. Take more frequent tallies of the cattle. We can't let this problem get away from us, Ben.''

"It'll be done,'' he agreed.

They fell silent. Each day he reported to her and she made decisions, always asking his advice and usually taking it. Over the past four weeks, she discovered Ben had indeed listened to Old Clay's teachings; he never drew conclusions until all facts were in. Prudently, he thought ahead to next years' calf crop, which old cows to cull, which pastures to prepare for good barley and alfalfa harvests. He considered the best use of the men's time and talents, and then let them get on with their work without interference.

She'd noticed his easy manner. He made no overt commands, but rather he quietly encouraged men to feel they were part of a team whose goals were the same—efficiency and prosperity for the ranch. Considering how some might feel about taking orders from a "breed," Harmony thought this particularly clever of him.

Watching him work, she felt her admiration grow. But not her trust.

Ben waited for orders. Since she had none, she started for the barn, saying, "I'll talk with you later."

The sun overhead was hotter than a branding iron, but since the incident at the creek she'd eliminated her private baths, promising herself it would be only temporary until she could figure something out. She would take no chance of allowing him any more glimpses of her naked self. Most upsetting of all, she discovered, was that each time she recalled his incredible, emotion-filled gaze as he'd looked upon her, she felt…aroused.

Each night she thrashed her bedclothes into a tangle. Blood pulsed in unmentionable places. Never before had she had such wicked images of Ben Panau. And why him? Some day, she fully expected to fall in love and marry some local rancher's son. A man of good family, sophistication. Someone different. Someone *else*.

Her parents would surely object to her interest, however reluctant, in Ben, and their condemnation she could not bear. Always, Harmony had been a good, obedient daughter. Good, because William and Josie were strict and loving, stern and indulgent all at once. It was easy to be a model child to parents such as hers. How could she cope with their disappointment?

Distressed by her thoughts, she told herself to get

busy and jerked open the gate. As she strode across the corral, her boots sent up explosions of dust. Inside the dusty shed, she busied herself rummaging for a long strip of leather. She had to sift through a jumble of dusty halters, hackamores and bridles.

"What are you muttering about?" Ben said from behind her.

She jumped. "I thought you'd left. Why are you always coming up behind me? You're going to give me heart failure."

He grinned, a flash of white against his bronzed skin. "Sorry." He didn't look the least bit sorry, she thought crossly.

He wore his hat low over his eyes, but as a concession to the heat, instead of his felt Stetson, he'd taken to wearing a wide-brimmed straw. As always, his faded shirt was rolled to the elbows, and *Lordy*, it did fit nicely across his deep chest. His worn-soft jeans molded his muscular thighs and intimately cupped his sex.

"What are you looking for?" he asked.

Harmony jerked her gaze up. She felt a slow burn suffuse her cheeks until she realized what he meant.

Averting her face, she answered, "Apache's old bridle reins broke yesterday. I thought I'd fashion new ones. There's got to be some pieces of leather in here somewhere."

Lazily he reached up. "Here you go." Following his hand, she saw a dozen strips hanging right before her nose. She also noticed again that Ben smelled nice—not a citified soapy cologne scent, but an out-doorsy, country scent.

Annoyed with her straying thoughts, she snatched the leather from him. "Thanks."

"Are you all right, Harmony?" Ben asked quietly.

"Of course." She held the leather tight in her hands. "Why wouldn't I be?"

He shrugged. "Your parents left you with a big responsibility, even without having to deal with fire and rustling. I want to make sure you're eating well—sleeping good."

"I—certainly, I…" It was on the tip of her tongue to assure him that everything was fine, when she read genuine concern in his face. She *wasn't* sleeping well. And lately food held little appeal for her. The Wilker-sons were providing an additional burden. Entertain-ing them was a full-time chore; she'd had no idea being a good hostess could be such a strain. In recent days Harmony had acquired a new appreciation for her mother's skills.

Her gaze fell away from his as she fought an urge to break down and tell him her worries. She settled for an evasion. "All my life I've been trained to over-see the ranch."

"I know."

"Yes," she conceded slowly, "you would. You've had much of the same training from Old Clay, haven't you?"

He nodded, waiting.

She bit her lip, her reserve warring with the need to confide. Ben had always been there for her, always rescued her. His patient, interested expression won her over. "The truth is…I'm a little worried. There's so much to think about, so many decisions to make. What if I neglect something, make stupid oversights or outright errors?"

He was shaking his head before she'd finished. "Won't happen."

She couldn't help a tremulous smile. "You're so certain."

"You're an intelligent woman. As you've said, you're well trained. And nobody loves this ranch more. But most of all, you're strong-minded."

At his praise, her smile grew. "I guess I come from good stock. For all her quiet manners, my mother is iron-willed beneath. And my Grandmother Amy— well, she was the daughter of a San Francisco madam. They had to be strong to survive."

"The rumors are true?" Ben was surprised. "I thought it was all talk about the madam."

"No, indeed." Harmony lifted her chin proudly. "By all accounts, Bella was quite a character. She lived…boldly."

He snorted. "A Barbary Coast madam? I guess so."

"She was much more than just a lady of the night. She won this ranch in a faro game as revenge against the man who broke her heart. And she kept a journal—a book. My mother has it somewhere. She says it's a very special journal handed down to each Heart daughter when she needs it." She shrugged. "Whenever that is."

"She sounds like a resourceful woman. Just like you. Don't worry about the ranch—it'll be fine."

She looked at him and remarked lightly, "I've got you to help me, right?"

Ben's lips curved into a smile as sultry and hot as the summer day that surrounded them. "I'm yours, Harmony. I've always been yours."

She drew a quick breath. "I didn't mean—"

"It's all right, sweetheart. I know what's inside you, the way you think, what you feel." He made an effortless movement of his shoulders that spoke of his certainty.

"Don't patronize me, Ben. And *don't* call me sweetheart."

He made no reply, merely slanted her a knowing glance which prodded her further. "I mean it, Ben," she warned.

He spread his hands. "You're the boss."

"That's right. We have a business relationship, nothing more."

His dark eyes dropped to her mouth. Against the wall beside her head, he leaned on one hand, boxing her in. "Sure."

Despite herself, her heart leaped at the lambent heat in his gaze. His black eyes were like shiny charcoal stones glittering in the sun. Was he thinking about kissing her? Images of being swept into his arms burst into her mind. She swallowed hard and decided to escape the confines of the tack shed. But hastily darting by him, she felt her breasts inadvertently brush his arm.

Her gaze flew to his face in time to catch his infuriating grin. It was as if he thought she'd done it deliberately, as if he knew the role he played in her nighttime dreams.

The idea galled. He could *not* read her mind. Why did this one man have the power to send her into a frenzy? How was it he could infuriate her with merely a sly comment or arrogant twist of his mouth? She stormed to the house, her temper flaring. Stomping up the steps, she ignored a puzzled Edna Wilkerson.

She went to her bedroom, slammed the door and sat on her bed. She needed a few minutes alone.

It was not to be.

A tapping sounded, and Edna's voice called. "Harmony, dear, are you feeling poorly?"

Sighing, Harmony rose to open the door. To her surprise, Randolf stood in the hall beside his wife. The gaunt man started right in. "That Indian foreman upset you, missy? I've been tellin' you for weeks to get rid of him. William would surely be livid if he knew. Why—"

"She knows your view about Indians, Randolf," Edna interrupted. "You've told her often enough, so don't go on about it. Can't you see the poor dear is feeling ill?"

"I feel fine," Harmony said, guessing her high color was misleading the woman. Then she wished her words back. If Randolf thought she was sick then maybe she wouldn't need to listen to another of his sermons. Ever since he'd discovered Ben was acting foreman, he'd been on a campaign to get Ben fired.

He could expound for hours on the evils of allowing a "lowborn savage" a position of authority. "Give them a bit of power, they get impertinent and disrespectful," he'd boomed more than once.

How shocked they'd be, Harmony thought, if they knew of her midnight fantasies, how appalled if they knew she was wildly attracted to the half-breed foreman.

"Randolf, you know there's nothing to be done until William and Josie return," Edna said. "Why, Harmony isn't in charge here, are you dear?" She gave Harmony no chance to reply, but continued to address her husband. "You're going to addle her brains, making her think about business matters that don't concern her. Now, go on downstairs and read that magazine you're forever perusing, why don't you?"

"I'm all right, honestly." Harmony tried not to listen to them. They were naive, perhaps even ignorant. They didn't realize how offensive their remarks sounded. Though their notions were often wrongheaded, they *did* mean well. They were only looking out for her.

Head and shoulders thrust forward, Randolf resembled nothing so much as an aggravated stork. "I still say this is a sad state of affairs," he grumbled. "I only hope William won't hold *me* responsible, since I'm the only capable white man here."

In exasperation, Harmony put a palm to her forehead and felt the beginnings of a headache coming on. Maybe she *was* sick.

"I'm going to get Magdalena to prepare you a nice pot of tea," Edna soothed. "You just lie down and put a cool compress over your eyes. Your skin is looking—well, I don't want you to become alarmed, dear—but it's looking a bit *tanned.* I've noticed you never wear a hat, as a lady should. Perhaps you've had too much sun."

When Edna hurried off to find Magdalena, Harmony sighed in resignation. This was definitely not the most restful summer she'd ever spent.

ROUNDUP WAS ALWAYS HELD at the end of summer. Neighbors, friends and hired hands came from miles around to help gather the fattened yearlings and to brand late calves. It was several days of hard sweaty labor, culminating in a fiesta at week's end. Everyone pulled their weight, because the sale of cattle determined whether it would be a comfortable winter or a lean one.

No one worked harder than Ben Panau. He was up long before dawn, spent the hot hours hunting difficult brush-hidden steers, riding, roping, handling red-hot branding irons. Ben slaved as if the success of the entire roundup rested solely upon his shoulders.

The neighboring ranchers took Ben's direction grudgingly, unaccustomed to doing a "digger Injun's" bidding. Some grumbled outright, and two flatly refused, turning their mounts around when they discovered Old Clay was still bedridden.

Harmony had a panicked several moments, but to

Ben's credit, he forced no confrontations, gritted his jaw and pushed ahead with the work.

"What's driving him?" Harmony wondered, not realizing she'd spoken aloud until beside her Randolf Wilkerson sneered.

"He knows he'd best earn his keep. That Injun's on borrowed time—just wait till your daddy gets home."

Harmony turned to him. Not once during the long days of the roundup had he lifted a finger to help, preferring to recline in the salon, offering unsolicited instructions and criticisms. "Mr. Wilkerson," she asked evenly, "do you realize there's a bit of sun on your face? You're in serious danger of getting *tan*. You'd best get under the shade of the veranda."

"It is hot," he agreed, mopping his brow. When he turned and hurried toward the veranda, calling Magdalena to bring him a lemonade, Harmony gave an unladylike snort. She sifted through her mind for a polite way to ask when he and Edna would be leaving, but none came to mind. It simply wasn't Western hospitality.

The next day Harmony rode out with the men, proving to them all once again that she could ride and rope as well as any cowboy. Ben stayed close by her side. Several times she felt the possessive weight of his gaze and wondered if others could see it, too. Around him, she felt more aware of everything, more alive. He complimented her on her skills and she found she liked his praise.

When they corralled their gather for the day, she

was the last to dismount and care for her horse. She called thank-yous and accepted good-natured teasing about a steer that had eluded her loop.

Pulling the saddle from her tired mount, she hadn't noticed that everyone had left but Ben until she saw him walking alone at the corner of the corral. He'd stripped to jeans, boots and hat and his legs were spread wide as he swung a hammer, pounding nails into a sagging end post.

Chest gleaming with perspiration, muscles contracting, Ben presented a picture of tensile strength and awesome masculine power.

Harmony's mouth went dry. For long seconds she was unable to breathe, blink or swallow. It was as if, suddenly, nothing existed but Ben. Every detail of him drew her fixed attention: the corded muscles beneath Ben's smooth skin, his bulging thighs, his ribbed abdomen, his flexing biceps.

Harmony took in the display of potent masculine virility like a slug from a forty-four. Every womanly part of her awoke and began to throb. Even her knees wobbled.

Sensual imagery flooded her mind—of his capable hands drifting over her skin, his large, work-hardened body covering hers in an explicit, physical act.

She was appalled and alarmed.

And completely incapable of not taking her eyes off of him.

Ben chose that moment to glance at her.

Before she could mask her feelings, he tossed the heavy hammer aside, straightened and sauntered over to her. With supreme nonchalance, he dipped his hand in the horse trough and slung water over his chest. Dipping his hand again, he scooped more and rubbed it over the back of his neck. Never once did he take his eyes off her. His gaze, steady and mesmerizing, held hers prisoner.

"Look all you want, Miz Harmony," he said, drawling her name.

She flushed. "I'm not looking." *Move,* she told her limbs. *Walk away.* But her traitorous feet remained rooted.

"Yes, you are," he contradicted. "That's all right. I sure enjoyed seeing *you* this way."

Flush deepening, Harmony knew she should disregard his reference to that day at the creek. She should storm off, ignore the tall cowboy. Yet, somehow, she was powerless to do so.

She forced out scathing words. "I've no interest in you."

"No? That why you can't stop lookin'?" he asked, and she realized with angry chagrin that her gaze had again dipped to his glistening chest.

"It's all right, Harmony." He abandoned his taunting tones and his voice became huskily encouraging. "You're a normal woman, with normal urges. I don't mind. How about we take a swim in the creek together, look our fill at each other?"

Scandalized, her gaze flew to his flashing eyes. A swim would feel heavenly on her perspiring skin. But she knew he was asking for more. "With no shirts on?" she gasped.

"With nothin' on." He smiled, his teeth very white. "Come on. You used to be fun. Remember as kids when we rode horses together through the fields, picked blackberries and fed each other? Remember swimming in the creek, splashing and yelling?"

Despite her shock, memories rushed back and Harmony thought longingly of those carefree times. The constant decision-making of running the cattle ranch had begun to wear on her. It was *hard*, damn it all. And now Ben offered a tantalizing freedom from responsibility and worry—if only temporarily.

She bit her lip. The temptation to take him up startled her even more than his offer.

"I'm still fun," she whispered, evading the issue.

"Prove it," he dared. "Come swimming. I won't touch you, if you don't want. I swear. You can trust me, can't you? Have I ever betrayed you? Lied to you?"

She was forced to admit he had not.

What devil goaded her into agreeing to meet him near sundown at the creek, she never knew.

SHE WOULD NOT ALLOW him to touch her, that Harmony vowed. As she slowly guided Apache closer, she watched Ben, already floating in the water. Dusk threw lingering shadows from the reeds and trees, but the heat of the day still endured. Ben's gelding cropped grass. Harmony dismounted, loosened her mare's cinch and picketed her nearby. Her hands went to the buttons of her blouse.

Was she really going to do this?

In the creek, Ben did not glance up. No man as alert as Ben could have missed her arrival. She could only assume he was giving her time to work up her courage. In the trees, two squirrels chattered a domestic argument. Higher up, doves nestled. Fading sunlight cast a dusky glow over the clearing.

In the water, Ben waited.

She shrugged to herself. She could be as cosmopolitan as the next woman. She could swim with a man and maintain control of the situation. To make certain, she would keep on her camisole and drawers. For insurance, she hid her clothing behind a rock.

At water's edge, she kept careful watch on Ben. The lure of his healthy sexuality pulled at her, but she had a virgin's natural fear. They would *not* be touching each other.

Still, he made no move to look, so she sank down and slipped off the grass-slick bank into the cool water. Like an otter, she submerged and kicked out, coming up with her hair sleeked back.

Keeping her shoulders carefully beneath the surface, she sighed. It felt wonderfully cool after the stifling day. Ben turned to her and smiled. With his long, wet ebony hair pushed away from his forehead, he suddenly looked younger, almost as he had when they were children. His black eyes danced with the same pleasure that swirled through her.

"Feels good, huh?" He moved a little closer.

"It's splendid," she sighed and closed her eyes. "Just what I needed."

When he touched her shoulders, her eyes flew

open. He was in front of her, his face level with hers. He filled her field of vision, yet his expression was nonthreatening, his hands gentle.

"You cheated," he said.

She raised one brow.

"Your underthings." He jerked his chin toward her body. "You're still wearing them."

She said nothing at all. Was he truly...*unclothed* beneath the water? Nervously, she kept her gaze fixed on his face.

"I would never hurt you, Harmony. You're safe with me. Do you understand that?"

She nodded, and Ben knew a falling away of the bitterness that he'd always been unable to shed. He couldn't believe Harmony had come. He couldn't quite grasp the fact that she was here, in the water with him, nearly nude. For how long had he yearned and dreamed to have her see him as an equal? How many bleak years had passed while he agonized over a way to make something of himself, so he'd be worthy of her?

If she thought the sleeveless white top she wore was preserving her modesty, she was dead wrong. The few inches of clear water did nothing to hide her, and through the thin fabric he could plainly see the outline of her rounded breasts and their rosy centers.

His hands were still curved over her upper arms. She wasn't shrinking away from him. She wasn't fighting him. He held his breath, terrified she'd lose her courage and flee. She was a skittish cat, all eyes and careful wariness. He stroked her slim arms, as he would a kitten, sought to allay her fears. He ran his hands down past her elbows and beneath the water to her wrists, then back to her upper arms. When she shivered, but stayed put, a thrill shot up his spine.

"I...wasn't going to let you touch me, Ben." Harmony bit her lip. She drew a deep breath that lifted her breasts. They bobbed in the water and Ben found his willpower sorely tested as he forced himself to maintain eye contact; it seemed of paramount importance to her. He must proceed slowly, he understood that. At all costs, he mustn't cause her to run.

She went on. "But you've always taken care of me. I can't imagine you forcing me into anything."

She's asking for reassurance.

"Never," he pledged. He drew a deep, lung-expanding breath of his own.

She blinked, and he could see the desire to trust him reflected in her huge violet eyes. Her evident vulnerability and virginal curiosity touched him.

"I want to kiss you, Harmony," he admitted. "To feel your mouth open under mine. For years I've wanted that, imagined it. I won't lie to you, I've kissed other women, had them in bed. But there's no one I've ever wanted as much as I want you."

Her lips curved a tiny bit. "Is that really true?"

He nodded solemnly. But he wasn't finished yet. "I want to kiss you and I want to touch your breasts, feel their weight in my hands. I want it so much, I'm shaking. Harmony, I ache for you. But I won't do anything at all...unless you want it."

When her eyed widened, he smiled tenderly. "You see? That's how I'll prove you can trust me."

Normally confident and impulsive, Harmony would never be labeled timid. Having her so uncertain for once was a novel experience. His heart expanded. He would go slow, very slow. In her innocence, she was adorable. "The touching—it's one way a man pleasures a woman."

"And himself?" she asked shyly.

Trying not to smile, he nodded. "And himself."

"Okay," she said matter-of-factly, and he was stunned.

"Okay...what?"

"You may kiss me and...um, touch me." She closed her eyes and lifted her chin.

Never in a hundred years would he be able to predict this woman. She was lovely, bold, generous, and he was bursting to have her. He found himself staring stupidly at her beautiful face. A gift from heaven, that's what she was, he decided, swallowing thickly. A precious gift.

Wasting no time, he leaned forward and touched his mouth to hers. She made a small start and he went perfectly still. Their lips a scant inch apart, she looked at him with wide eyes.

Suddenly she threw her arms around his neck and pressed her mouth to his. He was so startled and pleased at her unexpected daring he wanted to laugh aloud. Carefully he drew her forward, closing the last bit of space between their bodies until the tips of her full breasts grazed his bare chest. Her camisole's thin wet fabric acted as friction against his skin and he couldn't hold back a groan of agony.

Gently he kissed the corners of her mouth, then slid his tongue inside, deepening the caress. Molding her taut waist with his hand, he slipped his right palm up her rib cage to cup her breast. The nipple, already budding from the cool water, tightened at his touch.

Even with the chill of the creek reaching his waist, Ben felt beads of sweat break out on his forehead. His manhood was rigid, pulsing with need. Helpless, he couldn't stop from pressing himself against her soft belly. He needed to thrust himself inside her, claim her, love her. He needed it more than air. Harmony was his oxygen, his life. She always had been.

She responded by straining against him, folding her arms behind his neck, arching her body. Even in all his fantasies he hadn't believed he might truly elicit from her such a passionate response. Years of need thundered in his ears like the stampede of a thousand steers.

Only seconds had passed, yet he knew that if he allowed the passage of just a few more, he would be overpowered by his own desperate passion to push her too hard, too fast. She was untried, untouched; he must remember that.

It was his great regard for her that enabled him to break their kiss and rest his forehead against hers. His arms locked around her back. Breath coming in difficult gulps, he said roughly, "That's enough, Harmony. I can't take much more."

She blinked fuzzily, her eyes unfocused. "Goodness," she whispered. "Goodness."

He chuckled. "Yeah."

Harmony continued to look into Ben's dark features. In all her life, she'd remained in control of her senses, her thoughts. She was a proud descendant of the famous Heart lineage, an educated, intelligent, self-assured woman.

In one short kiss, Ben had wiped it all away.

It was the most dramatic, alarming experience she'd ever known. Like a storm moving off, the hazy sensuality fogging her brain slowly began to recede. She realized with shock that her arms were clamped around Ben's neck, every finger of one hand thrust into his wet, black hair. Her body was pushed up against his, her back bowed in a way that thrust her breasts into his smooth chest. His very naked smooth chest. Something beneath the water pressed hard against her. She couldn't allow herself to acknowledge the awesome tumescence resting against her stomach.

And yet it demanded acknowledgment. Harmony sucked in a breath.

Ben read her mind. He smiled knowingly, but somehow very sadly, like a man who'd suffered torments she'd never suspected. "Goodness."

Quickly she unwrapped her arms and sank down into the water. Her voice thin, toneless, panicked, she whispered, "I think it's time for me to go home."

EARLY THE NEXT AFTERNOON some one hundred men, women and children began arriving. Wagons, carriages and buggies drove up and horses were stripped of harnesses and saddles and turned into open pens. Wives brought covered casseroles of fragrant fried chicken, potato salads, watermelons and warm loaves of bread, while husbands gathered privately to smoke cigars, talk about range conditions and sample jugs of home-brewed moonshine.

An annual event, the gathering was held to thank everyone for their help in the roundup. Harmony had workers sweep out the barn where the dance would be held, directed others to hang streamers, put out chairs and arrange punch bowls. Magdalena covered long tables with cloths and shooed the errant rooster away. A four-piece country band tuned up in the corner. The cacophony of sound mingled with the excited chatter of children. The fiesta was beginning.

Before Harmony knew it, darkness was falling and Magdalena bustled into her bedroom to help her dress. Her special gown of rose moiré was embellished with a neckline of Mechlin lace and a fitted waist. Matching rose slippers covered her feet. Daringly, she left her hair down, with only a white ribbon threaded beneath her nape and tied in a small bow atop her head. A full moon glowed and Harmony paused a moment by her open window to breathe in the night. Crickets sang. A warm breeze glided over her skin and the darkness felt velvety, tactile. The evening emanated a bewitching, rife-with-possibilities aura.

In the barn, the band struck up "Li'l Liza Jane,"

and then "If You Were the Only Girl in the World." The music drew Harmony downstairs. Dozens of couples were dancing and she had no lack of partners. With her skirts swirling around her ankles, she laughed breathlessly.

Ben, she noticed, kept to the shadows. He ate heartily but did not dance, nor ask her to, but every moment she felt his dark eyes upon her. Tonight, he wore a high-collared white shirt with a blue silk vest. His trousers were black and cuffed. Combed off his forehead, his ebony hair touched his collar, all that was visible beneath his black Stetson.

His gaze smoldered, never letting Harmony forget his embrace, the incredible impulses that had raced through her body. Nor was it possible to forget how even the piercing rays of the lowering sun failed to match the intensity in his blazing eyes.

The weakness, the desire to succumb and sink down with him in the fragrant grasses beside the creek were entirely outside her realm of experience. She was totally and completely drawn to him, fascinated and yet frightened by her rampant emotions.

In the wee hours the party began to wind down. The band put their instruments into cases. Families hitched up wagons, loaded empty casseroles and sleepy children and rumbled home. Tired but pleased that she could report the success of the party to her parents, Harmony smiled indulgently as she spied teenagers stealing a last kiss. In the corner of the barn, two stove-up old cowhands snored, arms slung loosely around each other's shoulders, a jug empty on the floor beside them.

Warm and still, the night breathed with a life of its own. Silver moonlight dusted the buildings and cast intimate shadows. Picking up her skirts, she searched the back of the barn, glanced over the corrals, checked around the trees. Ben was not there. As she lingered beside the long horse trough, disappointment weighed down her heart.

She wanted to experience his kiss again. She admitted it. She wanted to feel his hard chest against her. She wanted to feel Ben's gentle hands sweep her body, to taste his mouth plundering hers, to hear his sweet words of praise and affection. She stared at the water, recalling the primal heat that had burned in her breasts and between her thighs at Ben's touch.

Over at the pens, a last family called from their wagon to their teenage daughter, who giggled as the boy kissed her again before she skipped away. Watching them, a yearning for a man of her own knifed through Harmony. She wanted the joy of belonging, the natural joining of a male and his woman. The mindlessness and overwhelming joy. She wanted Ben.

Her gaze dropped to the light of the moon glinting upon the water in the trough.

When his reflection appeared on the surface, she was not surprised. Moonlight clearly outlined Ben's black hat, his broad shoulders, his tall, silent frame. A force of nature, a man, a flesh-and-blood animal who called to his mate, Ben's simple masculine presence brought anticipatory tingles to her skin. In their shared image she saw the contrast of her blond hair with his dark-featured face. They were darkness and light, rising sun and waxing moon.

It was as if they were two halves of a whole.

Without speaking, he put a hand in her hair, burrowed it beneath the silky weight to caress her sensitive nape. She shivered and it seemed the most natural thing in the world to turn toward him.

Gathering her to him as though he'd waited a lifetime to do so, he kissed her and she melted in his arms.

This was right. This was fate, she mused dreamily. How silly she'd been, picturing herself with anyone else. Ben was the man she'd waited for all her life, and she'd found him, quite literally, in her own backyard. He wasn't a rancher's son—they'd all already made their offers. He wasn't terribly educated—but he was intelligent in more important ways. He wasn't wealthy. He wasn't white.

Ben's steady, enduring affection, his capability, his integrity far surpassed that of any man, white or Indian, she'd ever known.

Smiling to herself, she realized one thing more: no man but Ben had created such explosive sparks within her. The hot blood of accomplished courtesan Bella Duprey pumped through her veins, wild and uncontrolled. Harmony was the granddaughter of Bella's daughter—a throwback, a soulmate through time. Tonight, she decided with great certainty, she would give herself to Ben Panau. She clung to him.

Suddenly, a shocked cry rent the magical night air,

shattering it. Harmony and Ben jerked apart to find Randolf and Edna staring at them, mouths agape. Randolf held aloft a kerosene lantern.

"Harmony!" Edna gasped in shaming tones. "An *Indian?*"

Small eyes searing, Randolf scowled ferociously at Ben like a giant bird of prey. In hateful tones, Randolf spit out, "Take your filthy hands off her."

CHAPTER FOUR

"DON'T YOU MEAN my filthy *half-breed* hands?" Ben ground out hoarsely. Harmony let out a strangled cry. He ignored her. He could feel the familiar flush of helpless shame and fury coursing through him, rushing to his head until it crashed in a wave of futility and defeat. The bitterness and anger he'd known all his life came flooding back.

Randolf lifted the kerosene lantern high. He and Edna peered at Harmony. In the harsh, artificial light her hair was mussed, and curled about her face in wild tangles. Her lips were moist and rosy. He could even see pinkish marks on her arms where, in his passion, he'd clutched her. Her mouth trembled.

Self-hate engulfed him.

"How dare you?" Edna's agonized whisper sounded as loud as a shotgun blast.

Ben shook his head. "Guess I forgot my place." Though meant to be sarcastic, even Ben knew the truth of his statement. When had he begun to reach above his station, begun to covet the highborn Harmony Heart?

He took one last glance at her. Her eyes brimmed with tears. She'd been caught in the embrace of a no-account half-breed, a disgrace from which she might never recover. Lost in drowning guilt, Ben couldn't deny that he'd known that a relationship with him would put her in an untenable position. Had he killed any chance she might have for a suitable marriage with someone like herself—a white man of property and breeding? It had all been a dream, an impossible, damnable fantasy for which innocent Harmony would pay the price. He should have kept his hands to himself. He never should have done anything that might hurt her.

Bile rose in his throat. God, he despised himself.

Harmony began babbling now, making little sense. "It's not what you're saying. I don't want you thinking that Ben—"

"It's all right, missy," Randolf soothed, putting his scrawny winglike arm around her shoulders and urging her toward the house. "We'll keep the dirty savage away from you—"

Ben choked.

"No!" Harmony protested vehemently, digging in her heels. "He's not a savage. He didn't force me—"

"We'll try and be understanding, dear," Edna said, struggling with excuses she felt Harmony needed. "You're an impressionable young woman. You lost your head."

"No," Harmony insisted, "no. I know what I'm doing. Ben, tell them…Ben?"

He was gone, vanished from the circle of hostile light.

Randolf took hold of one arm, and Edna firmly

attached herself to Harmony's other. "Now, come to the house. I'll fix you some nice tea."

"Tea? *Tea?*" Harmony rolled her eyes and wrenched herself free. In an effort to calm herself, she drew quick, furious breaths. Fighting the impulse to chase after Ben and apologize for the Wilkersons, she decided she should fill them in on a few home truths first.

"Come to the house. Now," she commanded, forgetting they'd been trying to get her there all along. She marched up the steps, stormed in the house. Once in the parlor, she whirled to face them.

Edna kept wringing her hands and taking worried little glances at her husband as if hoping he would solve everything. Randolf set his lantern on a high table and strode to the stone fireplace. There, he placed an imperious arm along the mantel. Harmony frowned. She didn't like his assumed lord-of-the-manor air. She took her own position in the center of the room, arms akimbo.

"You both will listen to me," she stated, keeping her voice low. "There are some things you must know. I am *not,* as you like to think, an impressionable young girl. I know exactly what I'm doing. Do you understand? My father left me in a position of the highest authority when he and my mother left. I am ranch manager. As such, the foreman answers to me."

"What's this?" Randolf barked. "Manager? I don't believe it. I haven't seen William in twenty years, but I'm certain he would never countenance—''

Harmony ruthlessly cut him off. "I didn't tell you before because you seem...old-fashioned in your ideas about women. Furthermore, not that it's any of your business, but since I was sixteen, I've received offers of marriage from nearly every eligible male in Kern County. I've refused them all."

Edna gasped. The older woman put a steadying hand on the back of the sofa as if for support. Her skin went white.

"I didn't love them," Harmony explained, taking temporary pity on the woman. "I'm twenty-one now, well past the age of marriage, had I wished it before. Now, at last, I've found a man I can love. A man whose integrity and goodness of character—well— I've never encountered his equal."

"I hope to God," Randolf shouted, "that you're not talking about that digger Indian. He's beneath you, Harmony. He's trash. A man of no position, no wealth."

"In this house, you will not use those terms when mentioning Ben Panau," she shouted back.

But Randolf was working up a righteous sermon. "He can offer you nothing, nothing! And what will your parents say? Think, girl. Do you believe William would want you to consort with a redskin?"

Harmony flinched and firmed her lips. She could not let Randolf see how he'd put his finger on the wound. "My parents would never condone such hateful prejudice," she said, hoping against hope this would turn out to be true. "Ben Panau is a fine man any woman would be lucky to have. I only hope I'm worthy of him."

Edna came alive. "Oh, dear, what's come over you?" She fluttered her fingers anxiously. "You're settling for a man so—so *unsuitable*. Harmony—a mixed marriage? It's...disgusting."

No more, Harmony thought. She would take no more. Lifting her chin, she said, "I'm afraid I'll have to ask you to leave the ranch. You may stay until morning."

With as much dignity as she could muster, she gathered her skirts and swept from the room, outside and into the night. She needed no lantern to guide her to the bunkhouse and to Ben.

She rapped her knuckles sharply on the weathered wooden door.

It creaked open, Ben on the other side. Pushing past him, she charged in and glanced around. The long open room of bunks was empty. The men had chosen to continue the festivities elsewhere; even Old Clay had been driven to town after the fiesta.

Lit only by an oil lamp, the room was cast in shadows. She faced Ben, who remained near the open door, one fist still clamped around the latch. Flickering light threw his features into a tautly forbidding canvas of leather.

She drew a breath. The Wilkersons had wounded him deeply, but she was confident she could soothe the furious beast inside. Presenting him a soft smile, she held out her hand. "Ben, I don't care what those people say, you know that."

He said nothing, ignoring her outstretched hand.

She let it fall to her side. "I want you, Ben."

Still nothing.

"I...I love you. There. I've said it. I love you. Now you know the truth about how I feel. You love me, too, I know you do."

He snorted. "Love? You're playing at love, Miz Harmony. I'm just a summer romance to you. Somebody you can frolic in the creek with. Those people are right. You belong with a man of your own social position."

"I belong with you," she said quietly, determined to win him over. "I want to be your wife. And right now, I need to be held. Will you take me in your arms, Ben?"

"No," he said baldly. "Never again. You don't know what real love is. This—" he made a hand gesture between her and himself "—is just a game, just temporary. Soon enough, you'll forget about me."

The fuse of her anger ignited. "I wish everyone would stop treating me like a baby," she fumed. "I'm a grown woman. I can make my own decisions."

"The Wilkersons are right. I'm no good for you. I'm nothing but a poor breed."

"*I'm* a breed," she retorted, beginning to sense the depth of his implacability. "One quarter Hawaiian, remember?"

"It's not the same." He faced away from her, looking sightlessly out into the night, stoic and stubborn.

At a loss, Harmony tried again. And again. But Ben proved more resolute than she could have imagined. Where was the man who'd spoken so sweetly to her, held her like a precious treasure? And who was this cool, harsh man with his closed features and rigid stance?

"Ben," she whispered from a throat raw with emotion. *"Please."*

He remained adamant, unbending. "If you aren't humiliated, you should be. You don't know the slurs, the dishonor you'd have to endure as my wife. And you never should. Go on up to the house," he instructed with maddening control, "where you belong."

At last she had no choice but to leave him. Behind her he closed the door, its weathered pine as staunch and forbidding as a lead vault, so effectively did it shut her out. She choked back a sob.

It was dark and difficult to see her way home through the gathering moisture obscuring her vision. She stumbled up the stairs, then paused to take great, gulping breaths. In her heart the flame of hope wavered, despair threatening to extinguish its light. She had rejected the overtures of all other men, in favor of waiting for her true love. And now he wouldn't have her?

The bitter taste of loss filled her mouth. Without Ben's love, all the years ahead stretched out empty and miserable. She'd always known that once given, a Heart woman's devotion was forever.

Harmony would never love another man.

She lifted her head and swiped the tears away to look at the same moon that had shone down upon all the generations of Heart women. Somehow, its pale green light comforted her. *Oh, Ben,* her soul cried out. *I love you.* The moon continued to glow—a true and constant companion in an unpredictable world.

Gradually her vision cleared.

Her idols were resolute, confident females like Elizabeth Cady Stanton, Susan B. Anthony and Alice Paul. Those women fought through trial and adversity for the dignity and rights of women. They would be ashamed of her behavior now. And weren't the Heart women resolute in the pursuit of their goals and of the strong men they loved?

How could she not live up to their legacy?

With a deep breath, she raised her chin.

In their example, she would sally forth. Her motto would be: Never Give Up; her banner, love; her weapons, determination, her body, and her wits.

The battle, she swore to the moon, was joined.

THE WILKERSONS' indignant packing up and leave-taking barely registered with Harmony. In shrill voices they vowed to write her parents, complain about her insolent inhospitable treatment, inform them of her ill-advised liaison with "the Indian." Harmony merely shrugged.

During the long night, she struggled with the dilemma of how to win over Ben. When finally she lay down, hoping to sleep, she recalled the old stories. All her life Harmony had heard tales of the journal her great-grandmother had written. The diary, she'd been told, was for future generations of Heart women. The contents were unknown to her, but there to be read when in dire straits.

She must find the journal.

HARMONY SPENT DAYS searching the big house. She looked through cupboards and cabinets, scoured the attic, investigated crannies in her old nursery, nooks in the basement, closets in bedrooms.

Meanwhile, Ben continued to report to her each morning. But it was a new Ben, and nothing Harmony did or said had any effect on him. It was as if a cold, hard stranger had taken his place. He was scrupulously efficient, frostily aloof. The days passed and he did not relent. In agony Harmony lost sleep, and her search for Bella's journal became frantic.

At the end of the second interminable week, she found the precious journal exactly where she should have looked in the first place: at the bottom of her mother's beloved hope chest. The trunk was scarred and old, with metal bands clamped over the top.

Inside she found a wooden box with a beautiful tiger painted on the lid. The tiger's green-jeweled eyes gleamed. Also in the chest were a pack of playing cards, a gem-studded collar and several nearly empty bottles and vials. Gasping, she withdrew a crimson velvet gown and held it to her face. The beautiful fabric exuded an exotic circus fragrance, and in her mind rose the image of the formidable woman who'd worn it.

Above the big four-poster in her parents' bedroom hung a grand, opulent oil portrait of Bella Duprey. The Queen of the Courtesans reclined upon a velvet chaise. A satin wrap, draped over the back of the lounge, had obviously been rejected, for she lay in all her nude glory. An enigmatic smile barely touched the edges of her mouth, her blond hair curled thickly down her back, and in her violet eyes sparkled a mischievous light.

Harmony decided it was fitting to open the journal beneath her infamous great-grandmother's gilt-framed portrait. On the cover were the scripted words *The Art Of Fascination.* Sinking to a thick Aubusson rug, Harmony tucked her legs under her and began to read. In the yellowed pages, she was shocked and delighted to read Bella's innermost thoughts and secrets.

She skimmed a section containing exotic beauty tips—one called ''Bosom, a Beautiful One How Obtained''—tips on coquettish behavior and even sexual positions to maximize a couple's pleasure. Entitled ''The Texas Tongue Massage,'' and ''Around-the-World Switch'' and the confusingly designated ''Exotic Body Chew,'' they were meticulously detailed. At these last, Harmony felt every inch of her flesh blush.

But she read them avidly.

There was even a section on what appeared to be obedience training for dogs. Why dog training should be included, she couldn't fathom. She shrugged and skipped past it until a small section caught her attention.

Love Potions, etc. Beneath the heading were cata-
logued ingredients and directions for concocting and
administering several different elixirs. Including love
potions.

Harmony did not believe in love potions.

Yet she was too desperate not to try.

Biting her lip, she scanned the neatly lettered list.
The wartsworth she could dig up in the damp under-
growth where mushrooms grew behind the house. The
blood of a virgin would be no problem, she decided
ruefully, as only a drop was needed and she could
easily pierce her finger.

But elements such as "Jonquil, for Sexual Desire,"
"Azalea, for Passion," and "Cedar Wood, for
Love," would be harder to come by. And there was
"Wild Columbine" and "Purple Boneset" and others
she'd never heard of. Finally, "Vanilla, an Aphrodisi-
ac," was called for, and Harmony hoped Cook kept
some in the pantry. She needed all the help she could
get to penetrate Ben's awesome restraint.

She'd go into Caliente and try to purchase some of
the makings from the local healer. Outside the window, she heard Ben's voice calling orders from down
in the corral. Closing her eyes a brief moment, she
cradled the worn journal to her chest and whispered
a prayer for the potion to work.

When she opened her eyes, she studied Bella's
scandalous portrait. It seemed as if the woman were
looking back at her, the violet eyes hauntingly familiar. She supposed that was because she saw them
every day in her own mirror. For a moment, she fan-

cied that Bella, indeed, stared into her eyes and then
slowly closed one lid in a wink of encouragement.

Harmony shook her head at the silly notion. A
painting winking? Preposterous. Crazy. Impossible.

Rising to her feet, she closed the trunk but kept the
journal. She went to the door and paused there. On
impulse, she turned back to the painting…and winked
back.

THE SURREY BUMPED and bounced over every rut and
hole in the road. Harmony much preferred to ride
horseback, but she decided she might want extra room
for the items she needed in town.

Caliente consisted of a short row of wood buildings
in a rough but wide dirt street. The railroad, which
connected at Bakersfield, was built at one end, and a
lumberyard sprawled at the other, infusing the air with
the smell of wood shavings. Large roof overhangs
kept the weather off folks as they did their business
at the bank and the few shops.

Once there, she made quick work of visiting
Smith's General Mercantile and then the healer's hut.
She was vastly relieved to find the ingredients she
needed. She said polite hellos to the townspeople and
escaped as soon as she could. She placed the precious
bundle of herbs, essential oils and powders on the
leather seat of the surrey and headed home.

BEN TOILED steadily in the corrals with a half-broke
colt. He glanced up from his work and watched Harmony drive in. In a way, he understood better now

how the loss of a woman's love could nearly kill a man.

Or at least drive him to drink.

His father was drinking his life away, looking to the bottom of a whiskey bottle for relief from his sorrows.

Ben knew the story. His mother had been a fine lady from Chicago, a female of breeding and family. She'd impulsively married James Panau, and just as quickly regretted it. White society no longer accepted her, and the Kawaiisu were put off by her superior airs.

Discovering herself pregnant, she'd waited only long enough to deliver the baby, telling James that she was leaving him—but that she wasn't taking a half-breed brat with her.

Now, when Ben looked at Harmony's lovely face, he hurt. He could see she was suffering, too. But *he* was the cause of her pain, he must not forget that. If he selfishly pursued her, she would be disgraced, dishonored, even in marriage, by his Indian heritage. Her parents would never approve.

He forced himself to enter the barn and help Harmony unhitch the horse. She smiled at him and he felt a weakening and returning pain. Fists clenched, he knew one truth was certain: if he truly loved her, and every fiber of his being shouted it, he would care enough to leave her alone.

"We've news of the rustlers," he forced himself to say. "I've spoken with the McCandles, Bennetts and Furleys." They were all local people.

She was curiously uninterested. "That's good, Ben."

"The rustlers aren't Indian. They're white men who've been stealing cattle from all over the valley." He thought she'd be glad to know that. "It turns out the other ranchers have lost stock mysteriously, too. They're cooperating with me to set a trap. We'll get them."

Smiling halfheartedly, she thanked him and turned away, a bundle of something in her arms. At her lack of enthusiasm, he scratched his head.

SO BEN WOULD SET a trap? Well, she would be setting one of her own. A snare against which she hoped he would have no defense, from which he'd have no escape. She smiled. Tomorrow, it would be well and truly sprung.

IMPATIENTLY Harmony waited for the men to complain. Morning hours turned into noon, and then afternoon before Ben informed her of the broken waterline leading to the bunkhouse. "The men can't clean up until we get a new pipe from town. It's busted clear through—almost like with an ax." He shrugged, perplexed. "Anyway, I'll send a man to Caliente tomorrow for the pipe."

"So, in the meantime you'll have to bathe in the creek," she said eagerly. Then, hoping her tone hadn't given her away, she tried to look bored. "I guess you'll all live."

"Yeah."

She left him then, making sure he saw her go into the house. On the veranda, she took up her vigil upon the edge of a chair, toe nervously tapping, the moon-colored potion she'd carefully concocted warming in her palms. The bottle was one she'd found in her mother's trunk. An iridescent green, its smooth sides sloped to an elaborate silver stopper, shaped in the silhouette of a woman.

It was a vessel worthy of a love potion.

Late in the afternoon, her patience was rewarded when she saw Ben come out of the bunkhouse, a rough towel slung over one shoulder. She shrank into the shadows so he wouldn't see her. He went to the corrals and mounted his still-saddled gelding, then reined the horse through the meadow.

It was time.

When he had been gone less than a minute, she flew down the stairs and ran to the back of the barn where she'd hidden her mare. Apache blinked mildly as Harmony threw up a saddle and cinched it tight. She'd wrapped the vial in a cloth and now tied it into a saddlebag. Flinging herself upon Apache's back, she kicked her mare, who lurched into a surprised gallop.

Going the long way around, Harmony thanked the gods when she reached the creek ahead of Ben. Her mare was lathered and blowing, so she picketed her some distance away on a long line, hoping Ben wouldn't notice that the horse had been run hard.

She flung off her clothing, leaving only her sheer cotton drawers, loosened her hair until it hung heavily to her hips and charged into the water. Halfway to the middle, she remembered the vial and had to hurry back to Apache to collect it from the saddlebag.

Back in the hip-deep water, Harmony heard the whinny of an approaching horse and Apache's answer. Forcing her breathing to calm, she patted her shoulders and cheeks with water, took up a casual stance and widened her eyes as if surprised by Ben's appearance.

When he came into the clearing, she gave a soft little cry. "Oh, Ben, you're here." She feigned a maidenly blush, lowered her gaze and covered her breasts with her hands—careful to leave a good deal exposed. As she'd hoped, the sight of her partial nudity captured his attention.

Rigidly, he sat on his horse, staring. Water eddied around her hips and she allowed at least one pink nipple to peek out.

Why wasn't he dismounting, coming to her? Blast it, she thought, fearing his damnable pride would compel him to leave. She must act.

It took courage for her to lower her arms and untie the drawstring of her drawers, but she kept a vision of Bella's wanton painting firmly fixed in her mind.

If Great-grandmother could do it, then so can I.

"Were you going to bathe, Ben? I'm sorry, I didn't know." She lowered the drawers, drawing them off her feet beneath the surface. "It's all right. We can share the creek." She took a few steps into shallower water until the water lapped at the tops of her legs.

His gaze dropped to the junction of her thighs. She beckoned him forward. "Come closer."

"Harmony," he said in a strangled voice. "What the hell do you think you're doing?"

"Let's not fight," she coaxed, sensing a chink in the armor of his resolve. "Let's get along." Casually, though she was shaking, she tossed her wet undergarment onto the bank. "Did you bring soap? Wash my back, won't you?"

Gathering her hair to one side, she presented him with a view of her curving derriere, then peeked at him over her water-beaded shoulder. She still held the small vial.

When he made no move, she uncorked the vial and faced him again, desperately trying to assume Bella's mysterious smile. She tilted her head and took a drink, then accidentally-on-purpose dribbled some on her naked breasts.

The cool-green colored liquid trailed down to her nipples. As casually as a practiced *demimondaine*, she giggled so that her breasts bounced.

It was the last straw.

Ben slid from the saddle, forgetting his horse, which wandered over to Apache. Never taking his eyes off Harmony, he stripped off his boots and socks, and then, still fully clothed, plowed into the water.

He reached her, unable to stop himself. "God, Harmony, I'm a man, not a saint." He bent to sip the liquid from her skin, his lips laving her nipples of the sweet concoction. She thrust her hands into his hair and threw back her head. As she'd fervently hoped, he broke down and began to make wild and stormy love to her. It was fitting, she decided dreamily, that they make love *here* in this place; it had always been and would always remain special to her.

"Tell me to stop," he ground out, his lips stilling against her breast. "Tell me *now*."

Harmony responded by clinging to him with a strength that surprised him. Through his shirt, her nails raked his back. She arched into him, offering her breasts. A shudder passed through her body like a woman already lost in pleasure. Ben groaned in agony. *Too late,* he moaned inwardly, it was far too late to stop the impulses thundering through his veins to take her and make her his.

Today, he would have her, even if tomorrow she regretted everything.

The sight of her nude body mesmerized him. Her shoulders were smooth, her breasts rounded and high, her waist small. The line of her gently flared hips curved to straight, shapely legs. At the juncture of her thighs curls of dark blond hid the secrets he was desperate to know. Through half-closed eyes she gazed at him. Her mouth curved in a soft tempting smile he was completely powerless to resist. She was exquisitely fashioned, a creature of emotion, reaction and sheer wanton passion.

"Ben," she whispered, "love me."

Locked in her gaze, he tore at his shirt, spraying buttons into the creek as he ripped it off. It floated to the creekside. She was already working at his jeans, but with the fabric sopping wet, she struggled futilely.

He laughed aloud, and a great euphoria filled him.

Sweeping her up high against his chest, he kissed her. She locked her slim arms tightly about his neck as if afraid he would let her go. Striding from the water, he somehow made it to the bank and reverently laid her down on the long sweet grasses.

Beside them, the creek gurgled serenely.

For a timeless moment he hovered over her. *How long*, his spirit cried out, how long had he waited for this moment when Harmony would surrender to him? She was sweetly giving him her body, her heart, her soul. He could clearly read the messages of love and devotion in her lovely eyes, perhaps because they were all the things he gave so eagerly to her.

He couldn't believe this was real.

Lying beside her, he ran a worshiping palm from her collarbone to her breast, then bent to suckle her rosy nipple. With his hands, he stroked her waist, her belly, and then skimmed the curls shielding her womanhood. Gently he slipped his fingers past her tender petals to caress the growing bud of her passion. Her breath soughed over his shoulder and with wonder he felt the damp proof of her desire.

A moan wrenched from her throat and he lifted his head to see violet flames shimmering in her eyes. An answering conflagration roared through him. He was lost in the taste and scent and feel of her. In a futile effort to slow down he had to gulp in breaths of air, take time so that this first experience for her would be good.

He wanted nothing more than to tear off his jeans

and ravage her, take her with him into the very heart of the inferno. It was so difficult to go slow when she shivered in his arms, her eyes wide with shocked pleasure at each new caress.

Waning sunlight filtered through the willow leaves and dappled her skin ever-changing hues of gold. She pulled his head down to hers and kissed him with all the passion he could ever want.

He could wait no longer.

Getting his wet jeans off took some pulling, but she helped, delighting him as her slim fingers clawed at the fabric. Her eyes glittered, wild, and the sheer power of her hunger elated him. At last he was as nude as she, and she reached for his straining manhood with greedy hands. As her fingers closed around him, he felt himself expand, impossibly, even larger. Unable to wait another second, he lowered his body to hers and groaned in utter pleasure. Her legs shifted, opened for him and he was stunned at her generosity.

The musky, indescribably feminine scent of aroused woman tantalized him, taunted him. He breathed her in deeply, intoxicated by her.

Fitting himself to her felt like the most glorious homecoming, the most welcoming haven. At the barrier of her sheath, he probed gently, aching with effort, then as carefully as he could, slid inside. Though it almost killed him, he paused. She was tight, Lord, so wonderfully tight and wet. Sweat broke out on his forehead and gathered just above his taut buttocks.

"You okay?" he asked through gritted teeth.

She responded by lifting her thighs higher, pulling

him closer, her arms and hands mindlessly clutching him to her. Her small teeth nipped his neck. Beneath him, she moved, bucking against him like a wild mare, taking his turgid flesh, dear God, ever deeper inside.

He was lost. He rocked her, gently at first, but with her feminine strength, she asked for harder, faster, demanded *more* of him and he was thrilled to give in to her.

When the first delicate shudders began rippling from her deepest core she threw her head back and groaned, guttural and deep. He cried out, surged against her, and he felt his body spinning uncontrollably into the heat of the blaze.

IT WAS ONLY in the aftermath that Harmony was able to convince Ben she truly loved him. They lay together in the darkening meadow, splendidly unclothed, Ben's magnificent body stretched, satiated, beside hers. His palm rested possessively on her naked thigh.

She got up on one elbow and toyed with a strand of his ebony hair. "I'm willing to face them all, Ben. Even my parents. They'll—they'll accept my wishes." Had he heard her hesitation?

"Even if they disagree? Even if they hate the choice you've made?"

She smiled tenderly, the sensations of his passionate lovemaking still flowing over every surface of her skin. "Even so." *Please, God, let it be all right,* she prayed. But she let him see none of her gnawing doubts.

He said, "I...I have nothing to give you except my mother's earrings. I don't know, but I think they might be valuable—the only thing she left behind when she went back East. But to see the diamonds and little bells on you would make me proud."

"They sound perfect," Harmony replied.

Sparks of hope lit Ben's dark eyes, and the welling of happiness in her breast made her want to weep. On the grass beside her lay the empty green bottle. He hadn't asked about the sweet liquid and she'd wisely refrained from mentioning it. She tucked the bottle beneath her shirt, and to Bella sent up a fervent prayer of thanks.

IT WAS ALMOST DARK before they made their leisurely way back to ranch headquarters. Unable to bear being apart for even the short ride, they decided to lead Apache and ride double on Ben's sturdy bay. So engrossed in each other, neither noticed the two saddled horses standing at the hitch rail.

Ben saw them first, and Harmony, arms looped around his waist from her seat behind his saddle, felt him stiffen. Puzzled at his sudden change, she peered around his broad shoulder.

"Mother?" she gasped. "Papa?" Her parents had come home.

At the foot of the great house's stairs, William and Josie were evidently holding a conference with Old Clay, who stood before them supported by a cane.

Peering through the gloom of dusk, Josie recognized her daughter. "Harmony?" She looked at Ben. William came forward, arms outstretched.

Sliding off the horse's rump, Harmony ran to her mother and father, embracing them. "I'm so glad you're home!" she cried. "How is Grandma Nani? And the ship—was the crossing smooth?"

"Yes, Harmony," Josie said, smiling, arms linked around her daughter's waist. "Grandma is fine—she just wanted us to visit, the old phony. And the ocean trip was marvelous."

William touched Harmony's arm. "A lot has happened since we've been gone—Old Clay's been telling us."

Harmony thought of the fire, of the rustling and of Ben. Yes, a lot had happened. She glanced back at Ben, who had dismounted and was waiting behind her, quiet and diligently controlled. Waves of restless tension emanated from him. She said, "I think we handled things fairly well."

"*Very* well," William corrected. "Clay's just said a bunch of rustlers—the ones who set the fire—were caught today in a trap Ben had set up."

"They were caught?" Ben stepped forward. He nodded solemnly. "Good."

"Clay told us how you took over as foreman while he was recovering from his injuries," William went on. "In fact, when Josie and I got off the train in Caliente, we ran into Ralph Furley and the Bennett family. They had a lot of good things to say about your management, Ben."

"Did they?" Ben's expression remained neutral. He didn't appear to believe it.

"And when we started our ride up the hill, the McCandles were going down to Bakersfield. We had a real nice visit with them."

Josie nodded. "They raved about you, Ben. They said you ran the roundup better than ever. They said you're a natural leader, with a good head for business. They even recommended having you continue helping Old Clay."

"Oh, no," Clay protested. "I'm of retirement age, finally, you know. And Ben's done a great job—with Harmony's help, of course." He winked at her. "I think he should carry on."

"You're retiring, Clay?" William asked in surprise.

The old cowhand shrugged. "I'm eighty."

They all gasped. "No one knew," Harmony breathed. "You've certainly earned a good retirement."

William faced Ben. "Well, what about it? Want the job?"

Ben looked poleaxed.

Harmony smiled. "Of course he does." She took his arm. It was as inflexible and unresponsive as a tree branch. "He's an excellent foreman...with my help."

At last Ben cleared his throat. "There is a job I'd like to apply for, sir." His eyes narrowed with conviction. "I warn you, I won't take no for an answer."

William's eyes dipped to their two tightly joined

hands. He propped his fists on his hips. "Is that right?"

"Yes, sir." Ben stiffened his back, and only Harmony could sense the roiling tension inside him.

"I've asked your daughter to be my wife."

"She said yes," Harmony filled in eagerly.

Josie said nothing at all.

"You want to marry her?" William demanded. "Why?"

"Why?" Ben appeared momentarily nonplussed. It took only seconds to regain his composure. "I love her," he said simply. "I'll work harder than ever. I'll prove I'm worthy of her. If you'll give your blessing, I swear to honor her always."

Josie smiled then, an ancient, womanly expression that spoke directly to Harmony. "You've always been in love with her," she accused Ben gently.

He nodded once. "Yes."

A long moment passed, during which no one said anything.

Harmony couldn't stand even one minute of uncertainty. "You don't mind, do you? I know you expected me to marry, uh...somebody else."

William and Josie exchanged glances.

At last Josie stepped forward and took Harmony's hand. She drew her daughter off a step or two and looked deeply into her eyes. "It's not who a man's parents are or under what circumstances he was born—as your father and I learned more than twenty years ago—but what the man makes of himself that matters. We've known Ben since he was born, and we've always liked him. It won't be easy for you, but if you truly love and want him, you'll weather the storms together.''

Eyes brimming with glad tears, Harmony threw her arms around her mother and hugged her hard. ''Sometime soon,'' she said, ''I need to tell you about the Wilkersons' visit. It wasn't exactly…perfect.''

''Oh, dear.'' Josie smiled. ''They weren't too awful, were they?''

''Let's discuss it later,'' Harmony suggested prudently. She hugged her father, who grinned and patted her back awkwardly.

''Maybe I'll get some grandbabies now,'' he said, then pumped Ben's hand.

At last Harmony turned to Ben. ''Harmony Heart Panau,'' she breathed, gazing with love into her betrothed's gleaming eyes. ''French, white, Hawaiian and Indian. What a mix. I wonder what our children will look like?''

''They'll be beautiful,'' he assured her gruffly, taking her into his arms under the indulgent eyes of William and Josie. ''They'll never want for love.''

ARABELLA'S STORY
Fern Michaels

CHAPTER ONE

The present...

LIGHT FILTERED through the vertical blinds, casting golden stripes across the champagne-colored spread. Arabella could tell it was still early by the color of the lines crisscrossing the satin coverlet.

Should she get up or not?

For some reason, she didn't want to face the day and couldn't recall why not. Then she groaned when it suddenly all came flooding back.

She swung her legs over the side of the bed, a headache pounding at the back of her skull. Coffee and a bottle of aspirin might help, but chances were slim. Her gaze fell to the silky mess on the floor. The four-hundred-dollar designer chemise was nothing more than a thin black piece of material and two straps. Her glittery, sequined stiletto shoes sparkled in the corner of the room. She'd paid three hundred for them. She glared at the bare heel of the left shoe. Somewhere during the course of a long night of gambling, she'd lost the sequins.

If only a few paltry sequins were all she had to worry about now.

Arabella Collins was a professional gambler, a

hired gun, earning her living by playing games of chance with other people's money. Mr. Sandusky wasn't going to appreciate her poor decision to bet the two hundred thousand. Not only that, she lost her percentage. She'd walked away from the game at four in the morning a loser; Sandusky didn't like losers.

One more big loss like last night and she'd be drummed out of Vegas. When she thought of her credit card bills, maxed to the limits, she groaned again. She couldn't even charge a tube of toothpaste today.

What she ought to do was pack in this crazy life and take up a different profession. Something staid and calm. Secretarial work, perhaps. Or she could become a florist. Or an accountant. Anything but earn her living by remembering cards and bluffing others and maintaining cool composure in the face of tremendous pressure. It was just that she was so good at it.

Usually.

Las Vegas, with its brilliant, neon-lit streets, cosmopolitan crowd and exciting nightlife, appealed to her now just as much as it had when she'd moved here a decade ago. Or at least, almost as much. And she adored her penthouse apartment perched atop one of the most glamorous casinos.

She was a modern woman of the nineties and proud of it. And in her profession, she was a pro. On a normal night, few could match her skill with cards. Her natural talent had been honed years ago by rousing bunkhouse poker games with the men on the ranch, and she had thoroughly enjoyed fleecing the guys every chance she'd gotten.

For her, Vegas was a natural place to be.

At least, it had been.

Reminded of the disastrous night before, she felt her headache worsen.

In the kitchenette of her hotel apartment, Arabella stumbled toward the coffee maker. It was a feat, measuring ground beans into the filter with half-closed eyes, but she managed. Leaning on the tiled countertop, she stood impatiently before the machine until it dripped out a full mug. Before she could get a gulp, the shrill ringing of the telephone jarred her sensitive ears.

"What is it?" she demanded belligerently into the receiver. She was always belligerent before her first cup.

An old man's gravelly voice thundered in her ear. "Arabella Heart Collins, tell me you *have* read the reports I've sent you." Old Walt, the foreman, caretaker and general man-in-charge of Heartbreak Ranch.

She sighed and darted a guilty glance at the stack of unopened envelopes beside the telephone. "Hello, Walt. Of course I've read them. They're very... informative."

"I knew it!" he accused. "You haven't even looked at them."

She could easily picture him—an aging, bushy-gray-haired curmudgeon barking into the phone. He always held it awkwardly. If it were the reins of a difficult colt or the steering wheel of a combine, his grip would be far more expert.

"Arabella, it might not be my place—"

"It isn't—"

"But I don't think I'd be out of line to tell you how disappointed your parents would be if they knew how you've ignored the ranch—"

"Give it a rest, Walt. I'm not coming back. I live in Nevada now. I don't *want* to come back to California."

"The cows are starting to drop their new calves and the roundup will be—"

She cut him off ruthlessly. "It's all in the reports, isn't it? I'll read them, okay?" She had to cut him off—he reminded her of everything she fought so hard to forget.

There was a short silence. Then, "You belong here, Arabella. You know that. All Heart women belong *here*."

She stared at the ceiling. "All right, all right. At sixty-five, maybe I'll retire there. Will that satisfy you? Now, I've got to go."

With that she hung up, but as she walked into the small living room with her coffee, she felt like a heel. Old Walt was doing his best. He was a fine foreman and was only trying to include her in ranch decisions and events. She shouldn't have been so short with him. Blame it on the headache.

Dropping onto the ivory-patterned sofa, she stared up at the large gilt-framed painting hanging over the whitewashed fireplace mantel. Madam Bella Duprey lounged in all her naked glory, and the sight of the decadent pose always gave Arabella a lift. That woman had had guts, by God, and guts Arabella admired.

But going back was out of the question. After the dreadful nightmare that had occurred at Heartbreak Ranch ten years ago, she couldn't. Even after so much time, she still couldn't deal with thoughts of the fire and the toll it had taken on her life. When she'd run away from the ranch and all its horrific memories, she'd had Walt send her some clothes, the deed to the property and the heirloom painting. The scandalous piece of art had always been her favorite.

Bella gazed down upon her now with ancient feminine allure.

The old madam must have really known her stuff, Arabella reflected moodily. She'd spawned a dynasty. Vaguely, Arabella recalled tales her mother had told, tales that had been passed down from *her* mother, of how Bella had cleverly bamboozled Sam Heart, the original owner of the deed, and then had him conveniently shanghaied.

Into Arabella's mind came an image of her lovely mother and her soft voice recounting the delicious stories. Her beautiful blue-violet eyes, Arabella remembered well. But the vision was almost instantly clouded by sounds of her mother's frantic screams and images of destruction, and death.

For a brief moment, Arabella squeezed her eyes shut, and at the same time, shut out the memories. "Please," she whispered as the unwanted images came to her. "Please, no." Shuddering, she forced herself to put the thoughts aside. She would do as she had for years—turn her mind away, think of something else. She had enough to deal with without tearing herself apart over the past.

A big game was set for Friday evening—two days away. In spite of last night's loss, she didn't doubt that Sandusky would still want her to play for him. According to her calculations, he was still way ahead. Nevertheless, she was certain he would have a few choice remarks about her strategy. She'd just have to grin and bear it; when Sandusky made choice remarks, you listened.

Back in the kitchen for more coffee, she caught sight of her reflection on the shiny black refrigerator door. She might as well face it, she looked like hell. Her normally sleek blond hair was tangled beyond hope. Her eyes were bloodshot, the lids puffy. She gazed at the reflection of her expensive aqua silk nightgown and matching wrap and wondered how much she could get for them at the consignment shop off the Strip.

Blowing a strand of hair off her face, she knew she had to get her act together. Winning the big game was even more vital to her than the money she hoped to earn on her percentage. Whether or not she would ever again play in Vegas depended upon her performance.

IN THE PLUSH CASINO, the *ka-ching* of one-armed bandits could be heard over muted conversation, punctuated by occasional yelps of joy and groans of dismay from the craps tables. Scantily-clad cocktail waitresses juggling loaded trays canvassed the floor, faithfully dispensing alcohol twenty-four hours a day.

Up high, in the vaulted ceiling, a cloud of cigarette smoke hung near two-way mirrors, from which sharp unblinking eyes observed everything.

To Arabella the place felt, if not like home, then at least familiar. She'd showered and changed into a lavender cashmere sweater and matching slacks, and she felt a little better.

Now, placing herself behind an enormous potted palm near the lobby, she waited to see who her competition would be. She knew many of them would arrive this morning. The game would draw some of the most elite professionals from gambling hot spots all over the world: from the Costa del Sol, Atlantic City and Monte Carlo.

Monte Carlo.

She didn't want to think about the two months she'd spent there last year. At the time, combining work and a vacation seemed like a good idea. But her heart was still aching from memories of *him*—the man she couldn't get her mind off—and the fiasco of their relationship. If only things could have turned out differently.

Lost in thought, Arabella was taken by surprise at the sudden appearance of Lily Lake. Lily was like Arabella—a career girl who played with money from backers.

"Darling, *you're* here?" the elegant beauty inquired of Arabella in cultured tones.

"Hello, Lily." Arabella returned the greeting in tones as dry as the Nevada desert. She braced herself as the tall, leggy female glided closer. Lily glittered with oversize diamonds and something furry wrapped around her neck.

She looked lovely enough, but Arabella had learned by hard experience that one had to be on one's guard around Lily.

"Who are you playing for?" Lily asked in her sickly-sweet manner. "Raleigh? Or that Texas oil tycoon you were working for in Atlantic City?"

Arabella shook her head. "Neither. I have a new client. He's a local here. Into hotels and casinos."

"Sandusky?" Lily asked shrewdly, her obvious shock irritating Arabella.

"The very same."

"Well, *that* should make the game…interesting. For once you'll have a backer who actually has some *real* money." With that, she glided away, and Arabella realized the furry thing around the other woman's neck was an ermine stole.

A stole, Arabella rolled her eyes. As if anyone wore those things anymore. The frustrating thing was, on the stunning Lily Lake the fur collar looked great.

All at once Arabella's lavender outfit seemed plain. She grimaced. Next to Lily she always felt dowdy.

Arabella watched Lily slink toward the reception desk and observed the predictable gaping of the clerk. She scoffed. Men were such idiots, falling for every pretty face and impressive bust measurement.

Lily wielded her beauty like a club. Always in a dress cut to *there*, always perfectly coiffed and made up, always with a bold eye, Lily had won games by literally distracting her male opponents with her overblown physical charms. But Arabella was immune to such wiles, and knew that when it came to skill she was better than Lily and could outplay her at the table. She had before, she could do it again.

At the hotel entrance, a group of robed men, some sporting beards and balancing exotic turbans, flowed inside like an Arabian tide of rich oil. They surrounded a man with a hawk nose and piercing eyes. Faroud. *Well, well,* Arabella thought as she watched the flunkies flow smoothly around Faroud. The highstakes competition was certainly drawing in the very best.

Faroud was one of the only pros she knew who actually gambled with his own money. For him, winning a few hundred thousand, or losing a few, was merely a diverting hobby. His wealth came from Egyptian oil fields.

Suddenly, from the rows of glass doors that fronted the hotel, a lone man entered and paused just inside. His gray eyes flashed over the lobby with a mercurycolored gaze that missed nothing.

Arabella gasped and shrank back behind a broad palm leaf.

Zach.

Arabella ran an unsteady hand across her eyes. Lordy, what would she do? That Zachary Richards should come to town and participate in the big game hadn't occurred to her. After their time in Monte Carlo, she hadn't seem him in a year.

Eleven months, fourteen days, six hours, to be exact.

She would never forget Zach Richards. The starry nights, the sunny days on the Riviera. It had been magic, a world of heady romance, of laughter and lovemaking. It was the first time she had ever let herself open up that way to a man. She hadn't intended to let anything ever go that far, but Zach was so very caring, so seductive, so *perfect*, that she had begun to feel safe enough to open herself up. Safe enough to love and be loved in return.

But whenever Zach had looked at her with those steel-gray eyes, she'd felt as if he were looking into her very soul. When things really heated up between them, she realized she was in jeopardy of falling apart. Rather than risk her heart and leave herself open to eventual loss, she had run like a frightened jackrabbit, left him without any explanation.

She had walked out on Zach. But she hadn't been able to forget him.

Unable to help herself, Arabella peered through the palm leaves and saw him stride in his uniquely purposeful way to the reception desk. He gave a curt nod in Faroud's direction, acknowledging him, and then flashed a brilliant smile at Lily Lake.

That grin. That devastating smile. Arabella remembered it so very well. He had smiled into her eyes in the aftermath of their lovemaking. What was the expression, actually? A simple lifting of his lips? An easy showing of his teeth? But what lips. What teeth. A memory of what he could do to a woman's caress-warmed skin with those tools weakened her knees. Even from across a room he still had the power to make her feel as if thickened honey were spreading through her.

Zach Richards. Oh, Lord, not here, not now. Not

when the upcoming game was going to require all of her attention.

Behind her, in a tiny alcove off the lobby was a small grouping of chairs. She groped her way to them and sank into the overstuffed leather. Her hand trembled as she tried to rub away the tension that settled in her nape. Like her, Zach always used a backer's money, earning a percentage for himself; it was the way things were done. Naturally, his backer would want his best man to participate in the contest.

"Still hiding behind the hotel plants?" a masculine voice inquired behind her. She jumped, but he went on. "I thought I'd find you here, checking out the competition for Friday's game. You always did want to know who you were up against. You haven't changed at all." There was a note of disparagement in his voice.

Getting swiftly to her feet, Arabella faced him warily. "Zach," she said. "It's nice to see you. You... haven't changed, either." She took in his tall, broad-shouldered frame, thick dark hair, sharp gray eyes that seemed to laser right through her. His ebony suit was of expensive wool, expertly tailored. His shoes, Italian leather.

"No, I'm different now, Arabella," he replied. "Real different. I'm not the gullible fool you used last year in Monte Carlo."

"Used?" she blustered, unsettled by his wording. "What do you mean, used?"

"Don't play innocent, sweetheart. When you ran away from me I figured—wrongly as it turns out—

that you'd be back. When you never returned, I got the message.''

She lifted her chin, trying to brazen out the difficult situation. But he advanced on her and she took a step back, so that the huge pot came flush behind her. She felt one of the fronds jabbing her spine. There was nowhere else to go. "It wasn't like that," she informed him stiffly.

"We enjoyed each other well enough," he said, his tones bitter. He was so close she could see the cold anger in his eyes. "But I don't provide stud service—"

She gasped. "Don't," she said, her color rising. "Don't talk like that about what we...about our relationship."

"Why not? You used me, then dumped me. But maybe you underestimated me." Abruptly, he drew back and appraised her. "I'm a bad loser, Bell. I've been counting the days until I could get even. I'm going to best you Friday. Sandusky will be ticked. When the game's over, you'll be lucky to get a housekeeping job."

"*I'm* going to win that game, Zach," she promised. When cornered or threatened she always became stubborn and haughty. It was her defense mechanism, and it had worked very well for her for years. She hated nothing more than being on the defensive.

He tilted his head, confusing her for a moment. His eyes narrowed and she could swear his nostrils flared. He inhaled. Abruptly, she realized that he was *scenting* her, like an animal in the wild, searching for a mate. The thought shot an involuntary thrill through her. She remembered many times in Monte Carlo when he'd praised her fragrance. How often had he huskily whispered, ''I love your smell.''

Suddenly overwhelmed, she turned away. Back iron-rod stiff, she walked toward the bank of elevators. She couldn't believe Zach meant to blame her wholly for the way things had worked out between them. Ridiculous. Everyone knew it took two to tango.

She got into the elevator and faced forward. Before the doors closed, she saw that Zach was still watching her. She met his gaze with a level one of her own. Again, she lifted her chin. He'd best her, huh? Well, she would show him.

ZACH WATCHED Arabella until the elevator doors slid shut. He hadn't thought seeing her again would hurt this bad. He hadn't gambled on what one brief glimpse would do to his insides. At the first sight of her his gut had somehow twisted itself into a knot.

It had taken him a year to track her down after Monte Carlo—but he'd wasted half that time licking his wounds and brooding over the way she'd walked out on him. He could still taste her on his lips, remember how she felt in his arms, the way she looked into his eyes, cocky, yet wary and almost frightened at the same time.

When they were first together, she had seemed hesitant, even reserved. She'd given of herself and then pulled back, as if she was afraid to let go, afraid of what might happen if she opened up her emotions.

Just now, he had seen the familiar bold set of her

shoulders, the hard way she'd stared back at him from the elevator. Arabella Collins was an expert at being brash and flippant, as if she were ready to take on the world. But in those last few days they had been together, he had seen another side of her start to blossom, a glimpse of a vulnerability that she worked hard to keep hidden from the world.

She was the first woman who'd ever gotten to him. Arabella, with her violet eyes and teasing smile, had stolen his heart, then walked out and thrown it back in his face.

Just the sight of her, just the hint of her own special seductive scent still had the power to set him on fire. Tonight he'd told her that he was here to get even, but the truth went deeper.

He was here to win.

And she was the prize.

CHAPTER TWO

ARABELLA WAS in trouble.

She knew it the minute she opened the door early that evening. Sandusky stood poised at the head of a group of dark-suited men who looked like nothing less than a pack of Dobermans. *Damn*, she would have to brazen this out.

"Good evening, Miss Collins," Sandusky greeted her in his soft, cultured tones. He was a slim, elegant man of European descent. He spoke excellent English but with a faint accent that she had never quite placed. It didn't occur to her to ask. One did not question Sandusky.

"Howdy," she said with false enthusiasm. "Guys," she added, acknowledging the foursome surrounding Sandusky, "it's great to see you. Come in, please."

Two men prowled inside, fanning out. They stuck their snouts suspiciously into each corner of her penthouse, hunting for spies or killers or other sinister personages, Arabella supposed. When they were finally satisfied, Sandusky entered with the remaining two.

The "guard dogs," as she privately called them, all wore plain dark business suits, had their hair cut short, and had mustaches. Ominous, gun-shaped bulges were evident beneath their jackets and their faces were expressionless.

"I like your suit," she commented cheerfully to one. "You all go to the same groomer?"

He ignored her and took up a position beside the closed door. The others placed themselves strategically about the room. How wonderful, Arabella thought dryly. Even if an air-to-ground missile attack were launched she would be safe. What a load off.

"You are ready to play for me Friday, Miss Collins?" Sandusky inquired without preliminaries. He stood in front of the portrait of Bella, studying it.

She remained standing as well. "Never readier." Somehow, her reply had come out sounding like a battery commercial.

"And you are well?"

"Positively glowing with good health."

"Good. We want no repeats of your last game." He turned to face her. "Do we, Miss Collins?" Beneath his soft voice, a knife blade of warning nicked her.

She felt a twinge of fear and her color rose. "I'm sorry about that. But, Mr. Sandusky, you know I seldom lose—"

"But when it happens, you do it so spectacularly," he said. "In two nights' time you will be competing against Evan Hennessy's representative. I believe you have an acquaintance with Zachary Richards?"

She swallowed. "I know Zachary Richards, yes." She wondered if Sandusky knew exactly how well acquainted they were. Probably. He knew everything.

"I trust your prior...*association* with Richards will not affect your skill at the table." It was not a question, but a statement.

"No," she replied quickly. "My personal life is entirely separate from my professional one. You can rest assured that nothing will interfere with my card-playing ability on Friday. I will win."

"I'm glad to hear that because in recent years I have endured heavy losses to Evan Hennessy. I do not like the man." At this, the guard dogs bristled, their dark snapping eyes quartering the room as if an enemy had leaped into their midst.

"Whoa, down boys," Arabella said.

Sandusky withdrew a silver box from his pocket and lit a thin brown cigarette. "I do not plan to lose again. You understand?"

"Perfectly." She crossed her arms. The implied threat was as obvious as the cocking of a revolver.

"Very well. And to ensure your full attention to the game Friday night, I will advance you one hundred thousand dollars' credit at the table."

Her brow furrowed. "But that's not enough. Not by a long shot." She'd need at least three hundred thousand.

"Yes, I know. I expect you to put up the other two hundred thousand from your own pocket."

"*What?*" She couldn't have heard him correctly.

"That way I will be assured of your complete concentration. You will not allow yourself to become distracted if your own assets are at stake, hmm?"

"But—but I have no money. I don't own anything.

This penthouse is rented. My credit cards are maxed out.''

He remained unmoved. ''I am certain you have made investments—own stock certificates or maintain a healthy bank account.''

''No—I spend everything—''

Trailing cigarette smoke, he waved a negligent hand. ''Beg, borrow or steal. Do whatever is necessary. You will produce the needed capital.'' With a curt nod to the Dobies, he paced to the door. Two of the guards trotted ahead into the hallway, made a careful sweep, then indicated it was safe for him to come out.

During the ritual, Arabella merely stood gaping. How did he expect her to come up with money she didn't have? There was no one from whom she could borrow so much, and banks generally frowned on extending loans for use in poker games. Usually, a person making such a loan request was thrown out on her penniless ear.

At the door, Sandusky paused. ''Do not disappoint me, Miss Collins. It would not be...wise.'' The door closed with a soft, menacing hush.

Arabella was in trouble.

SHAKEN, SHE PACED her apartment trying to collect her thoughts. A drink—that was what she needed— but only an occasional drinker, she had next-to-nothing on hand. In her line of work, she could not afford to have any vital perceptions diminished, or her inhibitions lowered. To keep her wits sharp while working, she sipped only mineral water. A trip down-stairs to the hotel bar was in order.

Quickly she gathered her shoulder-length hair into a high ponytail and thrust her feet into silver sandals. She still wore the lavender sweater and slacks; they'd be fine for a quick jaunt to the bar.

The casino lobby, as always, hummed with activity. She barely noticed. Head down, she walked quickly past the reception desk toward the lounge. At the café adjoining the bar, a few people occupied tables. The café served appetizers and cocktails. As Arabella threaded her way through, one of the couples caught her eye.

Zach and Lily Lake were cozied up to a minuscule round table, sipping martinis and looking deeply into each other's eyes. A plate of half-eaten chicken wings sat between them.

Arabella's step faltered and something tightened in her chest. Though she'd inherited the violet eyes and blond hair of her ancestors, and some even called her beautiful, she knew she would never see the day when she matched Lily. The woman was cover-model gorgeous.

Too bad she was cold as ice inside.

Trust Zach not to have recognized that salient fact. The man was besotted, she could tell. Shrugging stiffly, she told herself it didn't matter to her if he chose to get frostbite. Zach and Lily were welcome to each other.

Pushing on, she hated how jerky her normally fluid stride had become. Her cheeks felt flushed and overly warm. She hated feeling anything. It left her too vulnerable. *Damn* that Zach Richards.

At the polished mahogany bar she placed her order. "I'll have a glass of chardonnay—no, make it the whole bottle."

The bartender, a young man in his early twenties, gave her the once-over and a slow, seductive smile. "And two glasses?"

"No. I drink alone." She purposely kept her tone firm and her level gaze cool.

"Whatever the lady wants," he replied, shrugging. He set a bottle of house chardonnay onto the bartop and a single wine goblet. As she collected them, she could not resist a last glance at Zach's table.

He was staring at her.

She stared right back, defiantly, as if she didn't care a whit *what* he did with the incomparable Lily Lake. He could do that thing with his lips and teeth to Lily and it wouldn't matter to Arabella at all. When a smile lifted the edges of Zach's hard mouth, an odd, pained sensation gripped her by the throat. Her eyes stung and the knowledge of just how badly he had gotten to her scared the hell out of her.

Arabella Collins *never* cried. She didn't dare. Since the fire and the hideous months that followed, she had trained herself not to show any emotion at all. It had taken her a long, hard-fought battle to retain her sanity. Her tough demeanor was all that stood between her and the nightmare of her loss.

But now she recognized that her control was slipping and it was all because of Zach Richards.

He made a small movement of his glass in a silent

toast to her. Lily turned and, spying Arabella, waggled her fingers. The diamond rings on two of her fingers caught the light and nearly blinded Arabella.

Without a backward glance, clutching the wine bottle like a lifeline, Arabella strode out.

AN HOUR AFTER he'd watched her leave the café downstairs, Zach stood outside the door to Arabella's penthouse. He'd already tried the doorbell and then the ornate brass knocker, but to no avail. So he resorted to pounding.

Finally the door whipped open. Arabella swayed inside and blinked up at him. A wineglass dangled forgotten from her fingers.

"What is it?" she demanded without even so much as a hello.

Zach stepped in without asking. He shut the door behind him. She gripped the glass and stepped back. Her eyes were glassy and she appeared to be having a hard time focusing.

"Imbibing alone, Arabella? As I recall, you weren't much of a drinker."

"I'm into it now," she told him a bit too brazenly. He followed her through the marble-tiled foyer into the living room. "I'm a real boozer. I drink all the time. Every night—days, too. Whiskey, gin, vodka, you name it."

His eyes narrowed and his gaze wandered from her glass to the bottle, misted with condensation, carelessly placed on the end table next to her white sofa. He could see through the green glass that the "real boozer" had polished off three glasses at the most.

In three strides he was at the chrome-and-glass entertainment center and wet bar, flinging open the doors to what he guessed was the most obvious place to store spirits. There was nothing inside but one dusty bottle of chocolate liqueur and three shot glasses.

"You're a real sot, all right. And what a way to go—death by chocolate liqueur."

She faced him boldly. "What are you doing here, Zach? You didn't come up here to find out what I'm drinking. If you did, you lead one hell of a boring life. Maybe you'd better get back to Lily."

"Lily? At least she's a woman who understands a man," he said, deciding to push her a little.

"Don't you mean, she knows how to *manipulate* a man?" she shot back. A challenge flared in her eyes.

At his sides his hands clenched. Deep inside, he felt an answer to her challenge urge him to reach for her, haul her into his arms and kiss the daylights out of her. He wanted to melt her tough outer shell with the heat that had always flared between them.

But first things first. "We've got some unfinished business, you and I. I intend to get the truth out of you here and now, Arabella. No more running."

"Chardonnay?" she offered, with a flip of her hair as she retreated toward the kitchen. "I'll get you a glass."

Not about to let her out of his sight, Zach moved so fast she had no time to guess his intent. He grasped her upper arms and held her in a firm grip.

"I'm glad you've had a little wine tonight, sweetheart. Maybe it's just the thing to loosen your tongue."

"Loosen my tongue? Why, Zach, I love it when you talk dirty." She held the wine goblet between them like a shield.

"Stop it." He tightened his grip, forced her to look him in the eyes. "You've always been a sassy little broad, haven't you? But I'm ready to call your bluff."

She didn't like that. She didn't like it at all. Suddenly, she looked away, as if she wanted to bolt again.

He tried to lighten his tone. "For a while there in Monte Carlo, I saw another side to you, Bell. I saw the real woman beneath this hard-as-nails act you like to put on."

She tried to twist free but he tightened his hold.

"Arabella." He kept his voice low and calm. "Tell me. I have to know. Why did you run away from me?"

"I didn't run away from you." She tossed off a careless shrug. "It...our relationship couldn't go any farther—"

"That's not true—"

"It was over between us. Surely you knew that."

"No," he ground out, "I didn't know any such thing. I thought what we had was more than a fling in some romantic seaside town. I thought there was something different between us, Bell, something special. You ruined it. You ran out on me. But I don't understand why. Why, Bell?"

Arabella closed her eyes and tried to think against the wine fogging her senses and the far more potent force of Zach's low, rumbling voice and his familiar touch. The way he spoke her nickname, Bell—no one had called her that in so long. Zach had used it when he'd whispered love words in her ear, thrilling her, bringing her to such incredible peaks of joy.

The yearning she had felt ever since she left him months before blossomed painfully in her chest. It hurt, this terrible longing. How she'd missed him.

His hard fingers on her upper arms moved slowly, became almost caressing. It both confused and excited her until she hardly knew her own mind.

She still wanted him.

Opening her eyes, she saw a tender light ignited in the depths of his gaze. Huskily, he said, "I remember your scent. Like jasmine and...spring rain." He leaned closer, drawing her in. He was going to kiss her.

Building emotions threatened to overwhelm her again—just as they had in Monte Carlo. Zach, so handsome, so incredibly intelligent, so attentive—he was perfect. The perfect male animal. Her own helpless response to him sent frightening spears of panic deep into her heart.

It was all too much.

She couldn't handle her feelings for him then and she couldn't handle them now.

With a quick wrench, she backed away. "Leave, Zach. Please. Just...leave."

The tender light in his eyes was extinguished as if it had never been, replaced by his customarily cool expression.

"That's fine, Bell, I'll leave. But we're not through yet, you and me. We're not through at all."

TWENTY-FOUR HOURS later, Sandusky paid Arabella another unexpected visit.

When she peered through her apartment's peephole and saw him, surrounded by his pack of mongrels, she groaned inwardly. Not again.

Pasting a brilliant smile on her face, she opened the door. She still had no idea what to do about the two hundred grand he'd insisted she produce, and the game was tomorrow evening. She'd spent much of the night pacing and fretting, and all day today making telephone calls. Not one of her friends or acquaintances could advance her anywhere near such a sum. A thousand here, a few thousand there, fell miserably short of the required amount.

The only item of value she owned was a pair of earrings left her by her great-grandmother Harmony, and she'd rather die than pawn them. Besides, they weren't worth anywhere near that much.

The small party streamed inside and she fell back. "How lovely to see you again. I should tell you, Mr. Sandusky, that I'm having the tiniest bit of trouble coming up with—"

He held up his hand to silence her. "Today I had my people investigate your financial position. It is true, you have little in the bank, no stock or bond investments and only a used sedan in the hotel garage."

Her lips tightened. All that stuff was supposed to be confidential. Anyway, now she could be relieved that he knew. Even Sandusky couldn't squeeze water from a rock. "There you have it."

"However, I've been informed that you do hold title to an interestingly large parcel of land in the mountains of California. Isn't that so, Miss Collins? In fact, on paper, you are quite wealthy."

Arabella felt the blood drain from her face. Even though she hadn't the courage to go home again, she had never once thought of Heartbreak Ranch as something she'd use as collateral, something she'd *gamble* with. The property had been in her family for generations.

"Mr. Sandusky," she began, determined to dissuade him, "there is no way I could—"

"I beg your pardon?" He lifted one slim eyebrow in the most threatening manner she'd ever seen. His dogs growled. She could swear one bared sharp incisors.

She quailed. Despite this, she was obliged to press on. "It's impossible. I simply won't play in the game. I'll withdraw. You can get another gambler to represent you."

"I think not," he informed her warningly. His voice began to rise in volume. "You've already been named and entered and the competition is closed. There can be no substitutions. I wish to make a showing in this game, and you will appear. Evan Hennessy will not be allowed to win by default!" His voice had risen to a near shout. It was amazing, considering that he always spoke softly.

Two of the guards advanced toward her. She

shrank back until Sandusky impatiently waved them off. They glared at her, unblinking and wolfish.

"Look," she tried in desperation, "ask me anything else. I'll play for you for a reduced percentage, or for nothing, whatever you want. But don't ask me to put up Heartbreak Ranch. I can't. I just…can't."

He glanced at her with disdain. "I have already informed Hennessy we shall be using this property deed in the game. You will have it with you when you sit at the table tomorrow evening. My sources tell me you've kept it here in the hotel safe deposit."

His sources? She moaned. As a last defense, she had been going to say the deed was back at the ranch, too far away to get by tomorrow night. But somehow he'd found out she kept the deed here. She'd forgotten that Sandusky, with his murky underworld ties, could find out anything.

Sandusky went on. "I do not wish to discuss the unpleasant personal ramifications to you if you do not appear at the game." With a flick of his hand, he summoned his pack and exited her apartment.

Her knees weak, she put a hand to her forehead and felt faint. Sandusky's warning was clear.

If she didn't show up with the deed, God knew what they'd do to her.

CHAPTER THREE

AT THE LOWEST EBB of her life, Arabella sat late into the night, thinking morosely that she'd had a good life, but not a great one. A great life wouldn't feel so hollow at its end. And it would *be* the end if she didn't produce the deed to Heartbreak Ranch tomorrow at the game.

A great life would have seen her in a loving relationship with a fine man.

She grimaced. It was what her parents had always wanted for her—to marry, settle down on the ranch and raise more blond, violet-eyed daughters to carry on the tradition. Well, if her parents had lived, wouldn't they be surprised?

Then again, if they had lived, their precious little Arabella would not have spent most of her adult life in smoky gambling joints manipulating cards and bluffing her way through mediocre hands.

Arabella glanced up at the painting of Bella over the fireplace. At least her namesake would have approved of her chosen profession. The old gal would probably be proud.

In the kitchen her clock struck 2:00 a.m. Four hours. She'd been sitting there four useless hours. She hadn't eaten all day and she felt light-headed, but she couldn't summon the energy to get up and fix something or even turn on a light. It was dark in the apartment. The only illumination in the room was a single fat candle that sat on the glass-and-chrome coffee table in front of the sofa. The candle sent unearthly shadows onto the walls, cast the corners of the room into eerie darkness.

She was hungry and tired and a new headache was coming on, when she noticed that the room suddenly felt cool. The damn air conditioner—it never had worked properly. Pulling her knees up to her chest and tucking her bare feet under her, she shivered. It really was *cold* in here.

Above her head, near the painting, a thin spiraling cone of gray mist swirled and Arabella gasped. Was the hotel on fire?

About to jump up, she realized that no smoke alarms had gone off, nor had her ceiling sprinkler system kicked on, either. And she smelled no smoke. Instead, a faint odor of lemon verbena wafted to her.

Something turned her attention to the life-size nude on the wall opposite where she sat. All around the gilt frame was a thin, ribbonlike stream of smoky vapor.

The smoky vapor began to take shape.

Heart thudding, Arabella put her hands to her eyes and rubbed. She really should have eaten something. When she removed her hands, she saw her ancestor's long, shapely legs slide off the red velvet settee and step right out of the painting. Reaching behind her, the vaporish woman gathered her satin robe from the back of the chaise and put it on. The vision's hair was blond, her curls upswept, her hands beringed. The woman was beautiful.

She hovered before the fireplace.

Arabella swallowed thickly and dragged a throw pillow into her lap. She hugged it to her chest and did not blink. Was she dreaming? That was it. She'd fallen asleep on the sofa and was dreaming that her painting had come alive. She pinched her leg. Hard. It hurt like hell but she did not wake.

Okay, so she wasn't dreaming. She was hallucinating. That explained things. Perhaps the tremendous stress she was under was playing tricks on her mind. She'd heard of such things happening. It came on people when they were sleep-deprived, or using drugs, or under the stress of death threats. Just last week she'd seen a television show depicting a bunch of sorry losers who claimed to see rivers flowing in their living rooms, tarantulas on the walls and monsters and…ghosts.

"Ma chère," the vision said, "I will have your attention now?"

Arabella gaped. Her hallucination was talking.

"S'il vous plaît, I know you are not stupid. You are my namesake, it is impossible. Now, listen, I have come to help guide you through your current difficulties."

The smoky vision wavered before Arabella. "I am imagining this," she whispered. "I am definitely not awake. You—you can't be real."

"I assure you, I am as real as you. Now, we are wasting time. You must return to the ranch, of course. This life you lead—" she waved her hand and her rings sparkled "—fandango palaces and gaming halls—they are fine for a few years. But then a woman must make a home for herself. You, Arabella, have reversed this order. First you had the home, then you went to gaming. This I do not understand."

Arabella stared at the woman. "Bella?" she asked. "Are you really Bella Duprey?"

If ghosts could preen, this one did.

"Naturally, I'm Bella Duprey. The most famous madam on the Barbary Coast, Queen of the Courtesans."

"I can't believe it!" Arabella exclaimed, deciding she might as well stop fighting this and go with it. "I don't care if I am dreaming. I've always wished I could meet you, talk with you. Wow, what a woman you were."

"*Oui*, I was an incredible woman," the vision agreed. "There were none who could match me. But we digress. You must return to the ranch and find my trunk. In the trunk, you will discover my journal. It will help you."

"Say, could you give me a few pointers? You were said to be a great gambler—my mom told me stories about you, probably most of them not true, but from you I could learn a lot—"

"Arabella," the ghost said sternly, "pay attention." She turned her head, as if glancing about the apartment. "Where is the dog? I can hardly work or think unless there is a dog present. They make such perfect companions, you know."

"Dog?" Arabella shrugged. "The closest thing to a canine around here would be Sandusky's curs." She shuddered. "Those guys would just as soon tear me limb from limb as look at me. And they will, too, if I don't produce Heartbreak Ranch's deed at tomorrow night's game."

"You have made many mistakes," Bella agreed sadly. "But it is not too late. Go back to the ranch. Oh, I almost forget myself—watch out for another."

"Another?"

"Since I have been granted this visit to you, then so may *he* also be allowed to return. Many years ago, I cheated him out of his ranch when he planned to humiliate me. Now, he may make a reappearance as well. If so, he will naturally be at cross-purpose with me—and will try to get to me through you."

"Cross-purposes?" Arabella echoed. "But who? The only one working against me is...Zach."

The older woman nodded and smiled wisely. "You see? You are not stupid, just slow. The spirit of Sam Heart may very well align himself with this Zach." The shifting mists that comprised her body began to dissipate. "Go back," she said, her voice now feathery and hard to hear. "Go back to the ranch."

"But, wait, don't leave." Arabella leaped to her feet and reached out a hand. She touched nothing but airy wisps of fog.

"And get a dog," a disembodied voice whispered.

Arabella sank back onto the sofa. It was becoming warmer in the apartment, as if the air conditioner had suddenly decided to regulate itself to an even temperature. Could all this really have happened? Could Bella have truly made an appearance in her apartment?

"OPEN THE DAMN DOOR, Bell!" Zach didn't care if he woke up everyone in the building as he stood outside Arabella's apartment again.

At last she opened the door.

He pushed past her, slammed the door behind him and leaned against it as he tried to catch his breath. With the elevators full, it had been a hard dash up the four flights of stairs from his room to hers.

"Well, do come in, Zach. Please, make yourself at home." Arabella's sassiness was back full force.

"Bell, I—" He didn't know quite how to phrase his thoughts. He had to clear his throat and start over. "I've got to talk to you about a visitor I had. Could we put aside what happened between us yesterday? Truce?"

Without waiting for an invitation, he threw himself onto the sofa and ran an unsteady hand through his hair.

"You're as white as a sheet," she said, watching him closely. All the animosity and distrust between them was set aside for the moment.

"I think I'm losing my mind. I don't even know where to start—"

"You had a visitor," she prompted. "A ghost, right?" She sat down beside him eagerly.

He stared at her. How could she know, unless—

"Did you have anything to do with this? I thought I was dreaming, that I was only—"

"Hallucinating? It's going around."

"I think I've got a bad case of jet lag. Either that or there was something in the midnight all-you-can-eat seafood buffet downstairs that didn't agree with me."

"Maybe that's what's wrong with me, too," she said absently. "But if all you have is a bad case of indigestion, then what are you doing here?"

He shook his head, unwilling to believe what he thought he'd just seen and heard in his room. Some old codger claiming to have been dead for more than a hundred years actually wanted to hire him professionally. He couldn't tell Arabella. She would either think he was losing his mind or that he was so desperate to see her that he had made the whole thing up. But after the strange experience, his first impulse had been to come and see Arabella.

She was still watching him, her eyes full of concern. He wondered if she was aware that her hand rested on his knee with unconscious familiarity.

"I didn't feel like being alone right now." He glanced over his shoulder, unable to shake the feeling that he was being watched. Damn that extra helping of Cajun shrimp.

"You're in denial, Zach."

"Damn it, Bell, I don't believe in ghosts. How about we just drop it. Forget I mentioned anything." He wanted to put the disturbing incident out of his mind. Besides, he had other things to think about. He couldn't believe Arabella had let him stay this long. Willing to press his luck, Zach said, "Maybe I'd better have some of that chocolate liqueur you keep around here, unless you've brought in something stronger?"

"Sorry, I'll get the liqueur." She crossed the room

to collect two shot glasses and the bottle. When she settled beside him again, she broke the seal and poured a measure of the thick, dark brown liquid into the glasses. Handing him one, she raised hers in a salute. He downed it like a shot of whisky.

"Some night, huh?" she asked, sipping her drink.

"Some life." He leaned back against the plush sofa cushions and closed his eyes. "Now ghosts. I guess gambling's finally getting to me. Lately I've been wondering how long I can keep it up."

"You mean, before you run screaming, stark raving mad into the night?"

"You sound like you know what you're talking about."

There was a faraway look in her eyes, as if she were gazing into the past. "Believe me, I do."

The shot glasses held no more than a thimble full. He poured another.

"How did you get into this life?" she asked softly. "I never asked before."

"We were too busy," he said, searching her eyes. They had spent their time together learning everything about each other's bodies, not their pasts. "I grew up on a farm."

She drew back in disbelief. "No way."

"I did. My folks still have the old place in Oklahoma. Cows and pigs and corn, the whole hayseed deal. But I couldn't wait to get out, see the world. I wanted to do things, be somebody." He rubbed the back of his neck. "But all of this is obviously getting to me. I'm tired—tonight's little episode back in my room proved that. I've been thinking about giving it all up."

In Monte Carlo he had thought about what it would be like to share a quieter, more settled life with Bell beside him. Now he waited for her reaction, waited to see if she could fathom his desire to get out of gambling. But trained by long hours at the gaming tables, her face was expressionless, unreadable.

"What would you do, if not this?" At least she sounded concerned.

"The truth is, I'm trained to crop-dust. When I was in high school, I helped out a pilot back in Oklahoma one summer and fell in love with flying. It's so peaceful up there, so quiet. I thought having a pilot's license was something I could always fall back on, so I keep one current."

"I would never have guessed you were born on a farm, not in a million years, Zach. You've always seemed so polished, so...worldly."

"How about you? How did you start gambling?"

He saw the shutters start to come down, then she shook her head and smiled at some long-ago remembrance. When she spoke, he barely heard the answer.

"In a bunkhouse."

"Care to explain?"

"My father ran a ranch with thousands of cattle. Cattle need cowboys and cowboys need bunkhouses. Our hands liked to gamble, mostly poker, gin, hearts, anything. I learned to play them all. Pretty soon, I was real good. By the time I was sixteen, none of the men could beat me anymore."

He shook his head, confused. "So, where's the

bridge? You had a fine home, it sounds like. Why'd you leave?"

For a heartbeat, he thought she was going to open up and tell him all of it. Softly, he urged her to go on.

"Bell? What happened?"

He saw her hands begin to shake. It appeared to take all her will to place the little glass on the table without breaking it. When she straightened her shoulders and looked into his eyes, he knew the moment had passed.

"I don't want to talk about—" Her voice broke.

"Let me guess. You ran away from home is that it? What happened? Daddy didn't let you use the pickup?"

"Let it go, Zach, please." More than her hands were trembling now. She pushed up off the couch and paced over to the wide bank of windows that looked out over the garish and beautiful lights of Las Vegas.

He knew that the key to unlocking her heart lay in the secret of her past.

"You turned tail and ran rather than face your feelings. Just like you ran away from me."

"You don't know anything about what happened. It wasn't like that—"

"Damn it, Bell. You're wound as tight as a drum right now. Look at you. You're shaking. Trust me. Explain it to me. Why do you have to keep running? What are you running from? Yourself?"

"Just get out," she whispered, dry-eyed, fragile.

He stood up and walked up to her. She drew back in a protective gesture that irritated him. He had never hurt her and never would. When he reached for her, she held her hands out in front of her as if to ward him off.

"Don't—"

Zach dropped his arms to his sides. They felt as empty as his soul. He and Bell might as well have been miles apart instead of mere inches.

"Someday, you'll have to stop running and face head-on whatever it is that's chasing you, Bell. And when that day comes, you'll have to face me, too, because I'll be there waiting for the truth."

AT PRECISELY ten o'clock the next morning, Arabella presented herself at the hotel desk and asked to be shown into the safe deposit box area. Her palm filmy with perspiration, she clutched the key, which she'd never used in the ten years since she'd put the papers into the safe.

A uniformed clerk appeared with the long locked box and verified with her that it was the correct number. Then he left her alone in a brightly lit cubicle. Her hands shaking, she unlocked the container and stared at the contents.

A yellowing document with old curling edges sat folded inside. The deed to Heartbreak Ranch. A rush of memories flowed through her mind. She saw herself riding horseback across sunlit fields, laughing with other ranch children. She recalled stories of the dilapidated branding shack, where Amy Duprey, her great-great-great-grandmother, had first met her husband, gruff Walker Heart. The shack was almost gone now, with wildflowers growing up around the weathered wood. But the spot still held a special aura.

How well Arabella knew the garden behind the first house the Hearts had built, the place where her great-great-grandmother Josie's engagement party had been held—and where she'd met her future husband when he'd ridden up and apologized for ruining her luau.

The stream beyond the ranch still gurgled and eddied near colorful poppies and lupine—the very place where her great-grandmother Harmony had fallen in love with her Indian beau.

All these stories Arabella held dear and precious in her heart. In the back of her mind she'd always known that someday she'd be telling her own beautiful daughter these very tales, passing them down to yet another generation.

But now, it might never happen. If she lost tonight, she'd lose not only her career, which now seemed insignificant, but the land of her heritage as well. Withdrawing the document, she quickly stuffed it into her purse. She was tempted to just cut and run. But she knew that Sandusky was far smarter than that. He was probably having her watched. He would know her every step. He meant to win tonight, to beat his nemesis, Evan Hennessy, and he meant for her to be the one to do it.

There was no way out.

IT WAS MIDNIGHT. The game was about to begin. Arabella stood in the doorway of the elegantly appointed private room off the regular casino, a room reserved for only the elite—those with money or those representing it.

Lily Lake was there, looking disgustingly lovely and serene. The scrap of gold spandex she called a dress molded each flat plane and lush curve of her fabulous body. At her ears and throat and wrists diamonds glittered, catching every beam and light in the room. She fingered the chips before her.

At the felt-covered table, Faroud crouched in his chair next to Lily, openly appreciating her many assets. He wore a freshly pressed tuxedo suit with a white cravat. In the shadowy corners of the room his turbaned cohorts lurked, dark-eyed and mysterious. Before him were several generous stacks of high-dollar chips.

Arabella turned her gaze to Zach Richards, and studied him intently. Of all the gamblers at the table, he was the most dangerous—and the most highly skilled. Besides herself, of course. He sat in a negligent sprawl, as if nothing in the world bothered him, not whether he won or lost, and not whether the sky suddenly fell, crushing them all.

Only she could see the bright spark in his clear eyes that revealed the passionate man beneath. He positively seethed with excitement and urgency. Like Faroud he wore a black tuxedo, but with a collarless white dress shirt and silver stud cuff links. His dark hair was brushed back off his forehead and his jaw shaved clean. Just looking at him weakened Arabella's knees. She could positively eat him alive, she thought wistfully. In Monte Carlo, she'd almost done so.

Monte Carlo. She couldn't let herself remember. She had to keep her mind sharp, concentrate on the moment, not the past.

When Zach spotted her in the doorway, his eyes gleamed. He got to his feet and held out a hand. "Arabella," he said gravely, "you look beautiful."

She shrugged, taking care that he couldn't see how his compliment warmed her. "Thank you, Zach." Her white sheath was set off only by the pair of earrings Great-grandmother Harmony had passed down. They were small diamonds with little bells.

"You outshine everyone here," he whispered. Strangely, impossibly, she almost had the feeling he was telling the truth. He seemed to have eyes only for her. She swallowed, accepting Faroud's and Lily's salutations, telling herself that while Zach might talk sweet to her now, he would have no compunctions about stripping her of every dollar *and* the deed if he could.

With a careless gesture, she tossed the small packet of papers onto the middle of the table. "You've all been told about this?" she asked the group.

"Somewhat unusual," Faroud remarked. "But acceptable. My people inform me that your ranch is quite valuable, possibly worth millions."

"I wouldn't go that far," Arabella said, frowning. She didn't know what it was worth, but losing it tonight—when it represented a mere two hundred thousand—that would be a crime.

"I'd love to own a piece of country property," Lily offered. "It would be wonderful to have a quiet place to retreat to occasionally. I've made a deal with my backer—he keeps all the money I win, I get the deed.''

"*If* you win," Arabella reminded her.

"Of course."

"I've made the same deal with Hennessy," Zach said, surprising Arabella. Why would these people want a *ranch,* for Pete's sake?

She'd arranged with Sandusky that if she won, she would keep Heartbreak Ranch and get her regular cut of the money. However, there was always the danger that she would lose the money *and* the ranch. God forbid.

"I could learn to ride a horse there, couldn't I, darling?" Lily asked Arabella. "I'd want a stallion, I think. A large black one. It would be delicious— straddling such a magnificent stud."

Faroud's dark eyes widened and he leaned closer to Lily. Arabella rolled her eyes. So, Lily was starting in on him already. Faroud didn't know it yet, but he'd already lost the game.

"I could do other countrified things." She waved her elegant fingers. "Like feed chickens, I suppose. You *do* have animals there, don't you?"

An unwilling smile briefly touched Arabella's mouth at the vision of Lily Lake, wearing spike heels and ermine, tossing corncobs to clucking hens.

"Absolutely," she replied. "Pigs, too. You'd be right in your element." Out of the corner of her eye, Arabella saw Zach bite back a smile. Clearing her throat, she sat up straight in her chair and concentrated on assuming her best poker face.

"If you're all ready, we can begin."

OUTSIDE, IT WAS almost dawn, but time was irrelevant in the false glitter of the casino lights of Las Vegas. Too exhausted and shattered to manage the walk to the bank of elevators, Arabella dragged herself into the hotel café and ordered coffee.

"Leave the pot," she ordered the waitress brusquely, then quickly added, "please."

At five in the morning, anyone in her right mind would be asleep, or headed there, but she doubted she would ever know peaceful slumber again.

She'd blown it, big time.

The first sip of steaming coffee burned her lip. The pain was welcome; she deserved it. But it couldn't compare to the hurt and loss caused by what had transpired that night. Losing Heartbreak Ranch was like losing her mother and father all over again. Now, even the tangible proof that they had once laughed, loved or even existed together was all gone.

She'd lost big, all right.

If there was one consolation, it was that Lily Lake hadn't gotten her hands on the ranch. But it was still a hard pill to swallow, knowing that Zach Richards had been the one to take it all away.

Sandusky had been violently unhappy. She would never be able to gamble for him again—but he'd said he would not have her killed. There was that, at least, she thought morosely. She'd live.

Bella Duprey must be rolling over in her grave, Arabella thought as she slumped over the small table. Bella would probably haunt her for the rest of her life—rattling chains and howling her rage. The truly ironic thing was, Arabella couldn't blame her.

"Share a cup?"

"No," she said.

Zach ignored her scowl and slipped into the seat across from her. He even had the audacity to look as elegantly charming and sophisticated, as perfectly pressed and composed as he had when he'd first sat down at the poker table hours ago.

Before Arabella could protest, the waitress set down another mug on the table in front of Zach. He poured himself a full serving and stirred four packets of sugar and at least two ounces of cream into the steaming liquid.

"The fat and cholesterol will kill you." Her tone was frigid, even if her voice wavered. It was the best she could do.

"Don't sound so happy about it." He leaned back and hooked one arm over the back of his chair.

"Why don't you go celebrate with Lily?"

He ignored her question. "Feel like talking about it?" He watched her as if he were just waiting for her to break—as if he wanted to witness her final humiliation.

"Shut up," she mumbled into her cup. "And get lost."

"I've got something to tell you, Bell."

"I knew you were here to lord it over me," she whispered. Somehow, some way, she had to find the strength to stand up and leave him sitting there gloating.

"The most incredible thing happened at that table." He actually had the nerve to shake his head and laugh, even though she had lost the ranch. He was killing her slowly, but she wasn't about to give him the satisfaction of seeing her break down.

"Yeah." She tilted her chin and looked him square in the eyes. "Incredible. You won."

"I cheated."

She stared at him. "You *what?*"

"You heard me. I cheated. I swindled you. You and the others were bilked. Chiseled. Duped." He took a big gulp from his steaming brew. "That about sums it up."

"You? I don't believe it." She sat back, stunned. "You have a sterling reputation for high principles. You're so good you don't need to cheat." It was unbelievable to think that he could hate her this much.

"I still don't understand how it happened, but I had a little help." He appeared thoughtfully confused, but was still smiling.

Then a niggling idea surfaced. Something Bella's ghost had said to her. Arabella searched his eyes. "It was Sam Heart, wasn't it?"

Zach frowned and slowly nodded. "That's what he called himself. He was behind me, telling me what cards all of you were holding. How could you possibly know? Did you see him, too?"

She shook her head. "No. I never saw Sam, but I know of him. Let's just say you've been used, Zach. That ghost used you to get to me and one of my ancestors. He was after revenge."

It was too late to act on the information...as if anyone would believe her. There was no way she could go back to Lily and Faroud or their sponsors and tell them Zach beat them all with the help of a vindictive specter.

"I don't get it," he said.

"That was no hallucination at your shoulder telling you which cards to play last night. A man named Sam Heart came back from the dead and he used the situation to settle a real old score. Now you've got my ranch."

"That's right. I've got your ranch." He was actually grinning now.

Her heart went numb. Her eyes stung again. She knew she couldn't hold back much longer. Her throat hurt, her breath was shallow and painful, and her chest felt as if a great weight was crushing it. She didn't trust herself, couldn't bear to have Zach witness the onslaught of tears that she couldn't contain any longer.

She had to get out of the coffee shop and back to the safety of her apartment before she disgraced herself.

Zach was actually proud of the fact that he'd won. He had not only cheated her out of her ranch, but flaunted it in her face.

Dear Lord, had she hurt him *so* badly that he was happy about taking the only thing she had left? It was difficult, mustering enough control to put the question to him, but she had to ask.

"Do you hate me that much, Zach?"

If she hadn't known better, she would almost have thought he looked startled. "Hate you? Of course not. I—"

She cut him off with a wave of her hand. "I need

some rest. I'd like to go…home." She shuddered as she held back a sob. "That is, I'd like to go back to the ranch, with your permission, of course. There are a few personal items I'd like to keep…."

He regarded her carefully, as if afraid that any word or move on his part might set her off. Speaking softly, in the controlled, refined tones she had come to know so well, Zach said, "Legally, the ranch won't be mine for at least thirty days. Take all the time you need."

Her throat working, she swallowed, unable to say a word. She dragged herself to her feet.

"Bell—"

She couldn't bear to hear the name he'd whispered in her ear during the most achingly beautiful moments she had ever experienced.

"Don't ever call me Bell again."

CHAPTER FOUR

BACK IN HER PENTHOUSE, Arabella cried until there were no tears left. Finally, she decided it was time to do as the ghost, hallucination, dream—whatever it was that had appeared to her—had suggested. She would return to Heartbreak Ranch. She had been running long enough.

The thought of returning after all these years filled her with conflicting emotions. She was scared and eager, both at once. How would she react to the sights and smells of her childhood? How would she feel, to see the place the barn fire had roared through, taking everything dear to her? Could she face Walt or walk the land again knowing it would be the last time? She didn't know, but she was determined to find out.

After unearthing several large suitcases, she threw them on the bed, yanked open drawers and jammed clothing inside. From her closet, she grabbed sequined dresses and crammed them into garment bags, then overfilled everything with her huge assortment of shoes. Strappy sandals, glittery mules, leather pumps, everything went in.

Since the penthouse had come furnished, all she really had collected over the years were clothes, which made packing easy. In the bathroom she swept her toilet articles into a small case. A toothbrush skittered off the marble countertop and flew across the floor. She left it there. With what little money she had left, she'd pay the cleaning crew to take care of everything.

She was going home.

Placing a quick call to Walt, she told him to expect her later in the day and hung up.

When the bellman came in for her bags, Arabella took a last look around the residence she'd kept for ten years. It wasn't much of a place, she decided. There were no lovely hills to look at, no fresh outdoor scents, no comforting animal noises. There was nothing *alive* here, not even a damn houseplant. She wouldn't miss it.

She had the bellman wrap the painting in blankets and wheel it out on his cart to her old sedan. Hard on his heels, she admonished him during the entire elevator ride downstairs to take care not to bump the frame or damage the canvas. She wasn't satisfied until he set it carefully in the back of her car.

At the desk she made the necessary arrangements, shocking the clerk, a longtime acquaintance. "You're moving out?" he asked.

"Yep. I'm outta here. I'm a country girl, you know."

He blinked at her. "A country girl?" He'd never seen her in anything but fashionable clothing and heels.

"The big city's not for me," she said. "It just took me a while to figure it out."

The drive from Las Vegas took five hours. When

she finally negotiated the winding road that led to the arching sign above the ranch gates, Old Walt was waiting for her. He stood beside a rangy roan gelding, holding the reins in his gnarled hands.

She stopped the car, got out stiff from the long drive and approached him. He held out his arms. Gratefully, she ran into his welcoming embrace. Walt smelled of cigar smoke and horse.

"Arabella," he said gruffly, smiling his gap-toothed grin, "I never thought I'd see the day. It's about time you came back. Hope it's for good."

"We have to talk about that," she evaded. "I'm scared, Walt. Walk with me."

Together they started for the corrals, where Walt would put up his horse. Spring rain had greened the hills, and the cattle were fat in the rich grazing pastures. Outbuildings of bunkhouses and branding sheds were spread about the area, but the big house and new barn couldn't be seen from this part of the road. A lizard scurried on the dirt before them, legs churning.

Walt ambled slowly beside her, leading the gelding, letting her take her time.

"I've decided I do want to stay in the area," she began the difficult admission. "That's the good news."

"And the bad?"

"There's no way to tell you this but to come out and say it. I, er…lost ownership of the ranch to another gambler."

His face twisted. "Poker?"

After a moment she nodded, then lowered her head. "I got myself into a bad situation. I—it was the biggest mistake of my life. I'm sorry, Walt. I'm so very sorry.'' She prayed Zach would keep Walt and the other employees on after he assumed ownership.

She expected recriminations, but Walt said nothing for a while, and they rounded a small curve in the road. She realized she was terrified. Slowly, the grand old ranch house was revealed. A two-story structure, the house featured tall stately pillars and a wrap-around veranda. Roses twined about the banister railing in bright hues of coral, yellow and ruby. The porch was broad and welcoming. Burned into the front door was the mark of the ranch, a deeply branded broken heart.

Arabella sighed in relief. Instead of the terrible memories she expected, a wonderful sense of home-coming infused her. As they approached, she saw that the white paint was peeling and weeds fought with the roses for the rich soil. Some of the nearby corral fences were rickety and needed posts replaced, but this slight evidence of disrepair didn't bother her. The place could be returned to its former glory with just a little money.

In her suddenly tight throat, her breath caught. She hoped Zach would make the investment. She hoped he would see the grandeur, feel the unique atmo-sphere, appreciate the many years of family customs that had made this place what it was. She hoped he could feel the love that had endured here for so very long.

"You said you're stayin' in the area?" Walt asked suddenly.

"Yes. I—I'll find work. I don't know what—

maybe clerking in a shop in Lake Isabella or Bakersfield. I'll get a room or an apartment. Someday, when I can afford it, I want to own horses again. Maybe even buy a piece of property near here."

Old Walt sighed. "I tried. I tried to bring you back sooner, but you wouldn't listen."

There was nothing she could say. He was right.

"But you want to stick around finally, and that's somethin'. I'll always be there for you, Arabella." He smiled at her then, kindly—when she didn't deserve kindness—and, at that moment, she almost broke into tears again.

In the following days, she hung the provocative painting of Bella in her bedroom and took long walks around the ranch. At last she screwed up the courage to go over the bare ground where the fire had claimed the old barn. She almost asked Walt to come along but then decided not to burden him. She had to face it alone.

To help her get through it, she focused on remembering the love she'd shared with her parents, and drew on memories of growing up wild and free and happy. It was a bittersweet exercise, but at last she admitted to herself that Zach had been right about her running away from her feelings. Once she'd started, it had been easy to continue.

It was why she'd run from Zach in Monte Carlo. The powerful emotions she'd felt for him had frightened her with their intensity. She hadn't known how to handle the vulnerability in herself, or how to accept love from him.

Now that she was home, she realized that what Old

Walt had told her so many times was indeed true: she belonged here. Without knowing it, she had healed, and coming back to the ranch had been proof of that. If only she had faced her fears sooner, the ranch and Zach might still be hers.

How many mistakes she'd made. How many wrong turns she'd taken—all of them leading her to sacrifice her extraordinary legacy and to lose the only man she had ever loved.

But it was too late to weep over the past.

She thought of Bella Duprey, her indomitable ancestor, and all the Heart women who came after her. None of them would have wasted a single moment dwelling on mistakes. It was time to get a grip, to trust in herself and the future.

"Get a dog," she recalled Bella advising. Maybe the old girl was on to something. There was no time like the present to start her new life—she might as well face it with man's best friend at her side.

That next morning she fired up her sedan and drove to Bakersfield. At a large, noisy pet store there were spotted beagles and limpid-eyed dachshunds, dignified German shepherds and shivering, bug-eyed Chihuahuas. She petted and cooed to them all, but the dog she knew she simply must have was a fluffy white standard poodle. The minute he'd seen her, he'd begun whining and jumping against the glass window of his display case. He was friendly, happy and sloppy, with no manners at all.

When they were introduced face-to-face, she realized he was a bigger dog than she originally wanted, but when he licked her face and then dropped and rolled onto his back, begging her to rub his belly, Arabella knew she couldn't walk out of the store without him.

She drove back to the ranch, where the dog bounded about madly, frightening the horses, scattering cattle and generally making a terrible nuisance of himself from the minute she let him out of the car. She loved him.

That afternoon, she went up to the attic to look for the trunk that Bella had insisted she find. She dug around until she located a dust-covered chest, banded by metal. It was heavy, but she dragged it out to the middle of the floor, where a shaft of sunlight shone through a high window.

After investigating the attic, her new dog flopped on the floor next to her and put his expressive face on top of his paws.

"Here it is," she said to him in wonder, "the book Bella told me about. There really *is* a journal. *The Art of Fascination.* Wow."

The dog whimpered his agreement.

"Look how old it is," she exclaimed. "The pages are brittle." The journal was divided into sections, one of them listing canine obedience training entitled "Toddy's Tricks and Commands."

She glanced at the poodle and he gave her a quizzical look.

"Yeah, you're right. Why would Bella write about dog training when she was a madam? I thought she'd have some really wicked sex tricks." Arabella shrugged and set aside the leather-bound book for a moment. Digging into the trunk again, she found a long crimson gown, its velvet fabric crumbly between her fingers. She held it up. The neckline plunged. "Wow," she said again.

Laying the gown aside, she drew out a deck of moldy playing cards and when she expertly cut them, a few broke apart in her hands. Next came a wooden box with a painted tiger on the lid. The tiger sported green gems for eyes, and the gambler in Arabella recognized it immediately as a faro box. Instinctively, she found and pressed the hidden lever and a card fell out onto the floor. She smiled. The old gal had cheated.

Next to where the box had been placed in the trunk, she found a jewel-studded dog collar. The stones appeared to be very good imitations. Suddenly, she remembered the small stone mausoleum that marked a grave site on the hillside. Engraved on the granite headstone was the inscription *Toddy: A faithful and loving companion.*

Getting to her feet, she fastened the collar around the poodle. "Your name is Toddy the Second," she announced. Petting the dog's cottony head, she crooned, "Good Toddy. Good dog." When she got the chance, she promised herself she'd read the journal section on dog training.

Waning sunlight glinted off a crimson stone on the dog collar, and something about the flashing light made Arabella pause. Bending over, she inspected the jewels more closely. During her many years of gambling, there had been times when her opponents had offered to wager various pieces of jewelry, and she had had to learn to distinguish real from fake.

A deep fire burned in the red stone. It was a ruby. Real. And probably worth a small fortune. Arabella gasped. The stone next to it glowed like the sea on a clear day. An emerald. And the next—a sapphire.

Slowly she straightened, and stared into space. So this was part of her legacy from Bella. The gems were real. Probably the tiger's eyes on the faro box were, too. All at once, she felt faint, and sank bonelessly to the floor.

How ironic. All along she had had the wherewithal to save Heartbreak Ranch, and she hadn't even known. For a moment, she thought she might cry again.

Sensing her mood, Toddy nudged her with his head.

"It's all right, Toddy," she said heavily. "Maybe it was meant to be this way."

Never a great believer in leaving matters to fate, Arabella wondered if she ought to, for once, trust in the future. Whatever the worth of the gems, she knew that Zach wouldn't sell the ranch back to her. He was far too proud, and too upset with her to simply hand the deed back over.

No, she had to find another path. She would stick with her plan to read Bella's journal and perhaps find a way to go on.

Finally, at the very bottom of the chest she found various vials and colored bottles. One greenish-colored one was in the shape of a nude woman; others were tall and thin, some squat and pear-shaped. Uncorking a short, fat amber bottle, Arabella took a careful sniff, then reeled back, her eyes watering. It smelled of herbs and chemicals and other odors she couldn't place. But she knew one thing—it was powerful stuff.

Putting everything back inside the trunk except the journal and the collar, which she left on Toddy, she closed the heavy lid and pushed the chest back against the wall.

That night, in her bed, she began to read. On a bedside table her lamp was turned low. Toddy snored, taking up most of her mattress.

If she'd been disappointed before, she was now shocked with delight. "The Texas Tongue Massage," she whispered aloud. She bolted up in bed as fantasies of performing the startling act with Zach flooded her mind. The possibilities were intriguing. Bella Duprey certainly knew her stuff. Arabella also liked the part entitled "Things to do with Champagne." There were sexual positions, recipes for aphrodisiacs and advice on manipulating the man of the lady's choice. By the time Arabella put the journal down, it was very late. It was an incredible manual by an incredible woman.

Except nothing in the yellowed pages seemed to be of any value to her. There was no hope for her. She rubbed her forehead tiredly as her heart sank. No hope at all.

She reached out to turn off the light when, just as before, she noticed the room had grown unnaturally cold. A ribbon of smoke began to frame the painting of Bella Duprey. Slowly the whorl of fog took shape.

Bella.

Toddy sat up and started whining.

"Très bien, ma chère, you have obtained a dog,"

she said, her voice warbly and soft. "And *such* an animal—he is exactly like *my* beloved Toddy!"

Arabella made a strangled sound in her throat. She couldn't believe this was happening again.

Bella went on. "But what is this that you have given up? You are a Heart woman. You are descended from a line of strong, courageous females. Will you dishonor their memories by abandoning the game?"

"Game?" Arabella whispered. She pulled the covers up to her chin and stared with wide eyes at the smoky vision. She was dreaming again. Or fantasizing. Or something.

The woman waved a hand. "Of course it is a game. Are not affairs of the heart played by strategy and wits? She who is the cleverest wins, *n'est-ce pas?*"

"Bella," Arabella began tentatively, "may I ask a question?"

"Questions are good. They mean you are thinking." The apparition nodded in approval.

"I've heard all kinds of stories about you from my mother and grandma. But neither of them seemed to know—did you really love Sam Heart?"

The spirit's aura seemed to take on a sorrowful glow. "I believed you would ask questions regarding your own love affair," she mourned. "I do not wish to speak about events that are long gone."

"I think you loved him," Arabella pressed. "That's why you reacted so strongly when you discovered he was going to humiliate you. A woman scorned—that sort of thing?"

Silence filled the room as Bella looked down at her

diaphanous hands. "It is true. I loved him in spite of what he planned to do." She raised her head and said with a Gallic shrug, "But there is nothing to be done now. We must concentrate on you."

Arabella drew a difficult breath. "Why shouldn't I give up? I've lost everything. I don't want to offend you, but losing the ranch doesn't hurt half as bad as losing Zach."

Bella brightened and the air around her began to shine with an incandescent light. "There is always a way to snare a man," she said with renewed confidence. "And he is coming very soon."

"Zach's coming? Here? But my time's not up. He said I had thirty days!"

"*Oui,* he comes tomorrow. But do not worry. You have only to use your wits and instinct," Bella said with an airy wave of her hand. "And a few of the suggestions found in my journal."

She made it sound so easy. Arabella frowned. "How can you be sure?"

Bella stretched. Her aura shimmered as she boasted, "I have friends in high places who are never wrong."

"What'll I do?" Arabella rubbed her temples. Was Zach really coming to take over the ranch so soon?

"Surely you found something in my journal that appeals to you? Did you read each section carefully?"

Arabella lowered her eyes. "Not all of it. But what I did read was of no use."

Bella frowned. "Impossible. What are this man's likes and dislikes? You have lain with him, *non?* What makes his blood run hot?"

Though Arabella thought of herself as a modern woman, she blushed. She wasn't used to discussing such things with other women, and when that other woman just happened to be her great-great-great-grandmother...

Reining in her embarrassment, Arabella tried to think back to when she and Zach had been together.

"My perfume!" she said suddenly. "He used to tell me how my scent aroused him. He said it made him think of making love to me."

"*Magnifique*," Bella trilled. "Everything is solved."

"How?" Arabella peered at her ancestor.

"Not to worry, *ma chère*. You yourself have come up with the answer. Now, you have only to find the relevant part in my journal and...*voilà!* You shall lead this Zach by the nose!"

CHAPTER FIVE

"AROMATICS," Arabella read aloud. As crazy as it seemed, she was going to try. She had nothing left to lose. Zach would be here tomorrow, no doubt, to claim the ranch and throw her out. But Bella's reminder had fired her resolve. She was a Heart woman, and Heart women had always done whatever it took to win the men they loved.

Hopefully, with the help of Bella's journal, she could win Zach's heart again.

Deep into the night she bent over the journal, her bedroom illuminated only by a single low-wattage bulb. "A delightful mix of aromas and fragrances formulated to bring joy and beauty into your private world." She looked up from the book to peer at Toddy. He sat, patiently panting, as she read. Bella had evaporated, or dissipated, or whatever it was that ghosts did when they disappeared.

Around Arabella were spread the bottles and vials from Bella's trunk, as well as bundles of brittle dried herbs she'd found at the bottom. The herbs were probably useless after all this time, but she used some anyway. She'd brought everything down from the attic to her bedroom.

In a pot set over an electric hot plate she'd taken

from the kitchen, she melted paraffin wax, which she mixed with a scented formula for candle-making. She laid out a clean handkerchief, to be anointed with fragrance, and a light bulb, which she would douse with her concoctions.

"Like lovers, the jasmine flower responds to the moon." Glancing out her bedroom window, Arabella was gratified to see a full moon shining down. She picked up a clear bottle with a few drops of amber liquid in the bottom. In Bella's careful handwriting it was labeled Essential Oils. Below that was a list of ingredients. Leaves, petals, roots, flowering tops and even bark, from at least a dozen plants, were mentioned. She unstoppered the top and took a shallow sniff.

A fragrant, pleasurable scent escaped from the bottle and drifted around the room. Without thinking, she smiled. The recipes in Bella's book explained that plants "inhabit the interface between dark and light, earth and sun, take energy from both and concentrate it into usable substances for the sensual woman."

She scrutinized the label of another bottle. It contained oil extracted from blossoms of the ylang-ylang tree of Madagascar, jasmine from the south of France, damask rose from the Balkan Mountains in Bulgaria. There was distilled lavender and chamomile and Palmarosa oil.

"Communicate to the man in question that you want him and that you *will* have him—and have him now. With his olfactory senses heightened, you must be sweetly demanding."

Arabella raised her brows. This looked good—she could do this. Zach was a man with an excellent sense of smell; he loved perfumes. For the first time since leaving him, she felt hope.

Frowning in concentration, she knew she needed a room, somewhere to use the aromatics on Zach. But where?

Not the house—too many people coming and going. The branding shack? Too far away and not enclosed enough to hold in the aromas. However, there was a rather large tack room in the aluminum barn. It had a door that shut tight and a small bed used for any bunkhouse overflow at branding time. Right now, the room was empty.

The longer she thought about it, the more it seemed like a fitting place—a new barn, a place for new beginnings.

It was nearly dawn when she crept downstairs, a silent Toddy keeping pace. Her arms full of her seduction implements, she let herself into the yard and crossed it to the barn. It was dark, but once inside the tack room, she set a small lamp on top of a counter and plugged it in.

With a broom, dust cloth and fresh bedding, she worked until the room was clean. Rows of oiled saddles gleamed on the walls next to neatly hung hackamores, bridles and harnesses. At last she surveyed the results with satisfaction. Her things were placed strategically about the room. Everything was ready.

Now all she needed was Zach.

LATE THE NEXT AFTERNOON, Old Walt caught Arabella dozing with her head on the kitchen table in the ranch house.

"We got company," Walt said as he hovered in the doorway with his hat in his hands.

Arabella sat up, rubbed her eyes and shoved her hair back from her face. She'd spent half the night getting ready for Zach and most of the morning fretting.

"What did you say?" she mumbled. Next to her empty coffee mug sat the remains of a half-eaten lunch.

"Company's here. Somebody just landed a plane out in the meadow."

"A plane?" Her heart began to beat triple time. Instantly she thought of Zach. He'd told her he'd kept his pilot's license current—could it be him?

Walt had a horse saddled and waiting for her, so in moments they were mounted and cantering toward the twin-engine Cessna that had been set down in the meadow. Tracks from the aircraft's landing gear had flattened the dried grass in a long furrow. Zach was lucky he hadn't hit anything, the nut. As she and Walt rode toward the plane, the pilot stepped out from beneath one of the wings.

The dark-haired man stood beside the aircraft and waited calmly. As she approached, she sensed his quiet intensity and couldn't help but be affected; her heart began a slow, measured thudding. As always around Zach she felt a hard tug of attraction.

She and Walt drew rein not far from the plane. The

old foreman dismounted but said nothing. Both men looked at her.

At a loss, she figured she ought to be outraged by Zach's audacity.

"What were you thinking—landing square in the middle of the pasture?" Arabella demanded, sounding more indignant than she really felt. "You could have killed yourself or some of the stock."

Zach glanced over at a few lazy head of cattle grazing not far away. "They don't seem as upset as you are. I told you I was a pilot. How do you like the little beauty I parlayed the rest of my winnings into?"

She spared the older-model red-and-white Cessna a quick glance. "I'm sure it'll come in handy."

"I hope so."

His smile tightened the strings about her heart.

"But what are you doing here so soon?"

"I own this place, remember?" He shot an appraising glance up toward the big house on the hill. "Thought it was time I came to have a look around."

Walt turned his back on Zach and began to mount.

"Walt, wait," Arabella cried. "This is Zachary Richards. He…he's the new owner of Heartbreak Ranch."

"So I heard." Walt nodded at Zach, who smiled in return. "I figure I'll be seeing enough of him as it is. You better show him around without me, Arabella." Without sparing Zach or her another glance, Walt headed back toward the corral.

"Zach, listen, Walt's really a wonderful man. He's

run this place for years, so I hope you don't hold his rude exit against him. It's just that—''

Zach shook his head. ''I know how he must be feeling. It hurts to lose something you love, doesn't it, Bell?''

Avoiding his gaze, she looked out over the meadow, toward the hills she had ridden over so many times in the past. ''Yes, yes it does.''

His smile faded. ''How about that tour? I've only got a few hours, then I have to get back to Vegas.''

A few hours? She had to work fast. This was what she had waited and planned for. But now, face-to-face with Zach, she suddenly had terrible doubts.

What if he didn't respond to her aromatic seduction? What if she was wrong and should have chosen another chapter in the journal? What if he laughed at her, scorned her? What if nothing on earth could make him want her again?

''Well?'' he prodded.

He was waiting for her to do something, say something, but all she could do was sit there on her horse and stare down at him. He was wearing faded jeans, boots and an open-necked shirt. A dark lock of hair fell across his forehead in an incredibly sexy curl. She swallowed hard.

If Bella says I can do this, then I can, she told herself. She would just have to brazen things out.

ZACH WAS STUNNED by the difference only a few days at the ranch had made in Arabella. He had been concerned enough about what losing the place might do to her that he'd flown down to make sure she was all right. Now that he was here, he could see there was an openness about her that hadn't been there before, a glow in her eyes coupled with a confidence that wasn't all false bravado. She truly was at home here. She looked as if she could take on the world again.

They had reached the sprawling white ranch house and she was telling him something about his needing to paint when she opened the door, branded with a broken heart, and a huge white dog came bounding up. The dog nearly knocked him down. "Whoa," Zach said, laughing. He looked up at Arabella. "Does he come with the place?"

The dog barked joyously and licked Zach's hand. Arabella scratched the traitor's head. "Definitely not. This is Toddy and he's mine."

"I never figured you to be a dog lover," Zach said, studying her carefully.

For the first time since he'd found her again, her dynamite smile lit up her face. "Come on in, I'll show you the house."

It was strange, but the minute they walked through the door he felt immediately at home. Toddy ran ahead and then back, to be certain they were following, as Arabella led Zach from room to room, telling him about each one, letting him linger at each window to take in the varied, spectacular views.

Finally, they came to her own room. He indicated the scandalous painting of a nude on the wall.

"I saw that in your apartment. It's not you, is it?" He squinted and peered close. The likeness was uncanny, but the oils had a yellow cast that only came with time.

"You think it could be?" She wondered, sounding almost coy.

"There's a definite likeness."

"That's Bella, my great-great-great-grandmother."

"Some grandmother!"

He walked around the room, his gaze drifting hungrily to her bed. It didn't take much of an imagination to picture the two of them together tangled in the sheets, but it was going to take plenty of patience, and more than a little explaining, to wind up in bed with her again. He hoped he still had a chance.

It was past the time he had set for himself to leave, but whenever he mentioned taking off again, Arabella would suggest they tour the new barn. She was getting to sound like a broken record. A barn was just a barn, wasn't it?

"It's past time I leave," he told her, glancing over to the meadow to where his plane sat waiting.

"There's a lot more you haven't seen," she told him. "You really, really, *really* should see the new barn."

"If I don't get out of here while it's still light, I'll have to spend the night." He watched her closely, waiting for an argument, but she appeared distracted as she stared off toward the barn.

"It won't take long," she promised eagerly. "I think you'll find it interesting."

"I've seen barns before, Arabella."

"I want to show you the tack room before it gets too late."

She had already started off across the road, headed for what appeared to be a shining new aluminum structure. Zach sighed and hurried to catch up.

IT WAS TIME. Arabella wasn't going to accept any more delays. Already the sun was sinking behind the outbuildings as she led Zach up to the barn.

Sliding open the heavy aluminum doors, she gestured for Zach to go first. After leading him past rows of stalls and agricultural equipment, she stopped at the door to the tack room.

"This barn is state-of-the-art," she said. "You should be pleased to have it."

"Listen, Bell—"

"My dad's roping saddle is in here," she said. "You should see it."

"I've seen saddles before, too."

"Not like this. This one's really wonderful. Good leather and, um, stitching. Great, uh, stirrups." She ushered him inside and closed the door. Behind her back, she silently turned the lock.

"Hey. It's dark in here," he protested.

"I'll get the light." She flipped the switch but the room was barely lit by the low-wattage bulb. As it warmed, the essential oils drifted out.

"Oh, that's not enough light, is it? You can't really see the saddle very well. Here." With a hand that shook, she lit several candles she had made herself, using Bella's ingredients. Their delicious aroma soon wafted about the room. She prayed they weren't too obvious, but she wanted to inundate him with scents. If her plan was to work, she had to practically suffocate him with her fragrances.

"Candles in a barn?" he asked skeptically, studying the saddle.

"It's aluminum, don't worry. This barn won't burn." Turned away from him, she put her finger into a bowl of dried flower petals, stirring up the scents. Then, facing him, she loosened the neckline of her Western shirt, and tied a liberally doused red handkerchief around her neck. "Zach, I wanted to thank you for something. You were right. I...have been escaping my problems."

"I know." He blinked. "What's that smell?"

She waved her hand, anxious to divert him. "Oh, the candles are sort of scented."

"Those candles—they smell really good. What is that?"

She edged toward him until she was standing very close. "Just Egyptian rose, rose Maroc and a little Turkish rose."

"Hmm, it's fantastic." He took a deep breath and his gaze dropped to her breasts. She could feel her nipples responding to his avid perusal, stiffening against the light denim of her shirt. "Where'd you get the...uh...candles?"

"Here and there," she answered vaguely, not about to tell him. "You like the saddle?"

He turned his head to glance at her and said politely, "Yeah, sure." Then he added, "It's double-cinched, that's good. And the high swells make long hours on horseback more comfortable.''

She'd almost forgotten his country background. But she realized she really didn't want him focusing on the saddle. She wanted him focusing on *her*. Taking one of his hands, she massaged the palm. "Zach," she whispered, "I've missed you.''

He blinked at her, and when another whiff of the mysterious scent drifted by, his eyes went a little fuzzy. "I missed you, too, Bell.''

At his admission, her heart leaped into her throat. "Did you? Oh, Zach, it was the hardest thing I've ever done, leaving you—both in Monte Carlo and in Vegas, but I was so afraid.''

Around them floated warm currents of heady fragrance. Arabella reached a hand toward the lamp, flicking it off. The room was bathed in a golden glow from the candlelight.

He shrugged. "Vegas wasn't the same after you left. All the life went out of the town when you did.''

Arabella smiled tremulously. It was one of the most arousing declarations she'd ever heard. With slow steps, she backed toward the small bed, tugging him with her. "Maybe we could try again?''

He nodded, gaze unfocused. "That fragrance. It makes me—'' He pulled her into his arms. "I want you, Bell. You smell so damn good.''

"And I want you, Zach. I've always wanted you, but I was afraid to follow my heart.''

"Afraid of what?''

"Of loving you too much and losing you.'' She ran

her hands through his hair. "Kiss me," she demanded, sinking onto the bed.

Eagerly, he followed. "You're always so bossy, Bell," he teased. "Say please."

He unbuttoned his shirt and pulled it off his magnificent shoulders. She smiled.

"Please," she whispered.

His hands worked on her own buttons, then went to her naked breasts.

She hesitated, looking down at his hands as he cupped her. "They're not as big as Lily's."

"Whose?"

"When I saw you together in the café, I thought you were falling for her."

"That little scene in the lounge?" He worked her jeans off until she lay gloriously naked. All that remained was the red handkerchief tied at her throat. "I was desperate to get any kind of a rise out of you, Bell. I even thought making you jealous with Lily might work. I don't care about her. I never even touched her. All we ever shared was a plate of buffalo wings." He kissed her again. "I love you, dammit. I've loved you since the day I first laid eyes on you."

"Oh, Zach, I love you, too." Arabella let her head fall back as Zach kissed along the line of her throat. The candlelight danced against the walls, played over their entwined bodies. Tendrils of scented smoke wafted around them. He left her long enough to tear off his jeans and then he moved over her and nibbled her ear.

"Zach," she whispered, "do you suppose you could do that thing with your lips and teeth?"

His grin was white and very male in the candlelight. Moving his mouth down her body, he asked, "Like this?"

Arabella moaned, already lost in a heady swirl of sensuality and love.

EROTICALLY NAKED beneath the covers, Arabella nuzzled Zach's neck. Her head was cradled on his shoulder, their limbs entwined. The candles she'd arranged around the room had burned down, but not out. The teasing, aromatic scents still lingered in the air of the tack room.

"Can you tell me now, Bell?"

"Tell you what?" She traced his lips with her fingertips.

"Why you ran. I don't want any more secrets between us."

She stared at him. She had come home and faced her fears and memories and now they were behind her; it was time she told him all of it.

"My parents died when I was sixteen. There used to be an old wooden barn. Daddy always said he was going to tear it down and replace it with a modern aluminum structure. He said the old one was a fire hazard, said it was dangerous. He said somebody was going to get killed in there." The telling of it still hurt, but now it was a bittersweet ache, not a terrifying, soul-shattering nightmare.

A beat of time passed. "The barn fire took them both?" Zach stroked her bare shoulder.

"Mother ran in after Daddy when he wouldn't leave the horses inside to die. They were trapped—" She shuddered, but he was holding her so close, she felt his warmth seep into her. "I saw my mother run into the barn after Daddy, heard her screams. Walt held me back. It was hell, watching the fire, knowing they would never walk out of there alive. When it was over, I was in shock. They said I was traumatized. I was in and out of hospital therapy for two years and never came back to the ranch at all. When I was eighteen, I checked myself out of the hospital and took off on my own."

"That's when you started gambling?"

"That's right. It was the one skill I had outside of ranching and, luckily, I was real good at it. I wanted to leave every memory of my life here and the tragedy behind."

He placed his hand beneath her chin, raised it until he could look into her eyes. "God, Bell. You were so young to have suffered so much."

"When I fell in love with you in Monte Carlo, it all came back. The love, the loss. I don't know how to explain. All I know is that faced with the intense feelings that I had for you, I panicked and ran. Have you really forgiven me, Zach?"

His smile was heartbreakingly sweet. "Marry me and I'll spend the rest of my life assuring you that I have."

"I'll hold you to it," she said, smiling up into his eyes through unshed tears, "every day of my life."

"Bell, there's something I've got to tell you now, something that you have to know."

She laid her hand over his heart and felt it beating sure and strong. "You can tell me anything."

"I never intended to keep Heartbreak Ranch for myself. I won it for you."

Arabella raised herself on an elbow so that she could look him square in the eye. "What are you talking about?"

"You were playing like hell during the big game. You couldn't have beaten a five-year-old at a game of hopscotch that night. I could see what was happening, knew you stood in danger of losing the ranch. That was when I knew I had to beat you and everyone else just to get hold of the deed to give it back to you. Sam helped me win for you, Bell. After all, you're his descendant as well as Bella's. He wanted the ranch kept in the family."

She shook her head, astonished. "You used Sam Heart's advice to help win the ranch *for* me? That's unbelievable." She smiled, then laughed. "And it's wonderful. Bella would have loved it."

"Bella? The one with the nice tush in the portrait?" He kissed her soundly and gave her a swat on the bare bottom in the bargain. "I'm hungry," he said suddenly.

"You're always hungry."

"This time for food." He gave her a mock leer, slipped out of bed and stretched. "It's dark outside.

What do you say I sneak back to the house and grab us a plate of chicken or something?''

Arabella couldn't bear to be parted from him, even for a few minutes. She threw his boxer shorts at him and drew on a silk wrapper she'd hidden earlier. "We'll go together."

They held hands, scampering and laughing like naughty teenagers all the way across the yard and into the deserted house. Thankfully, everyone had retired, and they made it unnoticed. In the living room, Zach paused to gather Arabella into his arms and give her a long, luxurious kiss.

Arabella sighed, allowing him to lead her toward the kitchen. But when they were almost there, a creaky floorboard upstairs caught their attention. The house abruptly felt cold.

Zach and Arabella stilled and watched as a smoky mist took shape at the top of the stairs, and another at the bottom.

Bella Duprey, Queen of the Courtesans, stepped forward and paused at the top of the stairs. She wore a red velvet gown that hugged her impressive figure. She took the stairs slowly, regally, until she reached the middle landing. Then, she stopped and looked over the railing at the wavering vision below.

"Sam," she whispered. He was wearing the same checkered wool suit and gold brocade vest he'd worn that night so long ago.

Arabella gasped and clutched Zach. He put an arm around her and pulled her close to his side. They watched.

"Bella," came the masculine voice. "It's been a long time, but you're just as I remember you. Beautiful as ever."

"You always were a flatterer, Sam."

"I was also a fool. Listen, Bella, I admit I had plans to humiliate you—but those plans took a turn I could never have guessed. You see, my dear, while I was busy wooing you, I was falling in love with you. I never should have made that bet. I...wasn't going to go through with it." He put his foot on the first stair.

"And I've always regretted what I did to you," Bella said, emotion in her voice. She stepped down off the landing.

"What do you say we put it all behind us and start anew?" Sam suggested, taking another step up.

"I say...I love you, Sam Heart, for all eternity." Grabbing her skirt, Bella flew down the stairs and into her lover's arms.

Below them, Zach smiled in masculine appreciation and Arabella sighed.

And then, a strange and wonderful thing happened.

The broken-heart brand burned into the front door slowly cleaved together.

Harlequin® Historical

If you're a serious fan of historical romance,
then you're in luck!

Harlequin Historicals brings you
stories by bestselling authors, rising new stars
and talented first-timers.

Ruth Langan & Theresa Michaels
Mary McBride & Cheryl St.John
Margaret Moore & Merline Lovelace
Julie Tetel & Nina Beaumont
Susan Amarillas & Ana Seymour
Deborah Simmons & Linda Castle
Cassandra Austin & Emily French
Miranda Jarrett & Suzanne Barclay
DeLoras Scott & Laurie Grant...

You'll never run out of favorites.

Harlequin Historicals...they're too good to miss!

HH-GEN

LOVE *or* MONEY?
Why not Love *and* Money!
After all, millionaires
need love, too!

How to Marry a

MILLIONAIRE

**Suzanne Forster,
Muriel Jensen
and
Judith Arnold**

bring you three original stories
about finding that one-in-a million man!

Harlequin also brings you
a million-dollar sweepstakes—enter
for your chance to win a fortune!

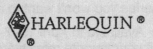

HARLEQUIN ®
®

HTMM

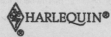

Take 4 bestselling love stories FREE

Plus get a FREE surprise gift!

Special Limited-time Offer

Mail to Harlequin Reader Service®

3010 Walden Avenue
P.O. Box 1867
Buffalo, N.Y. 14240-1867

YES! Please send me 4 free Harlequin Superromance® novels and my free surprise gift. Then send me 4 brand-new novels every month, which I will receive before they appear in bookstores. Bill me at the low price of $3.34 each plus 25¢ delivery and applicable sales tax, if any.* That's the complete price and a savings of over 10% off the cover prices—quite a bargain! I understand that accepting the books and gift places me under no obligation ever to buy any books. I can always return a shipment and cancel at any time. Even if I never buy another book from Harlequin, the 4 free books and the surprise gift are mine to keep forever.

134 BPA A3UN

Name	(PLEASE PRINT)	
Address		Apt. No.
City	State	Zip

This offer is limited to one order per household and not valid to present Harlequin Superromance® subscribers. *Terms and prices are subject to change without notice. Sales tax applicable in N.Y.

USUP-696   ©1990 Harlequin Enterprises Limited

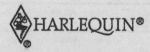

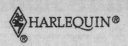 **HARLEQUIN®**

Not The Same Old Story!

 HARLEQUIN PRESENTS®
Exciting, emotionally intense romance stories that take readers around the world.

 *Harlequin Romance®*
Vibrant stories of captivating women and irresistible men experiencing the magic of falling in love!

 HARLEQUIN *Temptation.*
Bold and adventurous— Temptation is strong women, bad boys, great sex!

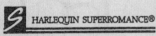 HARLEQUIN SUPERROMANCE®
Provocative, passionate, contemporary stories that celebrate life and love.

 AMERICAN ROMANCE®
Romantic adventure where anything is possible and where dreams come true.

 HARLEQUIN® INTRIGUE®
Heart-stopping, suspenseful adventures that combine the best of romance and mystery.

LOVE & LAUGHTER™ Entertaining and fun, humorous and romantic—stories that capture the lighter side of love.

You're About to Become a
Privileged Woman

Reap the rewards of fabulous free gifts and benefits with proofs-of-purchase from Harlequin and Silhouette books

Pages & Privileges™

It's our way of thanking you for buying our books at your favorite retail stores.

PROOF OF PURCHASE
HPT-PP23
Offer expires March 31,1997

Pages & Privileges ™

**Harlequin and Silhouette—
the most privileged readers in the world!**

For more information about Harlequin and Silhouette's **PAGES & PRIVILEGES** program call the Pages & Privileges Benefits Desk: **1-503-794-2499**

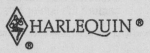

HARLEQUIN ®

HPT-PP23